BLOODLUST

By
Fran Heckrotte

ISBN 10: 1-933113-50-2
ISBN 13: 978-1-933113-50-0

First Printing: 2007

This Trade Paperback Is Published By
Intaglio Publications
Walker, LA USA
www.intagliopub.com

CREDITS
EXECUTIVE EDITOR: TARA YOUNG
COVER DESIGN BY SHERI (GRAPHICARTIST2020@HOTMAIL.COM)

DEDICATION

I would like to dedicate this book to my mom and dad, who introduced me to the worlds of fact and fiction and for encouraging me to take the journeys and visit the places of the heart and the mind when the body is at rest. Their lesson taught me that each story is an experience to be savored before moving on to the next.

Et à Annabelle Lamarre. Mon Français peux ne pas être correct mais ...Merci beaucoup, mon amie. Je ne sais pas combien d'heures à la plage et au téléphone j'ai faites un brainstorm avec toi des développements de caractère d'excédent et le storyline. Vous m'avez commencé sur ce voyage de l'écriture et m'avez encouragé avec chaque étape. And thanks for helping with the French translations. As you can see, I needed it.

And to Howie, who still doesn't know why he gets named here and has yet to ask. One day, he'll figure it out, though.

ACKNOWLEDGMENTS

There are many people I would like to thank for their assistance in helping me write this story.

A special thanks to my beta readers who read and dissected *Bloodlust*. Their detailed critiques were essential to the finished product. Thank you, Alex D'Brassis, Lee McLean, Jove Belle, Chris Limbach, and Carolyn.

To my alpha readers who have been with me from the very beginning, Mary K Bosshart and Remy.

Pam, my proofreader and so much more. The amount of energy expended searching for grammatical and punctuation errors made my copy editor's life a lot easier, making me look good.

Sheri Dragon, my cover artist. All I can say is, "Wow!" You're an amazingly talented woman who captured the essence of my story. I'm in awe of you and your skills.

Tara Young, copy editor extraordinaire. Once again, you provided the polish that makes my finished product shine. I don't know how you do it.

Robin Alexander, I couldn't ask for a more dedicated, fun, or supportive publisher. It's been a pleasure working with you. I look forward to our next project.

CHAPTER ONE

Silent gray tentacles of fog crept stealthily through the darkened forest creating the illusion of shadows moving through the night. One by one, the trees disappeared into the swirling mass, hiding everything from the prying eyes of those who didn't belong in the small secluded valley.

Sarpe lay loosely coiled, resting amongst a thick carpet of leaves beneath an ancient oak tree. She was enjoying the solitude of her species and the warmth of the sunbaked earth. More importantly, she could dream undisturbed by the chattering of the minor spirits of her realm. Her recent journeys into the mortal world had depleted her spiritual essence, leaving her sluggish. Exhausted, eyes closed, she listened to the subtle sounds of the night.

In the distance, the wolf spirit, Vyushir, and her pack could be heard running amongst the trees, their high-pitched howls penetrating the stillness. The young wolves were enjoying the chase, probably pursuing a deer or some small woodland creature.

Sarpe knew that night was a special time for them. Rarely did their guardian take mortal form to run with her kin. Regina, the pack leader, had aged beyond the point of keeping up with her offspring during night forays. This night, as a reward for her years of wisdom and loyalty, Vyushir had granted her chosen renewed youth so she would once again remind her pack why she was queen.

"Welcome to my world," a soft bubbly voice whispered to her right, interrupting the serpent spirit's thoughts.

Half opening one eye, Sarpe stared lazily at the green-and-purple-haired spirit sitting beside her. *So much for peace and quiet.*

Catching the thought, Arbora laughed and the tree limbs above them swayed gently, sending a flurry of leaves to the ground. Sarpe gave an exasperated sigh as she found herself buried beneath a leafy pile. To most spirits, the golden elliptical eyes appeared cold and lifeless. Sarpe gave the intruder a perturbed look, sending Arbora into a small fit of giggles.

"Thank you," Sarpe hissed, pretending to be annoyed. The woodland spirit showed her no respect at times. "I sssee you have not lossst your sssense of humor or your penchant for changing hair color."

"Why, Sarpe, age doesn't diminish a sense of humor." Arbora smirked and reached over to stroke the smooth golden forehead of the other spirit. "At least for some of us. I'm surprised you didn't hear me. You must be growing old."

"I am old..." Sarpe sighed indignantly. "But I heard you. You may move quietly like a sssummer breeze, but you ssstill disssturb the night. Perhapsss it is you who have grown old," she countered before changing the subject. "I like it here. It'ss peaceful, at leassst mossst of the time. I come to thisss meadow to enjoy the sssolitude and to feel the warmth of the earth and to replenish my energies."

"Ah, poor Sarpe, and here I am disturbing you," Arbora said sympathetically, trying to appear serious. "I'll leave you alone. Enjoy your peace and quiet, old friend. This is a magical place, one for resting. My forest soothes the soul, as well as the body, even those of our world. Relax and partake of all it has to offer. Me, I'm off to meet Ursa. We promised Maopa and Mari we'd attend the preparations for their union at the Great Falls. You're more than welcome to join us if you feel up to it. We can always use another hand, figuratively speaking, of course." Arbora chuckled, her lavender eyes twinkling with mischief.

"Of courssse. Sssomething I would obviously exsssel at." Sarpe rolled her eyes in disgust and shook her head in exasperation.

Arbora's laughter echoed through the forest like a gentle wind chime. For the normally stoic spirit to show any emotion was amusing.

"Not thiss night. I wish to ressst, but ssssooon. My bessst to the Earth Mother and Maopa."

"I'll be sure to give them your message."

A faint breeze caressed the exhausted spirit's body as her friend departed. Arbora was one of the few whose touch was tolerated by the serpent.

Alone once again, Sarpe sighed contentedly and closed her

eyes. Her thoughts wandered to others of her world. She was happy Mari and Maopa were joining. The Earth Mother's renewed interest in the spirit and mortal worlds was welcomed by everyone. Even Intunecat was more approachable.

Ursa and Arbora, they were an odd couple but had been together for several hundred years. Sarpe still didn't understand the attraction between the huge bear spirit and the dainty forest spirit. Ursa was always grumpy, except in the presence of the easygoing Arbora, who never lost her zest for life. Perhaps that was the secret to their success. Ursa's somber nature needed Arbora's exuberance. Sarpe wasn't sure what Arbora got from the relationship, but apparently both were quite happy.

Sarpe's musings were interrupted by the faint rustle of leaves as something moved amongst the trees. Raising her head slightly, she stared into the darkness and flicked her tongue, lightly tasting the air. To her left, a shadow moved, unaware of the spirit's presence. It was a woman.

Knowing humans rarely wandered the forests at night, Sarpe became curious. Uncoiling her long body, she followed the human silently through the undergrowth without disturbing the debris littering the forest floor. When the woman stopped near the edge of the town, Sarpe coiled into her favorite position and watched. Soon, another woman stepped from an alleyway and walked to the figure standing in the shadows.

Jussst a tryssst, Sarpe thought, quickly losing interest until she saw the taller woman wrap her arms around her companion and sway sinuously back and forth. Her movements reminded the spirit of her own kind. Fascinated, she decided to stay a while longer.

The woman pressed her companion close to her own supple body. Their hips moved seductively from side to side in a slight circular motion. She combed her fingers through her partner's hair and let them travel down the woman's cheek and along her neck before resting on her left breast. Twisting and turning, the two bodies writhed sensually in a mating dance not unlike that of snakes.

Slow, deliberate, hypnotic body rubbing against body, arms and legs intertwined as the tempo increased. She was a predator who had mastered the art of seduction.

Sarpe could feel the heat from their bodies and smell the scent of their passion. She heard the low humming as the seductress first inflamed then soothed her prey, only to repeat the cycle until her victim no longer had the strength or the will to resist. Hands lightly caressed sensitive areas, leaving the woman weak and vulnerable.

Twirling around, the human faced Sarpe, making unexpected eye contact with her. The spirit jerked back and hissed. Eyes the color of pale blue ice glowed unnaturally bright, red flames flickering mysteriously in their depths. The woman spotted the snake and frowned. Sarpe quickly closed her eyes, startled by the unnatural gaze.

Lowering her head, Sarpe nestled into the leaves and feigned a sleepy indifference. When she finally reopened them, the stranger's back was turned toward her.

Deciding to leave, Sarpe hesitated when she noticed the woman's lips curling upward, exposing slightly elongated canine teeth. As swift as a cobra's strike, she sank them deep into the other woman's neck. Seconds later, the attacker withdrew her fangs, leaned down, and effortlessly picked up her victim. She carried her to a dimly lit area and gently lowered the unconscious woman to the ground, making sure she rested comfortably against a stone wall.

After adjusting her blouse, she stepped away, walked back into the forest, and stopped. For over an hour, she waited and watched. Only after the body was discovered did she leave. Passing within a few feet of the spirit, the woman hesitated, then moved on.

Troubled by her discovery, Sarpe returned to the Eternal Fire, no longer comfortable in the mortal world. This female was human in appearance but different. As one of the eldest spirits, Sarpe knew most living things. Still, the world was changing. That a species could evolve for so long and constantly go unnoticed was disturbing but not necessarily unusual. One day soon, she would track this one down and learn more.

CHAPTER TWO

She was Ekimmu, born in ancient Babylon. Her father was Elil, reputed to be one of the great ancient gods of Mesopotamia. Her mother, Inanna, was thought to be from the land of Sumeria. In truth, they were neither.

Elil and Inanna came to Babylon during the reign of King Nebuchadnezzar. The king had married a young woman, Amyitis, to form an alliance with the land of Medes. To make her feel more at home, he wanted part of the city rebuilt with mountains and gardens. A call went out to the people offering a fortune to anyone who could accomplish the task.

Elil and Inanna appeared a few days later. Impressed by their innovative ideas, the king hired them immediately.

During their stay, an unusual plague spread across the land. Young women were discovered unconscious and remained comatose for days, sometimes weeks. Eventually, they recovered, though they often remained pale and weak for months. Several spoke of strange dreams, dreams never quite remembered but never completely forgotten. Although no one suffered permanent damage, these women were shunned out of fear that they had been violated by evil spirits. Many left, never to be seen again.

By now, as chief adviser to the king, Inanna assured the people that the plague would end…and in time, it did. Shortly afterward, Inanna gave birth to an infant girl with dark skin and pale blue eyes.

Ekimmu was three when her family was forced to leave Babylon, but she remembered the happy days spent playing in the hanging gardens above the roofs of the city. Her mother would chase her through the shrubs while her father watched in amusement as he sat on a bench beneath the flower-laden vines under recently imported trees.

Elil was tall with broad shoulders, golden hair, pale skin, and bright blue eyes that twinkled when he smiled or laughed. Inanna was the complete opposite—dark skinned with honey golden eyes. Both were an anomaly to their own people, who were dark-haired with eyes the color of coal. Although several inches shorter than Elil, Inanna still towered above the Babylonians. Beautiful beyond imagination, neither of them showed any signs of aging.

In time, it provided a fertile environment for planting the seeds of fear amongst the king's less favored subjects. When the whispers began, Elil and Inanna knew their time in the great city was over. To protect their daughter, their friends, and their adopted homeland, they would sacrifice their own happiness. One night, the three simply disappeared, leaving everything behind except what could be carried by hand. The next day, many of the people of Babylon wept.

For centuries, they traveled like gypsies, stopping for short periods in remote villages, then moving on. It was in the land of Daci around 82 B.C. that they once again settled down. The Dacians were a loosely knit group of tribes occupying Eastern Europe.

Ekimmu fondly remembered her time with the Carpi, an unusual people who chose to isolate themselves from the other Daci. The arrival of Ekimmu and her parents proved fortuitous for the Carpi. The people had been plagued by mysterious deaths. Young men and women had been disappearing in the night only to have their mutilated bodies turn up in the light of day. Ekimmu was horrified when she discovered that one of her own kind, a man named Ramus, was committing the atrocities, and it troubled her that her parents refused to stop him.

When Ekimmu confronted her mother about him, Inanna tried to reassure her that Ramus was an aberration.

"Why do you permit this to continue, Mother? He's destroying lives and families."

"We have no way of stopping him." Inanna shrugged.

"So you simply ignore him and the deaths of our adopted people?

They trust us. Is this how we reward them or for their trust?"

Sighing, Inanna took Ekimmu's hand and pulled her down onto the bench next to her.

"It's complicated, daughter," she said, rubbing her temples tiredly. "Our people aren't perfect. We have rules to guide us, and most follow them willingly. Others..." Shrugging again, Inanna left the sentence unfinished.

"*Others* do as they wish, free of consequences. Is that what you're saying? If this is what we are, I hope I don't meet any more of our kind. We're no better than him. Perhaps worse. To do nothing is condoning everything that he is."

"You're overreacting, dear. What would you have us do? Kill him? Lower ourselves to his standards? We aspire to greater things."

"Doing nothing is not an aspiration. I hope one day we *will* be greater, instead of *aspiring* to be." Ekimmu stood and walked away, leaving Inanna deeply troubled.

A few days later, Ramus did move on. Ekimmu questioned her mother about his departure, but Inanna merely waved her hand dismissively saying Elil had talked to him. The deaths ceased and the Carpi tribe again lived in relative peace. Ekimmu and her parents lived amongst them for many years sharing their skills and knowledge.

It was during those years the villagers declared war against the mountain wolves. For several seasons, the winters were unusually harsh, making it difficult for the wolves to find prey. The Carpi cattle were an easy target.

In retaliation, the Carpi hunted the beasts almost to extinction. Strangely, the wolves didn't retaliate, although there was ample opportunity to exact revenge. Knowing the situation would escalate to a point of no return, Inanna decided to intervene. She and Elil called a meeting of the village fathers.

"It's time we ended this," she said, making eye contact with each of the elders.

"Yes," Toria, the tribal leader, agreed. "We must destroy these beasts once and for all before they wipe out our entire herd."

"No!" Inanna countered angrily. "That is unacceptable. You

15

blame every death on the wolves and yet only a few cattle are lost each winter. It's a small price for the benefits we gain from them during the rest of the year. Our vermin population is down, giving us more than enough grain to compensate for our loss."

"Bah! You give them too much credit, woman. Their destruction ensures our survival," Toria argued. "I see no other solution."

"Then you are blind," Inanna countered, trying to calm her anger. "There's always another way."

"Wolves have been a pestilence here for many seasons. In the beginning, we ignored them, hoping they would go away. They haven't. Now our lambs and calves are slaughtered."

"Much like their young and old. They take only enough to survive the hard times and leave us alone. You, however, kill every wolf you see."

"True, and we'll continue to do so until there are no more on our land. Let them go into the mountains where they came from," Toria declared arrogantly, looking at the others for support. Heads nodded in agreement.

"*You will not!*" Inanna rose slowly to her feet. Her icy gaze sent a chill down the elder's spine. There was a fire in her eyes that he had never seen before and hoped to never see again.

"The wolves were here long before us. We are the intruders, not them."

Toria glanced nervously at the others and rolled his eyes, feigning a courage he didn't feel. As it sometimes happens, fear made him brave, but arrogance made him stupid.

"Inanna, you've lived amongst us a long time. We're grateful for your help, but you're still an outsider. Of course, we welcome you at our council, but really, *child*, it's only a courtesy that we permit you to attend these meetings."

Toria smiled gently, trying to soften the words, more for the sake of image than anything else. Several council members frowned uneasily, recognizing that their leader had overstepped his position, but they were unwilling to chastise him openly.

"Outsider? You dare to call me *outsider*?" Inanna advanced on the elder councilman. The old man cringed, breaking eye contact with the tall, angry woman standing before him. "I am more than that. This has been my family's home for many years. I believed you had accepted us as equals, but I see I'm mistaken."

Toria glanced at Elil, his eyes begging him to intervene. The amused smirk he received wasn't reassuring.

"Forgive us, Inanna," Lysium pleaded, trying to calm the tension before it escalated further. "Toria means no disrespect. You and your family are loved by all. Every day, we thank the gods for bringing you here," he said, sweeping his arm around the room to include the others. "Of course, you're one of us."

"Yes, yes," Toria piped in. His leadership was dependent on the support of the council. Alienating them could jeopardize that position. "I spoke without thinking. Forgive me."

Inanna relaxed, choosing to let the verbal slight pass.

"Fear makes us do and say things we don't mean, Toria."

"Thank you," Toria replied, bowing his head humbly. Through lowered lids, he quickly scanned the room to assure himself his repentance was noticed. When a few nodded approvingly, he relaxed. "What would you have us do?"

"A truce."

"Truce? With animals? Have you lost your senses?"

Inanna laughed. "No, these are not the ignorant beasts you believe them to be. If you'll trust me with some of your youngest children and your best cow, I believe I can make peace with the wolves."

The tribal elders looked at one another with skepticism but reluctantly agreed. It wouldn't do to inflame their wisest healer and adviser at this point. Once she was proved wrong, they would be magnanimous in their forgiveness.

The next day, Inanna and six young Carpi traveled deep into the forest. Leading a fat, healthy cow, they searched for signs of the packs and their leader.

Sonia was the most ancient of wolves. She had lived longer than most and was familiar with the humans. Captured as a pup, she had spent many seasons as a pet with a Carpi family. Although they were loving and kind, the mountains constantly called to her. Eventually, she fled the security of her human home for the wildness of the forests.

Rica, a lone male, discovered her two weeks later and taught her the way of the wolves. Within the year, they had bonded and she gave birth to their first litter. For more than a decade, they

17

raised many pups until Rica was killed by the same farmer who had captured her.

Sonia mourned her loss but never retaliated. All packs, human and wolf, struggled to survive. Death was never easy, but it was inevitable. This she accepted as a part of life.

It had taken Inanna two days to locate the spot where the wolves' energies were strongest. Instructing the children to set up camp, she relaxed beneath an ancient oak bordering a small meadow and waited. A narrow stream meandered lazily through its center. The cow was staked nearby.

Long before they showed themselves, Inanna felt their presence. As the wolves approached, the cow tugged frantically at the rope. Aware of the animal's nervousness, the lead wolf halted, lowering her tired body to the ground. Her pack immediately followed her example.

Inanna rose to her feet but didn't approach the wary animals.

"Welcome, Sonia, and thank you for coming. The winter has been long and hard on both of our people. I bring you the gift of food for your pack."

Other than a slight lowering of her gray muzzle, Sonia remained motionless. She too had learned the art of patience.

"This one-sided war has caused great sorrow for all. The time has come to end it. Let this be the place. Let now be the time," Inanna offered, raising her arms to encompass the meadow surrounding them.

Unmoved, Sonia continued to stare at the woman standing between her and the frightened animal. The wolf's eyes were clouded with the opaqueness of age.

Inanna was not fooled into thinking the old she-wolf was handicapped by her infirmity.

"I bring you these children," she continued softly. "Three are yours to do with as you wish. If forfeiture of their lives brings peace to your pack for our injustices, they die willingly. However, spare them, teach them, show them your ways, and they will serve your people well, as will their children and their children's children. You will become as one family, each guardian and caretaker of the other. Will you accept this offering, my queen?"

With those words, Inanna knelt on cool grass and lowered her head humbly in a gesture of trust.

The old she-wolf closed her eyes. Her pack couldn't understand the words, but she did. Patiently, they waited. After several minutes, she opened them and stared at the human pups. Unflinchingly, they returned her gaze.

As Sonia rose, the pain of age was like a fire in her joints. Slowly, she approached each child and sniffed, giving no sign of her intentions. Finally stopping in front of a young female, she nuzzled her hand. The girl fell to her knees and stroked the gray forehead of the old queen. She stared into opaque eyes, smiled, then pressed her cheek against the wolf's shoulder.

"You remember me, don't you? Mama told me about you." Turning to Inanna, she grinned shyly. "She agrees to your terms. Her young don't hunger this day. They have no need of the cow. You can return it to the villagers but must remind them that she may collect the debt in a time of need."

"Granted. Thank you, Sonia. From this day forward, Carpi and wolf are one. The child will go with you now. The others will follow in three moons."

Inanna turned to the young girl and smiled.

"Your children will be blessed from this moment on, Yemaya. Learn your duties well."

Grinning, her blue eyes twinkling with mischief, the child nodded enthusiastically.

Standing, Inanna walked to the old queen, bowed, and turned. She and the other children left, their cow in tow.

Yemaya, her hand clutching the gray fur on Sonia's neck, walked into the woods eager to begin her new life.

CHAPTER THREE

D akota's nose twitched. "Mmm," she murmured drowsily. "Food!"

Yemaya laughed. "Wake up, sweetie. Maria made breakfast for us. Your favorites: eggs, bacon, homemade biscuits, fresh fruit, and juice."

Dakota yawned and opened one eye. "God, you're beautiful," she whispered, her voice gravelly from sleep.

"Flattery will get you everywhere." Yemaya chuckled. "Now sit up so I can serve you."

"Now there's an offer I'd like to pursue."

"Behave. You know what I mean."

"Damn. Can't a girl dream?" Dakota pushed herself into a sitting position and slid backward, leaning against the headboard. Yemaya put the tray on her lap, then climbed in next to her. Picking up a piece of bacon, she placed it against Dakota's lips. Dakota smiled and took the offering before leaning forward to give her a quick kiss.

"Did you sleep okay?"

"Yes, how about you?"

"Me too. I'm glad to be home."

Yemaya smiled. They had only known each other a few months. She was happy Dakota felt she belonged here.

A light knock on the door interrupted them.

"Come in," Yemaya said, knowing Maria wouldn't bother them if it wasn't important.

"I'm sorry to interrupt, mistress. Andrei is downstairs with Kenyon. They need to talk to you about a young woman who was found unconscious early this morning."

"Tell him I will be right down," Yemaya said, sliding off the bed.

"Wait for me," Dakota yelled. "Damn, she moves fast!" Muttering a few swear words, she scooted off the oversized bed and grabbed her jeans and yanked them on along with a T-shirt.

Andrei and Kenyon paced restlessly near the front door. When Yemaya appeared, closely followed by Dakota, both men bowed respectfully.

"We're sorry to intrude, Ms. Lysanne, but we may have a problem developing," Kenyon began. "This morning, a young woman was found unconscious on the edge of town. She's the seventh this month. Thankfully, she's alive. Two weren't as fortunate."

"And the others?"

"They're recovering. We're not sure if there's any connection between the dead women and the others, but all of them are of our blood."

Yemaya frowned. "All?"

Kenyon nodded.

"Has this girl regained consciousness yet?"

"It may be a few days before she wakes up. That's why I've come here. The doctor says this might be the start of an epidemic, perhaps a virus."

"Hmm. I assume they have run the necessary tests."

"Yes, the victims are slightly anemic but healthy. There's one other thing. Each woman talked about strange dreams."

"Nightmares?"

"They couldn't say. They remember bits and pieces but nothing more. What's strange is that they each described variations of the same dream. Dr. Lichy thinks it might be the result of the sickness and sent blood samples to Cahul for additional testing."

"What about the dead women? Why was I not informed of this earlier?"

"You were in the States."

"I am always reachable, Kenyon. You know that better than anyone. What do the authorities say about this?"

"They think the women may have been attacked by a wild animal. Their throats were ripped open and there was considerable blood lost."

"Animal? Are you saying we might have a feral dog or something running loose again? Has anyone reported other attacks in town or neighboring villages?"

"None that I've heard about. Just these two. At first, we thought there might be a connection between the five injured women and them. All had marks on their throats, but Dr. Lichy has decided it's unrelated."

"Thanks. Andrei and I will drive into town later today. Please, tell Dr. Lichy I will be in touch with her."

"Thank you, Ms. Lysanne. Everyone will feel better knowing you're involved in the investigation."

Bowing again, Kenyon left.

"Andrei, bring the car around. I will be ready to leave in an hour."

"*We'll* be ready," Dakota corrected.

Rolling her eyes, Yemaya chuckled and shook her head. "Yes, *we'll* be ready."

Andrei nodded and left.

"Are you always going to be this way?"

"Nah. Only when you try to exclude me from the good stuff. Otherwise, I'm quite easy, you know." Dakota grinned impishly.

"Yes, I know."

Slapping her arm, Dakota ran up the steps and disappeared into the bedroom. Yemaya shook her head again and sighed.

I am definitely whipped, she thought, following her lover up the stairs.

CHAPTER FOUR

The darkness called to her. Like the voice of a long lost lover, it demanded her presence and she felt compelled to respond. She had arrived in Teraclia three weeks before. It was a quiet town with a little over forty-five thousand inhabitants. Ekimmu knew she couldn't stay long without arousing suspicion, but something about these mountains soothed her loneliness. It was like returning home after a long trip. The nights were cool and the days not so sunny as to burn her sensitive skin. With a light, long-sleeved blouse and dark glasses, she could walk in the sun with little discomfort. It made choosing her next "subject" easier.

The night before, the young woman had been exceptionally sweet. She could still feel the warmth from the body pressed firmly against her own. Brown eyes had stared longingly at her, seeking answers to unknown questions. Ekimmu knew what the girl had wanted—to escape from the haunting reality of her meaningless life, if only temporarily. The spicy scent and salty taste of skin as she ran her tongue along the exposed neck had been intoxicating. Groaning softly, she had slowly pressed her teeth into the soft flesh, relishing the feel of warm skin beneath her lips. The coppery taste of blood, sliding thick and warm down her throat, was addictive, making her feel sluggish.

Taking only enough to sustain her own life, Ekimmu had found stopping difficult, but she wasn't a killer. It was forbidden by her people; at least that was what her parents had taught her.

Some, however, carried the feeding too far, enjoying the surge of energy as they felt the life force of their victims slipping away with each gulp. She had been warned about the seductive powers of bloodlust. Once she had almost succumbed to its lure of unimaginable pleasure. Had her mother not jerked her away, the young woman she was feeding from would have died. In the two thousand years since, she made sure she never repeated the mistake.

"Would you like something to eat? Perhaps your usual?" her waitress asked, interrupting Ekimmu's thoughts.

"Not now, Elana. Just tea," Ekimmu said, smiling at the dark-haired woman.

"Herbal tea. I'll be right back with it," Elana promised, hurrying away.

Ekimmu watched her disappear around the corner. It was a shame she suffered from Gaucher's disease, a genetic blood disorder not uncommon in Eastern Europe. Fortunately, Elana's disease hadn't progressed to its advanced stages, which included intense pain and bone disorders. Her blood would have been warm and sweet, like the woman from the previous night and Ekimmu would have rewarded her with pleasures she could only dream about.

Sipping her tea, Ekimmu frowned, remembering the strange snake that had temporarily distracted her during her "seduction." Their eye contact had left her uncomfortable for she had sensed an unnatural intelligence behind the emotionless cold stare. She should have investigated further but was in a hurry to return to her room. Shaking off the thought, she watched the people walking past the restaurant.

The Carpi intrigued her; they were sweeter and saltier than most humans and rich in nutrients. She had fed on her fifth. The taste had been both satisfying and addictive, renewing old cravings she thought she had suppressed long before. Soon she would have to move on before the temptation of their blood overwhelmed her need for anonymity.

"Would you like a refill?" Elana asked, returning with a large teapot.

Before she could respond, Ekimmu's attention was distracted by a tall, dark-haired woman stepping out of a Hummer. Behind her followed a small blonde.

Definitely Carpi, she thought, her gaze lingering appreciatively on the sleek figure of the taller one. "And definitely not," she added, looking at her golden-haired companion.

"Ms. Elil?"

Ekimmu glanced up and stared at the young waitress for a few seconds before answering.

"Umm. Sure. Who are they?" she asked, nodding toward the

two women disappearing into the building adjacent to the hotel.

"Oh, that's Ms. Lysanne and Ms. Devereaux."

"Locals, I take it."

"Well, Ms. Lysanne is, although she's away a lot. Her family has lived here forever. Ms. Devereaux is from America. I don't know much about her."

"They seem to be very good friends."

"Well, I've *heard* they're more than friends." Elana lowered her voice as if to confide some great secret. "I hope so."

"Are you a romantic?"

Elana blushed. "Ms. Lysanne always seemed so alone before she brought Ms. Devereaux here. The people love her, and Ms. Devereaux is such a nice person. She always asks how I'm doing when they come in for a meal...even remembers my name. She's a good tipper, too. They would make a great couple."

"Yes, I believe they would." Ekimmu didn't need to be told which one was the local woman. Her blood had given her away. "Ms. Lysanne is quite striking. The other complements her dark looks very well. Do they live near the hotel?"

"Not really. They have a place in the mountains. She's probably here because of that girl the police found this morning."

"What girl?"

"The one they discovered unconscious a few blocks away. She's the seventh one this month. Everyone's worried that there might be a plague or something going around. Ms. Lysanne and her brother are usually consulted on matters concerning the health and welfare of our people. Their opinions are highly respected by the council."

"Seventh?" Ekimmu asked, suddenly frowning.

"Yeah. Strange. I heard two were horribly mutilated. The others seem okay. The police think a wild animal is involved."

"You mean wolves or something?"

"Nah. We don't have any problems from wolves. There hasn't been a wolf attack here in over a thousand years. Legend says our people have some sort of pact with them," Elana whispered.

"That's a relief," Ekimmu said. It was the expected reply. "I'd hate to worry about being attacked. So if not wolves, what else could it be?"

"Mind you I'm not one to gossip, but some are saying it's a vampire or werewolf...or at least something supernatural. Not that

I believe in those things," Elana quickly added, although she knew it was a lie.

"Good for you. Only trouble comes from superstitions. So, since you don't believe it's something supernatural, what else could it be?"

"Probably a rabid dog. Once I was almost attacked by one. If it hadn't been for Ms. Lysanne, it would've killed me."

"That sounds frightening."

"Oh, it was awful. I was out late one evening when this huge mastiff charged me. I can still remember the look in its eyes and those fangs. They were huge. Ms. Lysanne told me afterward it was probably sick or something. Anyway, it was close to jumping me when she stepped in front of the dog and just stood there, staring at the beast. I tell you it was amazing. He stops dead in his tracks and just looks at us, confused like. I could tell it still wanted to attack but wasn't sure about her. Next thing I know, her driver walks up to the dog, snaps a leash around its neck, and leads it away."

"You were lucky. What happened to the dog?"

"I really don't know. Ms. Lysanne said it was probably sick and she'd make sure it was taken care of. Don't remember much after that. When I got home, I thought I'd be all shaky and nervous, but I was fine. I didn't even have nightmares from it."

"Good for you. It sounds like a horrible experience and one best forgotten. Apparently, you're stronger than you think. Should I be worried about these attacks?"

"I don't think so. I mean, you need to be careful if there's a wild animal out there, but I'm sure the papers or someone would let us know if there was a real danger…wouldn't they?"

Elana suddenly seemed doubtful.

"I'm sure they would. There's probably a good explanation. I imagine your Ms. Lysanne is being updated on everything at this very moment."

CHAPTER FIVE

Dakota and Yemaya arrived home late. Their initial meeting with Dr. Lichy was short. The doctor had nothing specific to tell them but had rescheduled a meeting with Yemaya the next morning, hoping the lab results would be in by then. Exhausted, they decided to call it a night.

Sleep came quickly to Dakota and along with it a recurring dream of Yemaya and her battle against the darkness raging within her mind. In the dream, Intunecat, the dark spirit she had encountered a few months before, was the *beast* trying to possess her lover. Dakota was fighting him to save Yemaya from herself. Every time she thought she had won, he laughed.

"She's mine, you know," the voice declared smugly.

"Never!" Dakota shouted, struggling for control.

"My dear, she has always been mine."

"No. She'll never be yours," Dakota screamed, tears streaming down her cheeks.

"But you promised, Little One. This is the price for my help. I've come to collect what's mine. You do remember your promise?"

"I don't know what you're talking about. I never promised you anything."

"It doesn't matter. When the time is right, you will, then she'll be mine."

"I won't give her up."

"It's the only way to save her from herself. She'll come willingly in time," Intunecat reasoned.

"No!" she cried.

"Dakota, Dakota, wake up." The voice was a gentle caress, leading her out of the darkness like a beacon guiding a ship from the reefs. "Come on, sweetie. You're having a bad dream."

Confused, Dakota opened her eyes. Concerned pale blue eyes

looked deeply into hers. Crying, she flung herself into Yemaya's arms and sobbed uncontrollably.

"What is it?" Yemaya whispered, holding her tightly. Dakota could feel her nerves calming.

"He can't have you."

"Who can't?"

"Intunecat. He wants you and he can't have you."

"Of course not! It was just a bad dream."

"No, it's more than that. I can't explain it, but I know it's more. It's like a premonition or something."

"With everything that has happened to you lately, I am not surprised you had this nightmare."

"Maybe," Dakota agreed reluctantly. "But I think there's more to it than just my imagination."

"If anything happens, we can handle it then. For now, how about we get some rest? I have to go into town in a few hours and you can sleep in," Yemaya said, seeming to dismiss the matter as unimportant.

"All right," Dakota said, irritated at Yemaya's attitude but not really sure why.

Several hours later, Yemaya eased out of bed. Looking down at her lover, she frowned. Something about Dakota's dream bothered her. It reminded her of her merging with the dead girl's memories and those of the dead wolf. The feeling that a dark force had tried to take control of her mind had been haunting her since the incident. If not for Dakota's and Regina's intervention, it might have succeeded. The thought frightened her.

Dakota awoke feeling slightly disoriented until she remembered the dream and Yemaya's apparent unconcern. She wanted to believe it was nothing but couldn't. She got up and paced back and forth restlessly.

I'm just overreacting, Dakota thought. *Yemaya's right. It was just a dream.*

Unfortunately, thinking it didn't mean she believed it. Feeling more agitated, Dakota realized she was blowing the whole dream thing out of proportion. It was a good indication that the last few months had taken a toll on her. Between almost being killed and falling in love, her life had been a roller coaster of emotions giving her little time to think about her future—their future. That was the real problem. She needed breathing room to put everything back in perspective and Yemaya was too much of a distraction.

As the first rays of daylight peeked through the window, Dakota decided to stay at a hotel for a few days. Being away from Yemaya would give her space to think more clearly about everything. With suitcase in hand, she informed Maria of her decision and handed her a note. "Would you give this to Yemaya?"

The housekeeper frowned and nodded but didn't comment. Simtire, the gray wolf, was waiting by the bridge. Kneeling, Dakota grabbed her cheek fur and pressed her own against the wolf's head.

"You can't go this time," she whispered. "No pets allowed," she joked.

The young wolf whined.

"I'm sure I won't be gone long." Ruffling the wolf's fur, she stood and walked to the small car Yemaya had given her for her personal use. The thirty-minute trip into town seemed to last forever.

Dakota was tired. The emotional drain had taken its toll physically and mentally. All she wanted now was to curl up and forget everything. Throwing her suitcase on the chair, she plopped down on the bed, pulled the blanket over her shoulders to reduce the chill of the cool room, and slept.

"So we meet at last," a bubbly voice whispered.

"Go away," Dakota muttered, too comfortable to talk with anyone at the moment.

Laughter tickled her mind. Dakota groaned and rolled over, searching for her pillow. If she could just bury her head in it…

"Come now. Aren't you the least bit curious about me?"

"No, I'm tired! Come back later," Dakota grumbled.

"Poor child! A lover's quarrel can be so stressful," the voice sympathized. "Unfortunately, we need to talk."

Opening her eyes, Dakota looked around. Once again, she was in the meadow with the small stream running through the middle. Before her stood a slender woman with green skin, lavender eyes, and bright green and purple hair. Blinking, Dakota sat up and rubbed her eyes tiredly.

Arbora's laughter swept across the meadow like a warm breeze. From the nearby woods songbirds joined together in a synchronous blend of chirping and whistles.

"I'm a very colorful girl," she boasted teasingly, her eyes twinkling, amused at Dakota's stunned expression.

"I'll say! I take it you're one of Grandma's friends."

"*Grandma*, such a strange word, but yes, I am. She's quite a character."

"That's her. Let me guess. Arbora, right?"

The forest spirit grinned impishly, displaying two small dimples.

"Right," she agreed, sitting down and crossing her legs. "I don't normally intervene in human affairs, but we need to talk. Or at least maybe you do. I'm a good listener, although some would disagree, I'm sure. Anyway, you and Yemaya seem to be at odds. This isn't good. Mari and Maopa are extremely concerned."

"So they sent you to talk to me?"

Laughing, Arbora shook her head. "My goodness, no! They'd have a fit if they knew I was here. I decided to intervene on their behalf. You can't *imagine* the grumblings going on in the spirit world. No one is able to get any peace and quiet."

"Grumblings?"

"Grumblings. Those two can't decide whether to step in or not. One moment they want to get both of you together to talk, the next moment they think they should stay out of it."

"Geez! I'm only taking a few days off to think things out. It's not like we've argued."

"Maybe not, but Yemaya won't understand why you left. Do you really believe leaving a note was the right way to handle things?"

Dakota looked down at her hands, suddenly feeling guilty.

"Probably not. I guess I was afraid." She sighed, taking a deep breath.

"Of what? Yemaya?"

"No. Never her."

"Well, if not her, then what?"

Dakota just shook her head, confused.

"I don't know. This dream I had is more than just a dream. I feel it. I know Yemaya wants me to believe it's nothing, but I don't, and I'm not so sure she does, either. I just needed some space to think without her trying to make me feel better. Is that so wrong?"

Sensing her confusion, Arbora pulled Dakota into her arms and gently held her. Dakota closed her eyes, leaned wearily against the warm, slender body, and relaxed.

"It's okay. We do what we have to. Fortunately, things usually turn out fine," she consoled, stroking the bent head resting against her breast.

"I hope so," Dakota whispered sadly.

"You're overthinking everything. Instead of worrying about what could happen, why not just take each day at a time and enjoy your moments together? The future has many paths. No one knows for sure which ones they'll travel."

"I guess you're right. It's just that I love her so much. I would never do anything to hurt her."

"I know, but you already have. Don't get me wrong. I'm not judging you. What's done is done, but you and Yemaya must get past your doubts. If you don't, it'll destroy both of you. Besides, Dakota, it *was* only a dream."

"I know."

"Then go home. She needs you to be there with her and for her, but mostly, to trust her. That means sharing your fears."

"She's going to be angry at me for leaving like I did." Dakota sighed.

"You're wrong. She'll be hurt and confused, and she'll be angry at herself for having failed you."

"Failed me?"

"Yes. She believes you left because you don't trust her enough to tell her your true feelings. Imagine how you'd feel if she did that to you. Also, there's this power inside of her that scares her. She doesn't understand it herself, but she knows it will consume her if she lets it. She can accept her own destruction, but she'll never survive anything happening to you, especially if she believes she caused it."

"That's absurd," Dakota said, sitting up to make eye contact with the spirit. "I make my own decisions. I love her, all of her. Well, not all exactly," she corrected. "But I accept her...the good and the bad, although I'll never believe she is capable of doing anything bad."

"Good. Now you just have to convince her of that and make her believe it. She will, but it won't be easy."

"I know. Can I ask you something?"

"You may ask. I won't guarantee an answer." Arbora tilted her head slightly, lavender eyes twinkling from her ever-present humor.

"This ability Yemaya has of reading the memories of the dead. Where did it come from? It worries me. It's sort of eerie. I'm not sure Yemaya even knows what to do about it. It's like she thinks it might be a darkness or evil. I just can't imagine someone as good as her having to live with something so awful."

"I don't have an answer to that one. Ideas, theories, yes, but that's all. Once I thought Intunecat controlled all the darkness. Maybe there was a time when he did, but now I'm not so sure."

"Why?"

The spirit's thoughts drifted to a distant time in the past. "Do you know the legend of the light and the darkness?" she asked.

"I know the big bang theory, if that's what you mean."

Laughing, Arbora leaned over and gave Dakota a hug. "You're too cute. No, I'm not talking scientific theory. Intunecat is the oldest of the spirits. We think he's our firstborn, but who can say? After all, where did he come from? Anyway, before his time, we believe there was only darkness, darker than anything you could ever imagine. Once Intunecat arrived, he ruled the darkness but felt an indescribable loneliness from the emptiness. While experimenting with some elements, he succeeded and light was born. It grew at an uncontrollable rate for a while. Eventually, it reached its own limitations and stopped expanding.

"For eons, Intunecat peered into the light from his realm, unable to leave his world. In time, he noticed shapes and movements. One day, Mari appeared. The Dark One was stunned by her beauty and wanted her badly. You really can't blame him for that, but Mari could no more live in his world than he in hers. It's said she created Earth to ease her own loneliness, although she denies it. Once Earth was born, life quickly followed. I believe the Earth now creates both the darkness and the light. After all, the Earth's mother is of one and her father the other."

"So you're saying Earth got its evil from Intunecat."

"No. Intunecat isn't evil. He's a spirit like me. His world is one of nothingness, void of life. It's a lonely place. His darkness is neither good nor bad. It just *is*. Besides, who's to say what is or isn't evil?"

"I don't know, although I think most people can differentiate between the two."

"Maybe," Arbora said, sounding skeptical, then she decided to change the subject.

She tilted her head, placed her palm on the ground, and closed her eyes. Entranced by her stillness, Dakota watched quietly. "Did you know the Earth hums when she's happy?"

"Hums?"

"Yes. About sixty days out of the year, she seems to find true happiness and hums. Of course few can hear her, but it's not too hard figuring out what days they are. There aren't any earthquakes."

"No earthquakes? You mean none? I thought there was always movement somewhere on the planet," Dakota said, awed by the revelation.

"There's movement of course, but that's all. Would you like to hear her humming? Today is one of her happier days."

"Oh, yes, please."

Taking her hands, Arbora pressed Dakota's palms against the ground.

"You must be very still. Take a deep breath, close your eyes, and listen with your body. The ears can't hear her."

Following Arbora's lead, Dakota did exactly as she was told.

At first there was nothing, then slowly, a faint grumbling sound was heard. Frowning, Dakota looked at Arbora, who merely smiled and nodded. The grumbling noise grew louder, reminding Dakota of a growling stomach. Only when it had reached a discernible level did she realize there was a familiar rhythm to the tone. It reminded her of a heartbeat, its pulsations low, slow, and soothing like that of a mother. Almost as if by magic, Dakota's own heartbeat slowed, her rhythm matching the Earth's. It was then that Arbora pulled both hands away.

"It wouldn't be good for you to join with her very long," the spirit advised. "When the Earth is happy, she can be deadly. That's why only a few can hear her."

Catching her breath, Dakota nodded. Her body felt lethargic. Never had she felt such calmness.

"I see what you mean. I'm not so sure I'd call that a hum,

though. It seems more tribal or something."

"To some. To others, it's a hum. I'm not sure why. We hear things differently. Speaking of which, I need to go. Mari and Maopa will be united in a few days. I've left Ursa in charge of the decorations. No doubt she has probably scared everyone off by now with her grumbling and growling," Arbora said, chuckling. "She can be such a bear sometimes."

"Bad joke, Arbora." Dakota smirked, then yawned. "I think I'd better get some rest. Thanks for your help and for caring. I'll think about what you said. Give Mari and Grandma my love."

"Sleep well, and have faith. I've existed a long time. I've learned that things usually end up as they are meant to."

Leaning over, she kissed Dakota on the cheek before disappearing. Exhausted, Dakota collapsed back onto the grass and fell asleep.

CHAPTER SIX

The sweat tickled as it slid slowly between her breasts before continuing its path down her stomach to her navel. Wiping the moisture away, she realized she was naked. Confusion and a sense of loss brought tears to her eyes. She closed them momentarily in an effort to regain some sense of being. Once again, she opened them and stared at the flames holding her captive. She had failed. Orange, red, and blue fiery tentacles swayed back and forth, moving in and out, beckoning her closer.

Occasionally, one long arm would snake out to caress her body. The coldness scorched her skin, causing her to withdraw into her corner, hoping to escape its searing touch. Each time the flames moved toward her, she felt an indescribable fear. Her heart beat furiously, which only intensified the terror that was already consuming her. If only she could scream, but the pain in her throat made it impossible. Exhausted, she sank to her knees, unable to fight any longer. Whatever her fate, it was better than this, she thought. Accepting defeat, she bowed her head, spread her arms, and surrendered herself to the inevitable.

The first touch was gentle, tentative, not icy hot like the crimson flames. It felt different from the flames that taunted her, which seemed extremely angry. They flared furiously but didn't advance. Another warm caress brought her to her feet. Spinning around, she saw behind her another fire burning brightly. Silvery blue in color, it moved gently back and forth.

Feeling hope, she stretched out her hand. The flame flickered momentarily then touched her fingertip hesitantly before running up and down her palm. Curiosity overcame her fear. She stepped closer. When it moved forward, she stopped. Mimicking her, it stopped. Gaining confidence, she approached the strange fire and felt its comforting warmth. Silver blue arms wrapped tenderly around her, enveloping her body in a soothing heat. A warm breath brushed her cheek as the sensation of lips pressed against her neck, then slid seductively downward. Breathless, she inhaled slowly, trying to cool the heat rushing through her body as invisible hips pressed sensually against her buttocks and arms pulled her firmly into fiery breasts.

Try as she would, she was unable to escape her captor, although in truth, her efforts lacked the will. Feelings and emotions she had only dreamed of coursed through her body as the flames slipped ever so tantalizingly over each breast, down her stomach, before resting warmly against the sensitive area at the apex of her thighs. Groaning, eyes shut, she leaned backward, giving herself entirely to the unknown entity wreaking havoc with her senses. Just as she was about to orgasm, the entity suddenly vanished. Crying out in frustration, she opened her eyes, only to discover she was alone with the fiery orange-red flames that had previously tortured her. Confusion and a sense of loss brought tears to her eyes. The cycle began again.

Yemaya released Lia's hand and withdrew from the strange images that inhabited the young woman's mind. The combination of terror and seduction—along with her inability to prevent or intervene on the victim's behalf—left Yemaya feeling disoriented and impotent; her inability to determine the meaning or source of the dream was frustrating.

The only clues to the woman's ailment were the flames. Yemaya felt there was a connection between the ones torturing Lia and the sensual one that protected her. She wondered if the doctor had learned anything more from the lab tests that would shed some light on the situation.

"I haven't gotten the actual paperwork yet, Ms. Lysanne, but the lab called," Dr. Lichy said, motioning for Yemaya to sit. "So far, everything seems to be within normal parameters, although they all are suffering from mild anemia. That's not unusual for women."

"Did you learn anything from your examination of Lia?"

"For the most part, she seems fine. She has some superficial scratches around her neck and two slightly deeper wounds. Nothing serious, though. Normally, I wouldn't think too much of them since the girl could have injured herself if she was having trouble breathing. It's not uncommon to clutch at your throat if you're in respiratory distress."

"So why do you think differently now?"

"She's the fifth case with that type of wound."

"You mean similar?"

"No. I mean the same. Depth, width, size. All match."

"Any theories as to the cause?"

Dr. Lichy stood and walked to the large window overlooking the main street, one of the busiest in Teraclia. Yemaya sat quietly, giving the other woman the chance to gather her thoughts. She could sense her uneasiness. Turning, the doctor half-reclined against the windowsill. Her buttocks rested on the ledge while her hands clasped the wood on each side of her hips. Yemaya watched her face closely.

Sylvia Lichy was a deceptively ordinary-looking woman. Mousy brown hair and brown eyes hidden behind bifocals reminded Yemaya of a librarian she had met at the university. Her smile was perhaps her best feature, something she rarely displayed.

"I'm not a superstitious person. I believe everything has a reasonable explanation. It's only a matter of finding it."

"But?" Yemaya prompted, leaning forward in her chair.

"Now I have data that say I'm wrong. Tell me, what are the odds of five women having identical wounds in precisely the same spot and suffering from the same symptoms? Or of it happening in a town the size of Teraclia within a three-week period? That is not coincidence."

"I agree. You mentioned superstition. Why?"

"Because if I were superstitious, I'd say this is the work of a vampire," the doctor said. "And we both know that's absurd."

"I would agree if we were talking about real vampires. Is there a chance someone out there believes they might be one? Perhaps some type of cult thing or mental illness?"

"Maybe. I hope that's what we're dealing with. I'm too old to start believing in the supernatural." Dr. Lichy chuckled.

"We are never too old to change our beliefs."

The doctor walked back to her desk and sat down, folded her arms across her chest, and leaned back in her chair. "Is that an opinion or an observation?" She smiled slightly.

"Both. The world is filled with things we know nothing about.

Things I would never have believed if I had not seen them myself. I no longer discount possibilities, even vampires. At least it would explain some of this and give us a place to start, which is more than we have at the moment."

"I guess that's one way to look at it. Personally, I'd feel better if the lab found something more substantial."

"I couldn't agree more. What about the two dead women? Is there any more information on them?"

"Not really. The police say it looks like a wild animal attack. They were badly mutilated—torn throats, lots of blood loss. They've put out a press release for the people to be alert for any suspicious acting dogs or wolf sightings."

"You can rule out wolves," Yemaya said, her tone edgy.

"Look, I know you have a special affinity to these animals, but it doesn't mean one of them hasn't gone rogue, maybe caught rabies or something. We have to consider all possibilities," the doctor stated reasonably, opening a folder on her desk. "These pictures show the extent of the damage done to victims."

Picking out two photos, she handed them to Yemaya then stepped next to her pointing to the victim's neck.

"These wounds are definitely caused by fangs. Notice the torn skin and muscles around the carotid artery and the esophagus. It's obvious that whatever attacked her bit here, then just ripped open her throat."

Yemaya frowned unaware of her teeth working her lower lip. "Were there any other injuries?"

"A few bruises on her upper arms. Other than that, nothing unusual."

"What kind of bruises?"

Handing her two more pictures, Dr. Lichy pointed to the dark smudges. Before she could say anything, Yemaya's cell phone rang.

"Excuse me…Lysanne…Yes, Maria…Did she say where she was going to be staying?…I see…Thanks. Goodbye."

Flipping the phone shut, she stared at it for a few moments, deep in thought.

"Is something wrong?"

"What? Oh, sorry. No. Where were we?"

The doctor pointed at another picture. "Look at these."

"Bruises? Someone was holding her tight to make these."

"Yes, and they're fresh. From their size and the way the thumb and fingers almost touch, I'd say they were probably made by a large man. She may have escaped from someone and was then attacked by an animal."

"Do you think we have a stalker out there using a dog to kill women?"

"It would explain the injuries."

"Perhaps," Yemaya said thoughtfully. "Could there be a connection between the five women and the two dead ones?"

"I doubt it. There aren't any similarities. The dead women had similar bruising and obviously struggled with someone before they were killed. The others showed no signs of a struggle."

Dr. Lichy decided to drop the issue of wolves for the moment. Yemaya Lysanne was a well-known advocate for their protection. It was a long family tradition. Even their coat of arms bore the image of a wolf and a woman's head. Between the two stood a sword and behind them a sun was either rising or setting. No one knew for sure. Perhaps the oddest thing was the shadowy image of a woman's eyes in the upper right quadrant of the sun. The ice blue stare was unforgettable.

"I hope everyone is right. A wild animal is easier to deal with." Yemaya looked at her watch. "Thank you for your time, Doctor. Now I need to see someone. Please keep me informed of any changes. The council will be notified of your findings."

"Certainly. Thanks for coming."

Rising, Yemaya shook the doctor's hand and left. Outside, she signaled to Andrei to get the Hummer and gave him instructions.

CHAPTER SEVEN

The caravan was parked outside of town on a small knoll bordering the forest. Several campfires burned even though nightfall was a few hours away. Children dressed in brightly colored clothing ran helter-skelter, screaming and yelling as they chased one another around the fires.

Romano looked up from his carving and laughed at their youthful exuberance. Arthritic fingers and joints prevented him from joining in the fun, but memories of his childhood brought a smile to his face. It was good to see the young free to play. There once was a time when he doubted he and his extended family had a future. Now life was good.

Glancing down at the small wooden carving in his hand, he remembered his first visit to Teraclia and what had brought him here. It was 1937 and Hitler had just declared that gypsies were no longer first-class citizens. He ordered them into concentration camps or the ghettos. Romano's tribe was not so lucky.

In 1941, the Einsatzgruppen rounded up several of his people and marched them to the outskirts of a small village in Moldova. There the Germans lined them up beside a large ditch and shot them one by one. Men, women, children—no one was spared. Had his mother not nagged his father to take him and his younger brother "scavenging" in a nearby town, they too would have died. News of the atrocity quickly spread to the surrounding villages.

Overhearing a conversation between two farmers, Romano's father ordered his sons to hide in a barn on an isolated farm while he went to check on his people. When his father failed to return after two days, Romano and his brother, Ota, slipped away from the farm under the cover of darkness. At the age of ten, he was quite capable of providing for the two of them. His father had taught him that stealing was a necessary skill for gypsies and was by far easier than working for a living.

For months, they journeyed westward through the mountains, making sure to stay well hidden during the day and traveling after the sun set. The Germans were like a plague on the land, spreading and destroying everything they didn't need. Unfortunately one evening, Romano and Ota grew careless and were caught by soldiers patrolling the area near their hiding place.

Ota had caught a cold, which developed into severe chest congestion. Breathing was difficult and frequently accompanied by a raspy cough. When the Germans heard him coughing, they sent their dogs into the rubble to flush them out. Terrified, the boys had no choice but to surrender, knowing it was a death sentence.

Then without warning, the wolves arrived. Outnumbered, the dogs backed away, whining with their tails tucked between their legs. After reaching a safe distance, they turned and ran, leaving their masters to fend for themselves. The soldiers looked around nervously. Something didn't feel right. Not wanting to chance a possible ambush, they quickly retreated, willing to sacrifice the two boys to the pack.

Romano and Ota watched, terrified they were going to be eaten by the fierce-looking animals. Several wolves circled them, growling softly, but none approached. Huddled together, they awaited their fate. It was then that they heard a voice. It flowed over them like the warm southerly breezes in late spring.

"Allo!"

They stared into the most incredible blue eyes. Romano remembered blinking a few times to make sure he wasn't dreaming. Before him, crouched a few meters away, was a woman. Her long black hair was being buffeted by a strong wind. When she smiled, Romano and Ota crossed themselves and said a silent prayer of thanks for sending them this beautiful angel to save them.

"*Ne rakesas tu Romanes?*" she asked slowly, tilting her head.

Nodding, Romano remembered feeling relieved that she spoke Rumanian.

Motioning to the two boys to follow her, the woman stood.

"She is a giant," Ota whispered to his older brother.

"But a beautiful one!" Romano said, feeling the first pangs of adolescent love.

Smiling faintly, she pretended she didn't hear the remark, but

Romano knew better and blushed.

"Come," she said quietly. Romano shivered. There was something unnaturally comforting about her voice. "We must leave here quickly."

Taking their hands, she pulled them from the rubble and away from the building. The wolves surrounded them as they disappeared into the woods. Neither Romano nor Ota feared the animals as long as the woman was with them. Once hidden by the trees, they followed a path that eventually ended at a large stone building. A wooden bridge led to the front door. Hustling them inside, an elderly woman greeted them and took their tattered coats before shooing them into a small room. Two glasses of milk and freshly baked cookies sat on a table near the fireplace.

"Sit! Eat!" she commanded, pushing them forward.

"Thank you, Sophie." Turning to the boys, she smiled gently. "So, my young friends, what am I to do with you?"

"There's nothing to do," Romano said. "We take care of ourselves."

"I see. And how do you survive?"

"We take what we need. Papa said that is the gypsy way."

"Ah, so you are gypsies."

"But of course," Romano said, thumping his chest with his fist. "Can you not tell by how we look, how we dress?"

"Forgive me. I haven't seen gypsies in this area for several years."

"That's because the Germans kill us," Romano said coldly. "They kill my people. Hitler is a pig. Papa says he wants all of us dead. Ota and I, we are the last of our tribe."

"I see. And what is your name?"

"I am Romano. What is yours?" he demanded arrogantly.

"I'm Illya."

A knock on the door interrupted their chat.

"Come in."

Romano knew immediately that the young girl entering the room was Illya's daughter. Black hair and blue eyes said everything.

"Ah, Anya, please come in and meet my two young friends. Ota, Romano, this is my daughter. Anya, they are gypsies."

"I'm the oldest," Romano said, stepping forward and bowing slightly. "Ota is three years younger. How old are you?"

"He's very bold, don't you think, Mama?" the girl asked, deliberately walking past him to stand next to her mother. "And lacks manners, too."

"Be nice now. They are guests in our home."

"If you wish, Mama." Anya turned back to Romano. "But only if he quits acting like such a pig."

Shaking her head, Illya laughed. "Behave."

Anya giggled and relented. "Oh. All right. Shall I show them to their room? I think they would like the one in the tower, being gypsies," she teased.

"Thank you, dear. Afterward, you can bring them to the dining room. Dinner will be ready shortly."

Romano never knew at what point they decided they would stay at the estate. Through the years of easy bantering, Anya, Ota, and he grew close. When she met and eventually married Vincente Lysanne, Romano was her best man, although having two best men at the wedding was awkward.

Shortly afterward, he and Ota decided to renew their gypsy ways and see the world. Perhaps with luck, they would find some of their family if any had survived the extermination. In time, they did. Soon he and Ota joined a caravan led by a distant cousin. There, he met Tania and married her after learning she was going to have his child.

Romano loved the caravan life and his people's carefree attitude but never relinquished the close bond he had with Anya. When he heard of her pregnancy, he gathered his wife and five children and returned to Teraclia.

Anya and Vincente were thrilled and offered them the entire north wing of their home for as long as Romano wanted. The sound of laughing children and running feet brought a new closeness to the group.

Unfortunately, shortly after his arrival, Illya, who had been widowed during the war, was thrown from a horse and died a week later from head injuries. Devastated, Anya never fully recovered from the loss of her mother, although she did her best to make everyone around her comfortable and happy.

Anya's firstborn was a girl. Vincente was ecstatic at seeing the miniature version of his wife and proudly displayed her to everyone from the top of the staircase.

"Behold!" He held up the infant with the curly black hair. "I proudly present to you my daughter, Yemaya."

Immediately, the gypsies bellowed out a toast. Violins and tambourines played as they danced merrily through the halls and rooms.

Folding his daughter in his arms, Vincente gazed adoringly at her face. As he carried her back to her mother, he hummed a lullaby, hoping to drown out the noisy crowd below.

It was then that Yemaya opened her eyes. Pale blue, almost the color of clear ice, they stared at the face above her for a few moments, then closed tiredly. Vincente would remember that moment for the rest of his life.

Several months later, Romano and his family decided it was time to rejoin their own family. Through the following years, he would stop in to see how Anya, Yemaya, and Vincente were doing. He missed the arrival of Anya's second child, Raidon. When Anya was killed a few years later in the same manner as her mother, he was in Italy. It was the only time in his life he chose to fly to a destination rather than drive. Most Gypsies had progressed to automobiles, especially large vans, instead of the old covered wagons.

Shaking his head, Romano didn't want to think any more about the past. Life moved on and so had he.

"Ola, Uncle Romano." She sounded so much like her mother the old gypsy dropped his knife. Looking up, he saw a younger version of Anya standing in front of him.

"Yemaya," he whispered. His throat felt tight from unshed tears.

Kneeling down just as her grandmother had done so many years before when she had saved them, Romano couldn't help but think about how much he had loved Illya. Of course in time, he outgrew the childhood infatuation, but never the love for her as his savior and protector.

"You look just like your mama and grandmama," he said, reaching up to touch her cheek. "I thought I was dying and their ghosts were here to take me," he joked.

Hugging him tightly, Yemaya placed her head on his shoulder while he wrapped his arms around her warmly.

"It has been too long, Uncle," she admonished. "I miss you and the children."

Looking around, Romano snorted. The loud screams and shouts of the young, the playful seriousness of the adults and older children made it impossible to have any peace and quiet.

"I find that hard to believe." He chuckled and pushed her slightly away so he could look into her eyes. "You have changed much, child."

"I am older," she said, her voice low and husky.

Romano shivered. *So much like her grandmama,* he thought again. "It's the way of things, but that isn't what I mean," he said. "Enough talk for now. Come. Join me in a meal."

Yemaya helped him to his feet, and they walked to a huge pot hanging over a large campfire. Picking up two plates, he dipped the ladle in, scooped out a large portion of stew, and poured it onto the tin dishes. Handing one to Yemaya, he sat on an old log and began eating.

"What is in this?" Yemaya asked, enjoying the savory flavor of meat, vegetables, and spices.

"A little of this, a little of that. Whatever we find lying around."

"I see. From the taste you managed to find a few chickens and a pig lying near here."

"Ah, yes. They were old and stringy, barely alive. We had just started the fires when they staggered into our camp and collapsed. Poor creatures. There was nothing we could do but put them out of their misery."

"Of course." Yemaya laughed. "What have you been doing for the past few years? You and the family disappeared."

"We almost did," he said solemnly.

"Almost?"

"Almost. Thankfully, the gods were with us, but it was a great adventure," he said with a grin.

"You have me hooked. Now out with it."

"I see you haven't changed as much as I thought. You're still too curious for your own good."

"You are one to talk."

Slapping his knee in delight, the old man laughed loudly, causing others to look in his direction.

"All right. Several years ago, Ota and I heard stories of a small group of nomads in Southeast Asia called sea gypsies. We were curious, so we decided to see if they really existed."

"Sea gypsies? I have heard of them but thought they were a myth. Are they real?"

"Very much so, but few people know about them, at least in the rest of the world. They call themselves the Salone or Moken and travel in small boats much like we do in our caravans."

"And they live on these boats?"

"For most of the year. They only stay on shore during the worst months, but even that doesn't stop them from diving for their food. Some can stay underwater for several minutes. It is unbelievable. They are fearless."

"How did you find them?"

"We wandered the coasts asking questions and searching. Finally, we found a small band in Myanmar. It took a lot of talk and bribery, but they agreed to let Ota and I join them for a few months. I think the worst part was the stench. Their boats have thatched roofs for shade and they dry all their catches on them. Phew!" he exclaimed dramatically, holding his nose.

Yemaya laughed. "Oh, it could not be that bad."

"Worse! You can't imagine. Still, they're good people and their lives are hard, unlike ours," he joked. "Saluzi and his family took me to a small village on an island to wait out the monsoons. I thought it would never stop raining. It drove Ota and me crazy."

"I can imagine. It looks like you survived the adventure, though."

"Barely! We were never so grateful to get back on solid land and home to our family."

"And a warm bath, no doubt," Yemaya teased.

"Several. It took weeks to wash off the fish smell. No one came near us. We were outcasts in our own tribe. They even burned our clothes."

Yemaya laughed. For several moments, both sat quietly by the fire lost in thought.

"So what brings you here?" he finally asked. "It's been a long time since you have shared a meal with us."

"Too long! I just heard of your return a few days ago."

"True, true. We only arrived last week. My body has grown old and lazy. Traveling is getting harder."

"Then build your home here. There is plenty of land for you and your family."

"I'll think about it, but that's not why you're here. Is there a problem?"

"No, not really." Yemaya said, leaning over to hug him. "But I need you to do me a favor."

"Anything. I have always served your family willingly."

"I know. Thank you."

Yemaya quickly outlined the conversation between her and the doctor. Listening quietly, Romano nodded but didn't interrupt.

"Have you ever heard of anything like this during your journeys?" she asked.

"There were stories a long time ago. Papa told them to scare us when we were bad. I remember one time being so afraid I hid in mama's old chest in our wagon. When she found me, she asked why I was there and I told her I was hiding from the drac. Mama told me there was nothing to be afraid of because her grandpapa told her the same stories when she was a girl."

"Then you think they are only stories?"

"Who's to say? In all legends, there's truth. From all truths come legends. The one great truth is that evil prowls the darkness looking for the weak."

"Yes," she agreed. "That is why I need your help."

"I'm yours to command, as are my people," Romano offered, motioning to those around them.

"Would you ask everyone to keep an eye out for anything unusual and let me know if they hear or see something? We need to find who or what is attacking these young women. Gypsies hear things that most people do not."

"I'll pass the word to the other caravans."

"I appreciate this," Yemaya said, leaning in to kiss his cheek. "Now I must go. I need to talk to someone."

"Perhaps you visit a young woman?" he asked hopefully.

"Perhaps," she chuckled, standing up. "Oh, and feel free to make use of anything you find on my land, but please, no more ...umm... *rescuing* the local livestock. There are some who still dislike and distrust gypsies. They will use any excuse to have you arrested."

"You wound me," he said, clutching his chest dramatically.

"I apologize if I have misjudged you...." Yemaya smirked, tipping her head. "But I am sure your heart will survive. Be safe and give my love to the family."

"The gods be with you."

Climbing into the Hummer, Yemaya waved good-bye.

"Take me to the Hotel Teraclia please, Andrei."

Once at the hotel, she sent him back to the estate with instructions to call her with any further developments about Lia.

CHAPTER EIGHT

D akota groaned when the phone rang. She had left a message at the front desk not to be disturbed.

"Surely they know that means no calls, too," she grumbled, reaching for the phone. "Hello?"

"Ms. Devereaux, I'm sorry to bother you, but Ms. Lysanne is here. She is asking you to meet her in the café," the receptionist said.

"Please tell Ms. Lysanne I'm resting. She can come to the room if she wants," Dakota said tiredly.

"As you wish. Again I apologize for disturbing you."

When the knock came, Dakota sighed and opened the door reluctantly, motioning Yemaya inside. "If you're here to give me a lecture, I'm not in the mood," she grumbled.

"Neither am I. In fact, I came here to see if you need anything. I understand your need to get away. I dismissed your concerns too lightly."

"No, it wasn't you. You're probably right. Maybe I'm just overreacting," Dakota conceded. "Look, Yemaya, I love you. Sometimes I'm going to do things you won't like or agree with or even approve of. They may seem stupid at the time, but I'll always have a reason and I'll always do what I think is best for you or us. There'll be times when I have to make decisions, right or wrong, without discussing them with you and I'm never going to ask your permission." Dakota took a deep breath and waited for Yemaya's reaction.

Wrapping her arms around her lover, Yemaya leaned her cheek against Dakota's head.

"I would not have it any other way. I know we will have disagreements, but never doubt my love for you. If something ever happened to you because of me, I, well, life…" Unable to finish the sentence, Yemaya leaned down to kiss Dakota.

"I know. I feel the same," Dakota whispered.

"We are quite pitiful, you know." Yemaya chuckled.

Laughing, Dakota pulled away and swatted Yemaya's arm. "Here we're having a Kodak moment and you go and make a comment like that."

"I was never very good at mush. However, I can be *very* good at making amends." Yemaya wiggled her eyebrows suggestively.

"Oh, really? Prove it," Dakota challenged, raising one eyebrow.

"My pleasure." Stooping to scoop the smaller woman into her arms, Yemaya tossed Dakota onto the bed.

Dakota giggled. "I'm hoping it'll be mine, too."

"Oh, you can be sure of that," Yemaya promised as she slowly unbuttoned her satin blouse. "In fact, that is my main objective," she added, slipping the blouse off her shoulders and letting it drop to the floor. Her purple satin bra glistened under the subdued light of the table lamp.

Dakota swallowed. She could feel her heart beating faster watching Yemaya undress. Each movement was slow, sensual, and deliberate. When she reached for the button on her slacks, she stopped and grinned.

"I wonder..." she mused. "Shall we make love slow and easy, or would you like it fast and hard? Hmm?"

Dakota caught her breath. "Umm...let's go slow. We have all night." Her stomach clenched at the images racing through her mind.

"All night it is." Yemaya unbuttoned her slacks and let them slide down her long legs. She stepped away from them, exposing smooth tanned skin. Shiny satin panties matched her bra. Yemaya could feel Dakota's eyes devouring her. Dakota could only stare at the long, lean body in the delicate shimmering material. Never in her life had she seen anything more stunning than the vision standing quietly in front of her.

"God, you are so beautiful," she whispered, her voice husky from the desire boiling up inside of her. "How did I ever get so lucky?"

Bending over her lover, her breasts swaying slightly beneath the bra, Yemaya's ice blue eyes gleamed. "We both got lucky, my love," she murmured, her lips inches away from Dakota's. Unable to stop herself, Dakota stretched up and caught them with her own, her right hand holding Yemaya's head as she supported her body with her left. Yemaya eased her body over the smaller woman's, rubbing her breasts against Dakota's T-shirt. She nudged her legs apart and nestled her hips against Dakota's. Dakota groaned when Yemaya pulled back. Staring into Dakota's eyes, Yemaya frowned.

"What is it?" Dakota asked.

Yemaya looked away, searching for the right words. "I look at you and I…I am afraid."

Dakota pulled her close and pressed the dark head against her chest. "Of what?"

"Of this. Of you. That this will end too soon."

"Too soon?"

"Yes. I believe we are given only the time we have and no more. I accept every minute may be my last, especially because of my work. But now…" Yemaya hesitated and swallowed nervously.

"But now?" Dakota asked softly, taking Yemaya's face between her hands and looking deeply into her lover's eyes.

"Now I am grateful for every minute we have, and it scares me to think I could lose you."

"It'll never happen," Dakota promised. "We're meant to be together, not just here and now, but tomorrow and every tomorrow after that. Call it fate, destiny, luck, or anything you want, but we are forever. You understand? Besides, as I recall, you're the one who likes to disappear," she teased, trying to lighten the mood.

"Funny." Yemaya chuckled. "And you accuse me of ruining a Kodak moment. Seriously, though. After this morning and all the things that have happened to you since we met, I worry that you will grow tired of me…of this, and I…I…"

"Stop it! I'm not going anywhere and you certainly aren't. I happen to like the sex too much and the fates can't be *that* cruel," Dakota joked. "Look, sweetie, we're going to have disagreements and there will always be the chance of something happening to you or me, but that's life. That's what makes every moment with you so precious to me. Don't you see, Yemaya, you're my life, my breath, my soul. You make me feel things I've never felt before."

"As you do me. I have never been good at expressing my feelings, at least not when it really counted, but I need for you to understand how much I love you. Losing you is unthinkable to me."

"As long as we can talk, we'll never lose what we have. Now why don't we get some sleep? We have a lifetime to make love. I think tonight we just need the reassurance of being together. Besides, I may have found a Web site that could give us a clue to these attacks or whatever is happening. I'm supposed to meet with a woman tomorrow evening about some research she's done on little-known cults and cultures."

"Really? You found something that quick?" Yemaya asked, awed by the news.

"I'm a journalist, dear," Dakota smirked, looking rather smug. "That's what I do. Now sleep."

Snuggling, the two slid farther beneath the sheets and drifted into a peaceful slumber but not before Dakota heard Yemaya say softly, "A lifetime will never be enough, you know."

CHAPTER NINE

Dakota wasn't sure what to expect when Constance Lorraine walked into the restaurant, but it certainly wasn't the stooped, withered old woman leaning heavily on a cane. Her silver hair was pulled tightly back into a bun, accentuating the sharp features of her face. Several strands managed to escape the knot falling loosely around her ears and neck.

The faded brown wool sweater draped loosely around bent shoulders, the tattered collar and holes in the elbows clear evidence of its importance. Standing, Dakota pulled the chair out and assisted the elderly woman as she slowly lowered her tired body onto the seat, placing the cane against the side of the table. Motioning for Dakota to sit, she leaned back and closed her eyes. Dakota returned to her seat and waited patiently while the woman caught her breath.

"Phew!" she gasped, opening her eyes to look at the young woman across the table. "I... didn't rea...lize it was so...far from the hotel."

Dakota had never seen eyes the color of coal before, except the one time the rage was in control of Yemaya. Black and shiny, the pupils and irises merged together to form small ebony pools of darkness that reflected the overhead lights. Dakota found them extremely disconcerting but refused to look away.

"Are you all right, Ms. Lorraine?" she asked, concerned about the older woman's pallid color and labored breathing.

"I'm fine, deary. Just need to catch my breath a bit."

"Can I order something for you to eat or drink?"

"Just a glass of water please. I don't normally eat out."

"I imagine it might be more of a hassle for you than room service," Dakota empathized, motioning to the waiter.

"I imagine so." The elderly woman chuckled.

"Oh, gosh. I didn't mean to imply," Dakota apologized,

embarrassed at how her remark sounded.

"Now, now. I knew what you meant, Ms. Devereaux. Besides, I'm well past the age of being insulted so easily. When you've lived as long as I have, you learn to read people pretty well and ignore those unworthy of attention."

"Well then, I hope I live that long. I sure haven't learned to do either yet." Dakota sighed, looking away for the first time. When a cool hand clasped hers, she stared at it for a few moments. The skin stretching across the bones looked like parchment, thin and transparent. Pulsating blue veins protruded across the back like miniature highways. The finger joints were slightly enlarged.

Probably arthritis, Dakota thought.

"No, just age."

"What?" Dakota asked, glancing up at the black eyes.

"I said it wasn't arthritis, just age."

"But how did..."

Shrugging, the older woman removed her hand and picked up the glass of water. She took a sip and stared at Dakota, assessing her looks, personality, and character.

"No, I don't read minds. It was the most logical conclusion, don't you think?"

"I guess," Dakota said hesitantly, not quite so willing to accept the explanation. "Oh, drat! Perhaps we should just get to know each other better. I'm Dakota Devereaux."

"I'm pleased to meet you. You may call me Constance, but for heaven's sake, not Connie. I hate that name," she added with a grimace. "It makes me sound like a brainless twit."

"Constance it is," Dakota agreed, laughing softly. "Before we begin, I should tell you I'm a journalist. A lot of people get very uncomfortable talking with my type."

"Oh, I don't think it's your *type* that's the problem, deary. Most likely, it's the profession," Constance joked.

Grinning, Dakota decided she liked the woman sitting in front of her. When Constance suddenly smiled, her eyes twinkling brightly, Dakota looked at her suspiciously but said nothing.

"I see you learn quickly."

Confused, Dakota couldn't think of an answer.

"Never mind. In time, you'll have all the answers to your questions. But as to being a journalist, are we on or off the record as your *type* say?"

"Oh, off. I asked to meet with you for personal reasons."

"Ah, yes. Your research into cults and vampires."

Nodding, Dakota told her about the five women and their symptoms. It was while she described the marks on their necks that she noticed the older woman look away momentarily, her gaze straying toward a tall, thin man staring through the restaurant window. The slight stiffening of her body accompanied by a frown made Dakota want to take a closer look at the stranger. Although a hat shaded his face, she couldn't mistake the color of his eyes—black, like those of Constance Lorraine.

"Do you know that man?" she asked, turning back to the elderly woman.

"Perhaps. He reminds me of someone I knew long ago," Constance replied, her voice cold and emotionless. "Let's hope it's not him."

Looking at the window, Dakota noticed he was gone. "Will he cause you trouble? Should I call the police?"

"No, there's nothing he can do to me. If it was him, he's just an unpleasant memory from my past. Now what were you saying about these young women?"

"So far, four of the five have recovered from their illness. Lia, the last victim, is still in a coma. Yemaya, my...uh...friend, said Lia was experiencing some sort of strange dream. I've contacted three of the other women, and they vaguely remember having some, too."

"What kind of dreams?"

"Yemaya described Lia's as both terrifying and erotic, something about fire and flames. She said it felt as if the flames were alive. Some tormented Lia while another seemed very protective and almost seductive. It was very bizarre. I'm not even sure I understood what she meant."

"This...Yemaya, your *friend*. She appears quite intuitive."

"That's one way of describing her." Dakota laughed. "She's one of the most remarkable people I've ever met."

"You're very fond of her, I see."

"Oh, well...umm..."

"No need to answer that. I can see it in your face. She's a very lucky woman."

Dakota blushed. "I'm the lucky one."

"I'll be the diplomat and say you both are." Constance laughed. "But I'm sure you've heard that before. So how is it that Yemaya knows about this dream if the woman is still unconscious?"

Dakota hesitated, realizing Constance was uncomfortably perceptive. "I...uh..."

"Never mind, child. Perhaps you need to get to know me a little better before giving away trade secrets, eh?" she teased, patting Dakota's hand.

"Thanks." Dakota sighed. "It's not that I don't trust you, but I don't think she'd like me talking about her like this. She's a pretty private person."

"Aren't we all? Besides, you're wise not to disclose such personal information to strangers, no matter how harmless they may seem."

"I guess so," Dakota agreed. Tilting her head, she stared at Constance pensively. "You kind of remind me of my great-great-grandmother."

Constance laughed. "I hope that's a compliment, although that would make me fairly old by human standards."

Dakota felt the blush all the way to her toes. "Oh, gosh! I didn't mean age. Grandma Dakota has been dead for a long time."

Shaking her head, Constance laughed softly. "It gets worse and worse, doesn't it?" she teased.

Putting her head on her hands, Dakota sighed again. "Me and my mouth. Sometimes it just doesn't say what I want it to. Anyway, Granny Dakota had this sort of wisdom about her, a worldliness, you could say. That's what I meant."

"I thought as much," Constance said, her black eyes twinkling with humor. "So how do you know so much about her?"

"I read her daughter's diary. She wrote a pretty detailed description of Grandma's antics. I have this mental image of what she must have been like. That's all."

"Ah. I see." Constance nodded knowingly. "Well, thank you. I'm sure your distant grandmother was a very wise woman. Country women usually are."

"How did—? Oh, never mind. I'm sure there's a logical explanation for guessing that, too," Dakota grumbled.

Smiling, Constance leaned back in her chair and relaxed. "There always is, if you think fast enough," she said mysteriously.

"But back to the reason we're here. Tell me about the dead women you mentioned in your e-mail. What do they have to do with the others?"

"We're not sure they do, but we don't want to overlook anything."

"Reasonable. So what have I got to do with all this?" Constance took another sip of water.

"Nothing directly, of course. It's just when Dr. Lichy mentioned vampires, mostly to make a point, Yemaya decided there may be more to this than everyone thinks. She asked me to research any case studies, legends, cults, etc. to see if I could come up with something. After 1,435 Web sites, I came across yours."

"Really? It took you that long to find mine?" Constance sounded perturbed.

"Actually, I was glad I found it so quickly. There were over a million more to go after yours."

"I guess you should be then, although I must be slipping. Normally, I can get people to find me in the first fifty tries. I'm not willing to pay those outrageous fees to get my Web site up to number one," she said.

"Speaking of which, that's quite a site you have. It must have taken you forever to upload all those pictures and data. How long have you been working with computers?"

"As long as they've been around, I'd say, maybe even longer if you count the abacus."

"You really know how to work that thing? I tried a slide rule in college and was totally lost."

"It takes getting used to. I had a long time to practice with one, but that's another story."

"I guess it goes along with being interested in history, huh? I got the impression you were either a history buff or a teacher from skimming through your site. Most of the information seems to be about little-known cultures and cults. Very interesting stuff."

"From a well-known journalist, I'll take that as a compliment."

"Well-known? Ha!" Dakota laughed.

"I believe your articles in the entertainment magazines have attracted a certain...how do you say it? Following?"

"You know about those? So you knew about me before I said anything."

"Of course. Like you, I do my homework. At my age, it isn't wise meeting strangers unless you check them out. There are a lot of nuts out there, but I'm glad you told me. It shows integrity."

For the third time, Dakota blushed profusely. "Thanks. Anyway, I saw something on your Web site that has me curious." Dakota tried to change the subject. "On one page, you referred to a people called Gebians. I was particularly interested in them."

"Ah, yes. A strange culture, mostly legend, though."

Constance shifted slightly in her chair. Dakota had the impression the woman was uncomfortable for more reasons than just age, but decided not to ask. Again, the old woman smiled.

"Maybe, but in my business, I've learned not to accept things at face value. Even legends hold a spark of truth. I couldn't find any reference to them on the other sites, so I was wondering where you got your information. There's a chance I might discover something that could help Yemaya."

"I doubt you'll find anything else on the Net. What do you want to know?"

"Mostly the rumors about their need for blood. If it's true, we may be dealing with someone who thinks he's a descendant and is copying their rituals."

"There's always that possibility, I suppose, although it seems a little farfetched. Most of the *stories* I came across in my travels, so there may be nothing to the legend."

"Maybe someone else knows something."

"I seriously doubt it. The places I've been, well, there wasn't an Internet back then. These were small remote villages. Sometimes it took weeks or even months by pack horse or walking to get to them, not to mention needing guides. Outsiders usually weren't welcomed. Besides, that was long ago."

"Hmm…still, it's worth a try. If you can tell me where the guides lived, I might be able to find a family member who knows something."

"Unfortunately, I can't tell you. I gave them my word. I can't disclose the locations of the villages. They didn't want civilization intruding in their lives then, and I doubt if they do now. That is if they even exist anymore. I must respect their wishes on this matter. Besides, as I said, they just told stories about the Gebians."

Dakota wasn't sure what to say. If Constance couldn't help her, she'd have to get back on the Internet and keep searching.

"Damn. Well, it was worth a try. I'll think of something else," she muttered to herself. "I appreciate you meeting with me, and I understand. Any idea how long it takes to scan a million sites?" She joked. "It was kind of you to come all this way on such short notice. I'm sure you're a busy woman."

"It was my pleasure. I'm sorry I couldn't be more helpful."

"That's okay. Your word is your word. I'd have been disappointed if you broke it because of me. So maybe you and I could have dinner before you go back home."

"I'd like that," Constance said, pushing off her chair. "Now I really must get back to my room. The sun's setting and I have to check my e-mails. You never know when a really important one might show up," she said, her eyes twinkling with humor.

"True." Standing, Dakota put some money on the table and walked Constance to the exit. "Thanks again. Please be careful. We still aren't exactly sure what killed the two women. There might be a feral dog out there."

"I'm not worried. No one would want an old woman like me," Constance joked, patting the hand holding her elbow. "After all, you did say the women were young. I passed that age long before you were ever born."

Waving good-bye, Constance leaned heavily on her cane as she moved slowly down the sidewalk toward her hotel. Dakota watched the stooped figure for several minutes, wanting to make sure she got there safely. Once she disappeared into the hotel lobby, Dakota walked to her car. When she opened the door, she saw the tall thin man from the restaurant enter Constance's hotel.

This isn't right, she thought, and decided to investigate. Inside, the lobby was empty except for the receptionist behind the counter.

"Excuse me. Could you please tell me what room Constance Lorraine is in?" Dakota asked. "We had dinner together and she forgot her scarf."

"I'm sorry, but I can't give out room numbers," the receptionist said. "If you want, I can get the porter to take it to her."

"No, I think I'd like to make sure she gets it. It's one of her favorites. Could you call her and ask if I can come up?"

"Certainly, Ms...."

"Devereaux."

"Ms. Devereaux." Picking up the phone, the receptionist punched in 432. When no one answered, she hung up.

"I'm sorry but she doesn't seem to be in her room. Are you sure you don't want to leave it with me?"

"No. I'll call her later. Thanks."

Dakota watched the receptionist resume her typing on the computer, then quickly walked to the elevator and pressed the button. When the door opened, she stepped inside, bumping into the solid figure of a man.

"Oh, I'm sor—" she began, only to stop as she stared into the gleaming black eyes of the stranger. Before she could back out, the door closed, trapping her in the small compartment.

"Good evening, Ms. Devereaux," he said, smiling complacently. "Finally, we meet."

"I don't think I know you. Have we met before?" she asked, reaching over to push the button to the nearest floor.

"No, but I've seen you around. You and your friend are very well-known in Teraclia." He stepped closer. Looking around, Dakota realized she was cornered.

"I don't know what you mean," she said, her back against the wall.

"I must be mistaken. I thought you were Dakota Devereaux, journalist and personal friend to Yemaya Lysanne."

"Well, yes. And would you mind backing up some?"

"Why, do I make you nervous? I certainly do apologize," he said, smiling smugly but not moving. "Perhaps if I introduce myself, you'll feel better. I am Ramus Falthama, at your service." Ramus bowed slightly at the introduction.

Dakota swallowed, not sure what to say. Staring into his glistening black eyes was like peeking through a doorway into a world she knew would make hell bearable. Not sure what to say, she only nodded.

"Nothing to say? No questions? Journalists always ask questions."

About to reply, Dakota was relieved when the elevator stopped and the door slid open. Ramus stepped away from her to confront the intruder. Dakota didn't miss the slight intake of his breath when Constance stepped inside.

"It's been a long time, Ramus," she said coldly, glancing

momentarily at Dakota. "I hope your business in Teraclia is concluded."

"Masa'a aLKair, Om Loh Rehn," Ramus replied, bowing slightly.

Dakota was amazed at the change in the man. Even if she didn't understand the language, his greeting was respectful, carrying a certain deference to the elderly woman, causing her to straighten her bent frame momentarily.

"I see you have retained your mother tongue well and your manners."

"It's all I have left of the good times, Om."

"Good times are made, not given. You've chosen to forget that in your lust for life," Constance reprimanded, moving to stand next to Dakota.

"I chose life. I was robbed of happiness a long time ago," he said, fully aware of the significance of the woman's actions.

Dakota felt invisible. Neither seemed aware of her presence until Constance and Ramus turned simultaneously to look at her. Both had eyes the color of polished onyx. Both were smiling, although apparently for different reasons. Dakota felt warmed by Constance. Ramus left her extremely cold.

"I believe you were about to say good night to Ms. Devereaux, Ramus."

"Ah, yes. So it seems, Om Loh Rehn." Bowing formally to Dakota, he stepped from the elevator. "Laila Tiaba, Om, Ms. Devereaux. Till we meet again."

When the doors closed, Dakota leaned back against the elevator wall and breathed a sigh of relief. "I don't like him."

"Your instincts are good. Stay as far away from Ramus as possible, although I fear it will be difficult now that he's met you. He has always been attracted to beauty and innocence. You, my dear, have both. So what brought you here anyway?"

"I saw him following you and thought you might be in danger. He's the same man looking through the restaurant window. You seemed surprised to see him."

"I was. Where Ramus goes, trouble follows. However, he would never harm me. I can't say the same for you or anyone else, though."

"Maybe we should call the police."

"No, there's nothing they can do. Ramus has been around for a long time. If the police haven't done anything about him by now, they never will. Now how about helping this old woman up to her room?"

"Oh, I'm so sorry. I can be such a flake sometimes." Dakota pushed the button to the fourth floor. "Do you mind if I ask you a question?"

"You can ask."

"Now you sound like Yemaya. Where'd you come from? I mean, the receptionist called your room and you weren't in it. Did you know Ramus was following you?"

"I knew. Actually, I was waiting for him. It was inevitable. Now let's go on in and call for room service. We might as well have that dinner now, if you have time."

"I have time."

"Good. I'll just call in the order for us. How do you like your steak? I prefer mine blue, so I hope it doesn't turn you off."

"Not a problem. Medium well works for me. I like my beef dead."

Smiling, Constance dialed room service and placed the order. Motioning for Dakota to sit on the couch, she lowered herself onto a nearby chair.

"I've been thinking. I haven't been exactly honest with you. If I tell you about the Gebians, in what capacity are you acting? Journalist?"

"Off the record, of course, but to be honest, I'd have to tell Yemaya. I don't keep secrets from her if I can help it."

"I don't have a problem with that. It's good to have someone to share things with, especially someone you love. It's been a long time since I had someone like that," Constance said wistfully.

Dakota could feel the woman's loneliness as her thoughts momentarily drifted to another time. Pushing aside her curiosity, she chose to ignore Constance's last comment.

"Yeah, Yemaya is that person for me. Anyway, what can you tell me about the Gebians?"

"I guess the beginning is as good a place as any, although much of what I have to tell is folklore, passed down from one person to another. Some of it, though, I know to be true. Let's see. Maybe a little history lesson is the best place to start. Have you ever heard of

Isis or Geb, the ancient gods of Egypt?"

"Isis yes. Geb I just found on the Net. He's the Earth god or something, isn't he?"

"That's right, but he supposedly also created the sun, but that was only a small part of his nature. Geb attempted to capture the souls of the dead to prevent them from achieving the afterlife. Although he was worshipped, he was also feared. Most followers thought Isis was his daughter, but some believe they were lovers. She was highly venerated in Egypt. She was referred to as the Great Lady and the giver of light. It's believed she made the sun rise."

A knock on the door interrupted them. Dakota took the tray from the porter and placed it on the table. As they ate, she picked up the conversation where they had left off.

"So I take it the Gebians named themselves in honor of this Egyptian god?"

"Not really. His Egyptian following came much later. Gebians are supposed to be direct descendants of both Geb and Isis, but the culture is, or rather was, very matriarchal. The people were ruled by women who were believed to be the direct descendents of Isis. Power passed from mother to daughter, then passed to the consort of the ruling female. Her chosen presided over the people but always under the watchful eye of his queen, thus making sure no male ever gained control of the people. Men were thought to be too warlike for the good of the race."

"Wow! That must have been quite a culture. I'd like to do a story on them one day."

"Maybe one day."

"What happened to them? Other than your Web site, it's like they never existed."

"It's a long story, too long for me to go into tonight. Like most cultures, they made mistakes that cost them dearly. I have an old manuscript for you to read, if you wish, but you must promise not to show it to anyone and to return it to me within three days. I need to return home soon."

"I would love to read it. Do you mind if I show it to Yemaya? I hate the thought of keeping something important from her."

"I would expect no less from you." The elderly woman pushed up from the chair and hobbled over to a tattered old suitcase. "I brought this just in case I thought you might be the one." She opened the lid and pulled out a small package. Carrying it back to Dakota, she placed it on her lap. "You must take good care of this. It's the partial history of a dying race, perhaps the last remaining record. I have several other documents at home you can read another time. For now, I think this one will interest you the most."

Staring at the worn cover, Dakota caressed it gently, almost afraid to accept the priceless gift. "I'll take good care of it."

"I know, child. We'll talk again after you've read it. Now I must rest. The years have sapped much of my energies."

Taking the hint, Dakota stood and walked to the door.

"Thank you. I'll get this back to you as quickly as possible," she promised, tucking it safely under her arm.

Dakota was climbing into her car when she felt a presence behind her.

"You should never be out alone so late in the evening, Ms. Devereaux. The night can be a dangerous place, especially for such a beautiful young woman."

Shivering suddenly, Dakota turned to look up at the tall man whose face was shadowed by the wide brimmed hat and light behind him. "I'm not afraid of the night, Mr....Mr..." she stammered, trying to remember his name.

Ramus smiled. Dakota blinked, stunned by its beauty. Glancing up into his shining black eyes, she noticed a glint of humor barely visible in the darkness.

"Ah. Such a brave young woman. A very modern trait, I must say. But then again, today's females have never experienced the horrors of those in the past, have they? Perhaps it's a good thing, eh, Ms. Devereaux?" He tilted his head slightly.

"I don't know what you're talking about, and I really don't have time now, so if you'll excuse me, I have to go, Mr... Falthamus," Dakota said, looking at her watch.

"Falthama."

"Sorry, Mr. Falthama."

"You may call me Ramus."

Dakota didn't like the satisfied grin on his face.

"Thanks but Mr. Falthama will do. Now if you'll excuse me."

"Of course. My apologies for detaining you. Om Loh Reyn must think very highly of you," he said, nodding toward the manuscript.

"I hope you find *our* history interesting. Until we meet again."

Backing up slowly, Ramus turned and disappeared into the shadows of the night. Dakota drove off feeling extremely uneasy. The "our history" hadn't escaped her notice.

CHAPTER TEN

For over three thousand years, Ramus had wandered the continents bringing death and destruction to those who were unfortunate enough to cross his path. Some called him immortal; most who knew of him called him monster. He didn't care. He was what he was—Gebian. His people were solitary except when coupled with another of their kind.

At one time, Ramus had loved, but it was long ago. The feeling was lost in the memories of time. Now he felt only the need to satisfy the hunger. The insatiable desire for warm, rich blood and the sadistic pleasure of feeling his victims dying was addictive. The power he felt from killing was exciting, but the dying was the real high. The bloodlust sustained him; death appeased the craving.

In ancient times, he had traveled from village to village, country to country, feeding his habit. There was a time when it didn't matter whether it was man, woman, or child, as long as the blood was hot and pure and his victims suffered. Depending on the size of the village, his stay could vary from a day to a few weeks. Rarely did he remain in one place longer. Attracting too much attention jeopardized his safety.

Only once had he actually been "asked" to leave but not by a local villager. Ramus remembered the incident well. He was finishing a late night *meal* when Elil appeared at his side, his disgust evident.

"Ramus, you continue to defy our laws," Elil accused coldly.

"Ah, the great Elil comes to preach to the damned." Ramus smiled cynically as he wiped the blood from his lips. "Or are you here to join me in the feast?"

"You disgust me!"

"Why? Because I choose to enjoy my meals *thoroughly* or because you wish you had the courage to indulge in the experience yourself? To throw away the rules and enjoy life as it was meant to be enjoyed?" Ramus laughed loudly. "You and the rest of our people treat these humans as equals instead of the animals they are. We are their masters. They're nothing more than a source of nourishment and entertainment for us, just as pigs and chickens are to them."

Elil ignored the crude humor. "We don't kill, Ramus. That's the law. You endanger everyone with your continued defiance."

"I endanger no one. They can't harm us and you know it. You and Inanna are the real threat. Your lack of leadership will be our destruction. These *decrees* were created eons ago when our race thrived. Now look at us. We barely exceed a thousand. Why do you continue this farce when they are so inferior to us?"

"You're a fool," Elil hissed. "You think us superior to everything. Look at you, standing there. You think you are a god or something more. We'll all be destroyed if you continue this path."

"It's you who is the fool. Humans are afraid of everything. They tell stories about us to scare their young. We are their boogeymen, their demons. Were they to discover we really existed, they would prostrate themselves before us and pray for their nonexistent god to save them," Ramus scoffed.

"I fear one day you'll discover there's more to this nonexistent god than you think. The humans and our people have much in common when it comes to our ancestry."

Ramus laughed. "You insult me and our people. They are spawn of the ocean. Their kind didn't evolve until millions of years after they crawled from the seas. We are of the Earth. They were our nourishment long before they evolved an intelligence."

"That may be so, but once they did, the rules changed. We have wisely followed those rules and will continue to follow them. If you can't, it's time you moved on…and feel lucky they exist or I would kill you myself. Those same rules are what stops me now."

"Bah! I'm not afraid of you nor that whore you bed. I'll leave when I *choose* to. Be warned, though. Don't you, Inanna, or that brat of yours ever cross my path. You may not be willing to kill, but as you can see…" Ramus kicked the body at his feet and chuckled. "I'm not in the least reluctant, human *or* otherwise."

Without another word, Ramus turned and walked away, his laughter penetrating the blackness as he disappeared into the shadowy night.

Inwardly, Ramus seethed. Older than Elil, he should have been the queen's chosen. Instead, Inanna had taken Elil as her consort. As the descendent of Isis, her bloodlines could be traced back thousands of years. Her consort would become the "Chosen One" of their people, giving Elil sovereignty over everyone except Inanna.

Ramus felt cheated of both the crown and the beautiful woman he had lusted after for centuries. Spurning his advances was bad enough. Being "asked" to leave by Elil was the ultimate humiliation. Aware that he lacked the courage or the strength to defeat Elil and Inanna, he decided to bide his time until the right moment for revenge presented itself. Its sweetness would be worth the wait.

CHAPTER ELEVEN

Time passed. During the fourteenth century, Europe was devastated by the plague. Many believed it began in Kaffa, a small town on the Crimean Coast. Soon it spread through Italy and France.

Ramus was in his glory, feasting on the healthy and finding humor when the locals blamed the deaths on the plague. Obsessed by his addiction, he captured flea-infested rats and transported them from town to town, ensuring the plague would continue to wreak havoc, thus providing him with an unlimited source of food and amusement.

It was in a small nameless village in France that he again crossed paths with Elil and Inanna. Ekimmu no longer traveled with her parents. Ramus didn't know where she was but knew in time, she would return to her family. Gebians needed that contact. It was in their blood.

Years might pass before a reunion, but inevitably, the *blooded* would find one another and renew their ties. When family members no longer existed, the last of the bloodline led solitary lives, unless they were fortunate enough to find a life partner or temporary companion.

Ramus had partnered with a few women and men through the centuries, but none lasted longer than a couple of years. Eventually, they fell victim to his rage and bloodlust. Time had not tempered his desire for revenge. France finally gave him that opportunity.

The plague had wiped out several townships, leaving only Verdeau untouched. Word spread that the village was protected by gods. Soon, the survivors flocked into Verdeau hoping to be saved or protected. When Ramus heard that the so-called gods were Inanna and Elil, he was furious. Memories of their last meeting were still fresh in his mind.

Within three weeks, eighty-three villagers contracted the plague. All were close to the two Gebians. The whispers began, born from the seeds of distrust that Ramus had planted in a few villagers' minds. Gleefully, he receded into the darkness and waited for the inevitable. Humans were so predictable.

"I tell you, they brung this on us," Franco declared, looking around fearfully.

"Hush. Someone will hear you," Phillipe said nervously.

"But he's right. We had no problems here. Then they showed up and our people is dyin'. What other reason could there be?" Raoul asked after eavesdropping on the conversation.

"Yes, Phillipe. You tell us that," Franco said.

"I did na say I disagrees, but they have friends. If what you says is true and someone heared us, we are dead men."

Overhearing the conversation, Ramus smirked. How simple-minded humans were, he thought. A few more killings and the people were sure to rise up against their "saviors." Within a week, they did.

The day was hot. The sun beat heavily upon the earth, scorching the crops and driving the living into the shelters of their homes. The air stank of decay as the bodies of eight missing children were discovered buried under a haystack near the edge of the village.

Wails of agony from mourning parents filled the air, causing the people to come out of their shelters into the sweltering heat. Tempers ran high as Franco worked the people into a frenzy with his suspicions.

Everyone knew Elil and Inanna slept during the hotter hours of the day.

"It's time, my friends, while they is sleepin'. These are not gods. Gods do na sleep. They is demons come to feed on our peoples. We must kill them before they destroys us," he shouted, his voice raw from yelling over the sounds of the wailing families.

"Yes, yes," another piped in. "Let's do it now. It's the only way to saves ourselves and our children."

The men of the village nodded in agreement.

"Are you sure it's them?" a young mother asked. "Perhaps it's something else. We must be sure, Franco."

"Go home, Jolie. This is men's work."

"You would do well to listen to her," an ancient voice advised. Looking around, the villagers parted as a stooped elderly woman leaning heavily on a cane limped slowly toward the gathering. Several of the men stepped away from her as she passed, each crossing their chests superstitiously. The woman smirked but said nothing until she stepped in front of Franco.

"They aren't the cause of your misfortunes, Franco."

"What do you knowed, old woman?" He straightened slightly in an effort to intimidate her.

"More than you'll ever know in a thousand lifetimes. Mark my words. If you carry out your plans, your village is doomed. They stand between you and this darkness," she warned.

"Bah. Go away. Ignore her. She's old and witless." He pushed her aside. Stumbling, she would have fallen if Jolie hadn't stepped forward to catch her.

"Franco, this is wrong," Jolie said. "Let's talk to them. At least give them a chance to defend themselves."

"Like they gives us? No. I say we kill them. Who's with me?"

Fearing they would look weak, several villagers joined the troublemakers. Picking up pitchforks and shovels, they moved toward the home of Inanna and Elil.

"Can we not stop them?" Jolie cried. "Is there no one willing to save them?" She looked at the remaining villagers who had stayed behind. Shaking their heads, they slowly moved away, not wanting to get involved.

"They fear the unknown," the old woman said sadly. "It will be the undoing of everyone who remains here. Take your children and leave quickly, Jolie. This village dies with Inanna and Elil."

"But we could at least warn them. Perhaps if we hurry, we can get there before the men and reason with them."

"You can't reason with fear. They'll kill you and anyone else who interferes. This is their destiny, child. The gods have their reasons for everything. Go! Gather your children and what little you can carry. Bring anyone who is willing to listen. We must leave this place by nightfall."

"But where can we go? I have no family, no relatives."

"Far away. To the west and over the mountains. It will be long and hard, but you can make it. I will show you the way."

"Are you able to make such a journey, Constancia? I can have a litter made to carry you."

Smiling, the old woman nodded. "There's no need for that. I'm stronger than I look. All who follow me will be safe. Now go quickly. There's no more time for talk."

Constancia wished she could have saved her queen and consort but was wise enough to accept the inevitable. Elil and Inanna would not have wanted her to sacrifice herself for a hopeless cause. It was better to have their deaths recorded than to just disappear into unmarked graves forever forgotten.

Elil and Inanna were asleep, exhausted from their nightly search for the killer. They suspected Ramus was behind the deaths but were unable to locate him. Arms wrapped tightly around each other in a lover's embrace, they were unaware of the villagers gathering outside of their home or the men stealing quietly into their bedroom.

Franco struck the first blow. The more cowardly stood back and watched. Spurred by his leader's courage, Phillipe attacked the sleeping woman, thrusting his pitchfork deep into her chest and twisting it viciously. Shocked awake from the burning pain, the lovers released their hold on each other.

Elil, the first to be attacked, yanked the pitchfork from his side and tossed it angrily on the floor. Tenderly, he removed the other fork from Inanna's body and threw it at a villager. Shielding Inanna with his own body, he faced his attackers, his face a strange mixture of pain, confusion, and anger.

"Kill them!" Franco yelled, shoving a farmer forward in front of him. "Before they works their evil. Kill them fast!"

The others pressed forward more terrified than ever. If the two were demons, they would surely destroy all of them if given the chance.

Outnumbered, Elil could do nothing to help Inanna. Although he knew she had died instantly from the initial assault, he didn't want her beautiful body or face mutilated further. Angrily, he surged upward, grabbing Franco by his shirt and used him as a shield.

"Why?" he demanded, tears of rage and sorrow streaming down his cheeks. "Why have you done this?"

"You kilt our people and you asks this?" Franco asked, fearful that the wounded man would vent his wrath on him first. "We knowed you and the woman is behind these killings."

"We killed no one," Elil hissed, shaking his head and glancing at his wife's lifeless body. "She was all goodness. She loved you as a mother would her children. She helped your families when they were ill or injured. You, Franco! Your daughter was bitten by a dog with the sickness. Did she not save her life? And you, Eduardo! Your mother was crippled from painful joints. Inanna gave her medicine to ease the pain. Your wives and sons and daughters benefited from her generosity. This is how you repaid her?" He shoved Franco away.

Some of the villagers began to have doubts. They stepped back, each looking at the others for direction. No one said a word. Growing fear increased their uncertainty.

"She was your only hope and my life. Now you have killed her," Elil accused sadly, turning to Franco. "Finish the job. Kill me now."

Hesitantly, Franco turned to look at the rest for support. There was none.

Leaning down, Elil picked up the pitchfork he had tossed away and held it out toward Franco.

"Why do you hesitate? Are you such a coward you can't complete the task? You were brave enough to sneak into our bedchamber as we slept. Surely, you are brave enough to kill me now." He pushed the implement against the other man's chest. "Take it! I won't resist. I go to join my beloved. You destroyed my reason for living. The least you can do is finish the job."

Franco took the pitchfork hesitantly, his hand shaking, but made no attempt to attack Elil. Disgusted, Elil turned to glare at the others. The villagers retreated slightly, fearing retribution.

"I see," he said, shaking his head sadly. "Now I must finish what you began. So be it."

Standing, he stepped toward Franco. Frightened, Franco raised the pitchfork. The stench of urine and the stain spreading down his leg betrayed his terror. Elil smiled slightly, pressing his chest against the sharp tines. Reaching out, he grabbed Franco's right hand, which was tightly wrapped around the handle.

"You will bury us together deep within the earth by the river near the old oak tree. It will not atone for your sins nor save you from your fate, but it is the least you can do for us."

Franco nodded nervously, swallowing the lump in his throat. "Good."

Before Franco could react, Elil pulled sharply on the fork, forcing the three points deep into his chest. A slight grimace was the only sign of pain he showed as he sank slowly onto the bed, causing Franco to lose his balance. Falling forward, Franco felt the pitchfork push farther into the wounded man's body.

Shaken, he leapt to his feet and yanked the fork out, dropping it to the floor. Elil gathered his wife to his chest and looked one more time at his killer.

"Thank you, Franco. My Inanna would have forgiven you for this. Unfortunately, our gods are not as understanding. They will demand a price for your betrayal. Now go and prepare our funeral. You haven't much time." Elil closed his eyes and pressed his cheek to Inanna's and died.

"What have we done?" a terrified villager asked.

"What did he mean?" another whispered, fear making his voice quiver.

"I do na know," Franco replied, looking at his hands for signs of blood. *Surely, there would be blood*, he thought. "They seem asleep," he muttered, looking at their lifeless bodies. "Hurry! We must do as he told us. Tell the women to wrap and prepare their bodies."

Hours later, a procession of villagers carried Elil and Inanna to the large grave they had dug near the river. Flowers covered their bodies as they were gently lowered into the earth, each embracing the other in death as they had in life.

The terrified villagers prayed for forgiveness, unaware of the small group of people leaving the village taking only what they could carry on their backs. A chilling laughter sent a shiver down the spines of those left behind. They knew their hopes faded with each shovelful of dirt falling on the bodies lying peacefully in the ground. In killing their saviors, they had released the very demon they feared. Within a few weeks, everyone was dead.

A month after the funeral, a dark-skinned woman arrived in the village shortly after sunset. Ignoring the swollen, maggot-infested bodies scattered along the abandoned streets, she walked straight to the gravesite of the two lovers. Kneeling, she placed her palm on the mound, bent her head, and silently cried. Afterward, she walked away, leaving the stench of death and the bloated human bodies behind, a final reminder of the tragedy.

Alone for the first time in her life, with no answer as to how her parents had died, Ekimmu felt empty. She was the last of her bloodline and Isis, their goddess.

Ramus watched from the shadows, smiling smugly. Revenge was indeed sweet. He would eventually discover that even it grew bitter with time. The loss of Inanna and her chosen would bring his race to the brink of destruction. Without leaders, there were few to enforce the laws or keep the traditions and history alive. Existence became their priority. Only a handful understood it was dependent on keeping true to the old ways.

Ramus had little interest in the decline of his own people. For centuries, he continued his path of destruction across the continents. Periodically, plagues sprang up, only to mysteriously vanish. Measles, smallpox, and influenza pandemics wiped out millions in the Old World, then were carried to the New World in the late fourteen hundreds. Unexplained ebola outbreaks in the Sudan, the Ivory Coast, and Zaire occurred as recently as the late nineteen nineties.

Ramus took great pleasure experimenting on the humans. Each new disease reconfirmed his belief in his superiority over them. His greatest achievement, though, was the transference of HIV from a small colony of monkeys to some male villagers in a tribe living in Africa. After discovering the virus, it was easy for him to ingest the infected blood from a few captured animals, knowing his own metabolism could resist it. He then transfused it into several human victims, then released them relatively unharmed. It was only a matter of time before the disease spread.

Even Ramus couldn't have foretold the enormity of his actions nor did he take much satisfaction in the final results. Gebians wanted pure, untainted blood. HIV spread across the land and seas unencumbered. Between the old diseases and the new ones, it became difficult for his people to feed without arousing the suspicions of the humans. Many, thought to be vampires by the superstitious, were hunted and killed; others were incarcerated as deviants or perverts.

Imprisonment was a death sentence. Ramus had counted on

human scientists to discover a cure within a few decades. Instead, it was more than twenty years before they were able to even identify the disease. When religious fanatics labeled the epidemic an act of god to punish the gays and immoral, he realized it would be a long time before a vaccine was discovered.

Over the centuries, Ramus would occasionally find one of his own people. Rarely did he seek their company. He knew many held him responsible for the decline in their numbers. When he saw Constancia Loh Rehn, he was stunned to learn that she still lived. His last memory was of her leading a small group of villagers from a long forgotten village. He believed she had died more than a hundred years before.

In truth, he was relieved to find her alive and well. Of all his people, Om Loh Rehn was the only person he respected. She was the last of the ancients, far older than him, and the sole guardian of their history. For all his faults, even Ramus didn't wish for the extinction of his race. It was, after all, forever. And the Om was a meticulous historian.

Feeling the urge to feed, Ramus's thoughts turned to Dakota Devereaux. Something about her intrigued the Om, otherwise she wouldn't have entrusted the journalist with one of the sacred manuscripts. They told the entire history of the Gebians. Giving them to another meant only one thing. The Om was dying and needed an heir, but choosing an outsider was unthinkable. Ramus needed to know what made this woman so special.

For now, though, a nice young human male or female would satisfy his immediate needs. Perhaps he would be generous and let his victim live, he thought, feeling magnanimous.

Strolling toward the edge of town, Ramus noticed a handsome dark-haired male standing in the shadows of an alley. Ramus estimated his age at eighteen or nineteen. It was obvious he was waiting for someone, maybe a lover or perhaps just preying on one of his own. Either way, he would find neither. Gliding slowly toward the shadowed figure, Ramus smiled when the young man turned to watch him approaching. Stepping into the darkness, Ramus focused on the honey brown eyes staring back at him.

He is a predator, Ramus thought, amused at the irony. "Good evening."

A slight nod was the only acknowledgment that he had been heard.

"Perhaps you will accompany me. I have use of your services," Ramus offered.

"I'm no *she'chorne* to suck your *kori*," the teen growled, grabbing his crotch to emphasize his meaning.

"You misjudge me, tanar baiat. I merely wish to hire you as a guide. I'm new to your town. Of course I'll pay you for your time." Ramus took out his wallet and removed several large bills.

The young man's eyes narrowed greedily. Glancing up at the stranger's face, he smiled. "What do you wish to see, domn?" he asked, wiping his palms on his thighs.

Ramus handed him the bills and shrugged nonchalantly. "Perhaps tonight we'll just walk and talk. You can tell me what I should see, then we can meet tomorrow. How does that sound?"

"Cu siguranta, domn. Lead the way."

Ramus smiled, turned, and walked toward the small church at the edge of the town. "What shall I call you?" he asked without looking back.

"Valeriu."

"An unusual name, Valeriu. I believe it means strong, does it not?"

"Yes, and what's your name?"

"Ramus."

"Ramus. It's not Rumanian. Does it mean anything?"

"I'm sure it does. What do you do? A handsome tanar om such as you must have many tanaras chasing after you."

"Cu sigaranta. I am much desired by the ladies," the young man boasted. "I can have any woman I want."

"I see. You must be very good with them then."

"They don't complain."

Ramus laughed softly. The night was late and the shadows long between the church and the forests bordering it.

"You laugh?"

"Not at you. You remind me of myself in a way. I too receive no complaints."

Valeriu snorted, thinking his 'employer' probably fucked old women or young boys as long as he paid them enough. Unfortunately, he didn't notice Ramus stiffen, nor the narrowing of his eyes as he glanced in the young man's direction.

"I see you doubt my *appeal*."

"Oh, no," Valeriu lied. "I can see you have...umm...how would you say it? Machismo?"

Ramus laughed. "I would never use that word to describe myself. Tell me, Valeriu, do you believe in god?"

"Pffft. Why should I? I see nothing of him around here." He spread his arms to signal his surroundings. "Do you?"

"Maybe you haven't looked close enough."

"A waste of time. I leave god to you old people."

"I'm trying to be patient with you, my young friend, but it seems you lack manners, something I will promptly correct."

Realizing he had gone too far, Valeriu gave Ramus a childish grin. "I meant no disrespect. I am young and reckless, as you can see."

"And a fool! Come here," Ramus ordered. "I will teach you respect and show you god."

Valeriu frowned, looking around suspiciously. "Where?"

Stepping close to him, Ramus grabbed his upper arms and jerked him forward. "Here," he growled, baring his teeth.

Valeriu pushed against the taller man's chest, trying to break the painful grip. When he realized Ramus was stronger, he kicked at his captor, trying to knee him in the groin. Ramus chuckled, bending his head and sniffing.

"Mmm. What's this I smell? Fear? Of an old man? You disappoint me. Where is the bravado you had only minutes ago? Do you feel your heart pounding? I can hear it." Ramus laughed, placing a hand on the young man's chest. "Perhaps if you pray," he suggested, smirking.

"Please, let me go. I meant no harm." *God help me*, he prayed. *He's a vampire!*

Ramus's laughter grew louder but held no humor. It sent a chill down the boy's spine. "Vampire? Don't insult me! You humans are superstitious fools. Do I look like the undead?" he growled, angered at being compared to the hideous creatures doomed to wander eternity as brainless feeding machines. "I'm no more a vampire than you."

Valeriu felt a sense of relief. Perhaps the stranger just wanted to teach him a lesson. If he asked politely... "I'm sorry. I meant no insult. Please let me go. I'll do anything you want."

Ramus cocked his head and stared at the panic-stricken face. Finally, he smiled. "Certainly. All you had to do was ask—but first a little remembrance. I wouldn't want you to forget me."

Bending his head slowly, he sank his teeth into his victim's neck, puncturing the muscles and vein. Drawing the warm fluid into his mouth, he swallowed several times. Valeriu's struggles weakened until eventually he slumped limply against his captor's chest. His last conscious thought was that he was dying.

Ramus lowered the body to the ground. That night, he wasn't in a mood to play or kill.

Seeing Om Loh Rehn with Dakota nagged at him. Giving an outsider the sacred books was forbidden. It was their primary edict, tantamount to treason. Only the queen or her chosen had the power. That there were now no leaders was of no consequence. The old woman was desperate if she was looking for a new guardian, especially if she was considering a human female.

For the first time, Ramus wondered if he had carried his thirst for revenge too far. It was one thing to destroy a few lives, but if his anger set in motion the destruction of his race, that was a different matter. It was a thought he preferred not to dwell on.

Tilting his head sideways, he looked down at Valeriu and nudged the body with his toe. Satisfied the human was still alive and wouldn't remember much of anything, he laughed loudly.

"Here's a gift for you, Ms. Devereaux," he murmured, walking into the darkness. "Tonight I'm feeling generous."

CHAPTER TWELVE

Ekimmu wasn't impulsive, but she felt the urge to indulge in an early brunch. Normally not a morning person, she rarely made an appearance before late afternoon or evening. For some reason, though, her stomach was complaining almost to the point of nausea, an unusual sensation. Putting on her sunglasses, she headed to her favorite spot outside of the restaurant.

Elana, her regular waitress, smiled when she saw the blue-eyed, dark-skinned woman. She had just begun her shift and was surprised to see Ekimmu so soon.

"You're early today, Ms. Elil. What would you like for lunch?"

"Just a bowl of fruit and a small croissant." Ekimmu returned the smile.

"Not your normal order," Elana teased, placing a cup of tea on the table. "I was beginning to wonder if you ate anything besides rare steaks and veggies. I'll be right back with your food."

Ekimmu chuckled and picked up the tea. She was growing fond of the young woman. Looking around, she saw several familiar faces sitting at the other tables. Distracted, she didn't notice the tall slender woman walking past her until a slight bump to her left shoulder jarred her. Hot tea spilled from her cup onto her lap, causing her to jump up, instinctively brushing at the stain with her napkin.

"Oh, my!" the blond woman with golden eyes said. "I'm ssoo ssorry." She grabbed the napkin and dabbed at the dark stain on Ekimmu's slacks.

"It's nothing," Ekimmu replied, watching the frantic actions of her assailant.

"Nothing! Don't be ssilly. Did the tea burn you? I'll pay for the cleaning, of coursse," the woman offered, opening her purse to pull out some money.

"Really, it's okay. I spilled something on them earlier."

"It'ss a nicce lie but unneccessary. I feel sso bad about thiss. Can I at leasst buy you another cup?"

"Now that's an offer I'll take you up on." Motioning to the chair across from her, Ekimmu sat back down. "I guess we should introduce ourselves. I'm Ekimmu."

"Ekimmu, I don't think I've ever heard that name before," the woman said, extending her right hand. "I am Ssarpe."

"A rather unusual name in itself, I'd say."

"I've never thought about it. I guesss it might be."

"If my memory serves me well, it's an old Rumanian name. I believe it means serpent or snake," Ekimmu said.

Laughing, Sarpe leaned close and whispered in a conspiratorial manner. "Actually, it'ss a lot older than that. But they do like to take credit for itss origin," she said jokingly. "You're right, though. It does mean sserpent. You're very asstute."

"Not really, just well traveled. I'd say your folks had a strange sense of humor."

"And I'd ssay you might be right."

Sensing Sarpe wasn't Carpi, Ekimmu was curious about the woman's origin. Her voice was soft but lacked an accent, her words lingering slightly on words with an S. Short golden hair glimmered while golden brown eyes glinted brightly but blinked rarely, even though the sun's glare was intense and shown directly in her face. Tanned skin added to her exotic appearance. Ekimmu's eyes roamed down the slender frame dressed in dark brown slacks and a cream-colored silk blouse before returning to the eyes.

Aware of the inspection, Sarpe sat motionless. When they made eye contact again, she smiled, showing even white teeth with slightly elongated canine teeth. Faint dimples crinkled the cheeks, causing Ekimmu to inhale slowly while licking her lips unconsciously.

Both became aware of a waiter standing silently by the table holding a pitcher of water.

"So, Sarpe, what would you like?"

"Whatever you're having. I sso rarely indulge in ssuch luxuries."

"You mean tea, right?"

"But of coursse. What elsse would I mean?" she asked innocently.

"What else indeed."

Turning to the waiter, Ekimmu ordered two cups of tea and another buttered croissant. Then she focused on the woman sitting across from her. Normally, Ekimmu could guess a person's nationality. There were subtle cellular differences that gave away many things about an individual's ethnicity, race, and lineage. Ekimmu's people had identified those subtleties eons before. Sarpe had none, which made Ekimmu both uneasy and fascinated.

Sarpe leaned back in her chair, silently studying Ekimmu. While in human form, the spirit found the other woman quite pleasing to look at. In the light of day, her brown skin glistened, giving it a healthy glow. It was the eyes, though, that she found the most compelling. Blue, the color of a glacial lake on a cloudy day, made it almost impossible to look away once she made eye contact. Even Sarpe felt their power. Only her own strength allowed her the opportunity to return the gaze unmoved.

"Well," Ekimmu said, suddenly feeling very uncomfortable. "Where do we go from here?"

Sarpe smiled. "Where would you like to go?" she countered, arching her right eyebrow.

The question caught Ekimmu off-guard. Adjusting her seat slightly to keep the sun's rays away from her skin, she laughed. Sarpe glanced at the angle of the light, making a mental note of the woman's action.

"I think this is one of the few times in my life I don't know what to say," Ekimmu confessed. "Perhaps if you told me something about yourself, it'd be a start. After all, it was you who assaulted me."

"Very true. Good manners would require me to sstart, I ssuppose," Sarpe agreed.

"I didn't mean it that way."

Waving her hand nonchalantly, Sarpe chuckled. "Fair is fair. Assk a quesstion and I'll try to answwer."

Shaking her head, Ekimmu relaxed. "Nicely done. Now the ball's back in my court. Let's see. How about you tell me a little about where you're from and what you do?"

"Hmm. If I were to choose my place of origin, I'd have to ssay here and I really don't do much of anything."

"Now that's informative," Ekimmu teased. "Place of origin is a strange way to describe where you're from. I'm assuming you mean you were born in Moldova."

Laughing softly, Sarpe leaned forward slightly and winked. "That would be the asssumption, yess."

"A woman of mystery, I see. Okay. I'll let that go for now. It's obvious you're not Carpi."

"Why obviouss?"

"You don't have the right accent. Nor do you have any of their physical characteristics. At best, you or your family are transplants."

"I ssee there is a very sharp mind behind those beautiful blue eyes."

Taken aback by the compliment, Ekimmu felt the blood rush to her face.

"Have I embarrasssed you? I do apologize," Sarpe said, reaching out and covering the other woman's hand with her own. "I tend to ssay what is on my mind when I'm around...*people*."

Ekimmu noticed the slight hesitation on the last word but was distracted by the cool hand holding her own. Enjoying the contact, Ekimmu turned her palm up and gently clasped the other woman's hand.

"So I see. I have the feeling you don't spend much time around people. You seem a little uncomfortable."

"Am I that obvious?"

Tilting her head to the side, she stared at Ekimmu curiously.

"As a matter of fact, yes, but don't worry. I'm sure no one notices," she smirked. "Maybe it would be easier if we started on less personal grounds," she suggested.

"A good idea. How do you like Teraclia and itss people?"

"I love it here. The climate is wonderful and the people are *fascinating*."

"I take it thiss is your first visit then."

"No, I've been here before, a long time ago."

Breaking eye contact, Ekimmu looked wistfully at their hands still clasped on the table.

"Ssad memories?"

Ekimmu looked into Sarpe's eyes, momentarily caught off-guard. "No, not really. Actually, they were good times. My parents and I stayed here a few years. That's how I learned the language. We moved around a lot, though. This is the first time I've been able to come back. It's changed a lot."

"Time does that. Sstill, you can't be more than thirty-three. There musst be ssome things that have remained the ssame."

Ekimmu laughed. "One would think. I guess I've just forgotten them."

The comment required no response, so Sarpe remained silent.

When the waiter arrived with their drinks and pastries, both were relieved at the distraction. Reluctantly, they released each other's hand and felt an immediate loneliness.

"They make the flakiest pastries here," Ekimmu said, wanting to change the subject.

"I'll take your word for it."

A sudden feeling of being watched made Sarpe uncomfortable. Looking around, she noticed a tall, pale-skinned man standing near a newsstand leafing through a magazine. Had it not been for the subtle glances he cast in their direction, she would have completely overlooked him. Sarpe knew he was the source of her uneasiness.

Pushing the untouched food away, she stood. "I'm sso ssorry, Ekimmu, but I didn't realize how late it is. I need to take care of ssome business while there's sstill enough daylight."

Ekimmu rose to her feet automatically. "Certainly! Perhaps another day," she stammered, clearly dissappointed.

"I would like that. Are you sstaying at the hotel?"

"For a few more days. Then I'll be moving on."

"Good. I'll be in contact. Oh, I'll need your lasst name when I call."

"Elil."

"Well, Ekimmu Elil. I've enjoyed our time together. I'll call."

Placing her napkin on the table, Sarpe walked away. Ekimmu watched the sway of her hips and how her body flowed easily with each step.

"Damn!" she muttered. "I could definitely get up close and personal with that one."

After Sarpe disappeared around the corner, Ekimmu realized she hadn't asked the woman her last name. Sarpe had subtly controlled the conversation. The thought left her feeling extremely vulnerable and restless.

"I need a good walk," she muttered, remembering the soothing coolness of the nearby forest.

Shortly after sunset, Ekimmu decided to return to her hotel room. It was then she heard the wolves baying. Recognizing the pain in their cries, she hurried in the direction of the howls.

CHAPTER THIRTEEN

Yemaya stared into the flames of the huge stone fireplace. Summer was approaching, but it didn't stop the nights from becoming cold and damp. Dakota had called to say she would be late, something Yemaya wasn't thrilled about but had refrained from commenting on.

Dakota was very independent, and after their recent argument, Yemaya didn't want to do or say anything to cause more problems. Still, she had sent Regina and her pack out to patrol the area in case there was something wandering around the woods.

In the meantime, her encounter with Lia had left her tired. Dreams normally told a story if they could be dissected and properly analyzed. This one was definitely saying something, but what she didn't know. Lia was being tormented. The orange flames terrified the young woman. The blue, however, seemed protective. Yemaya couldn't shake the feeling that the blue and orange flames were connected, perhaps even the same entity. It could be symptoms from a new strain of virus.

Rubbing her eyes, she decided she was just too tired to think about it. Perhaps when Dakota got home, she'd have something to add. A knock on the door interrupted her thoughts. "Come in."

"I'm sorry for the intrusion, but Mr. Marino called. He wants you to phone him tomorrow about your new show. He said he's trying to line up the European tour and needs to know what you'll require and a list of the cities you wish to perform in."

"Thanks, Maria."

"Oh, and he said Shezarra is on her way home, wherever that may be."

"A long way from civilization. I just hope she stays there. I would hate to have some fisherman killing or capturing her because she has no fear of humans. Go to bed."

"Yes, mistress, and I suggest you do the same. The wolves will let us know when Ms. Dakota arrives."

"In a few minutes."

After the housekeeper left, Yemaya thought about her new act. Now that Shezarra was free, she wanted to try something different but, so far, hadn't come up with any ideas.

Yawning, she decided it was time to call it a night. Sleep was impossible anyway until her lover was snuggled close to her. Just the thought of Dakota's warm body touching hers was enough to arouse Yemaya. If Dakota didn't make it home soon, she was definitely going to need a cold shower.

The ringing of the telephone interrupted her musings. Looking at the grandfather clock in the corner, she frowned wondering who would call so late. "Hello? Lysannes."

"Ms. Lysanne? This is Dr. Lichy. I'm sorry to bother you this late."

"No need to apologize, Doctor. What can I do for you?"

"I thought you'd be interested in the lab report that just came in."

"At this time of night? You keep late hours."

"I decided to wait for the test results, hoping something would show up. The techs just called it in."

"I take it they found something?"

"Yes and no. Most of the results are normal. The white cell count was a little high, but that's expected considering the blood loss. What was interesting, though, is an unusual bacteria found in her blood. So far, the lab hasn't identified it. It could be a new strain."

"You think this is causing the comas?"

"It's possible. Although the amount of bacteria is so small, I can't see how. If it is, though, this strain could be catastrophic if it becomes widespread. I'm more inclined to think it has something to do with the dreams, although I'm not discounting the coma part. Certainly, the toxins they released into the bloodstream could be affecting the neurological system. We're trying to isolate it to see how it affects mice, but it could take several weeks or months for those results."

"At least it sounds more promising. I would rather have a scientific explanation than deal with the supernatural."

"You and me both," Dr. Lichy said. "I'll let you know what the lab comes up with."

"Thank you. Anything will help. If they can figure out what strain this is, we might be able to discover its source and prevent a serious problem."

"I agree. Unfortunately, my experience has been that these things appear suddenly then disappear just as quickly. We may never discover the source."

"As long as it goes away with no further victims."

"Let's hope that's the case. Thankfully, it doesn't seem to cause permanent damage to the patients. Lia regained consciousness this evening and should be able to go home tomorrow. Other than losing a few pounds, she's in good health. She doesn't remember anything, though."

"Maybe she will later. Tell her Andrei will take her home tomorrow. Please make sure someone stays with her for a few days."

"I will. Have a good night, Ms. Lysanne."

"You too, Doctor."

Yemaya hung up the phone and sank back in the oversized leather chair. The news of the bacteria changed everything. With a possible scientific explanation, she felt better. Still, it was a good idea to keep all options open until they were sure. Glancing again at the clock, she yawned and decided to get some rest.

Running up the stairs, she began undressing when wolf howls broke the silence. Walking to the window, she opened it to listen. Something was definitely wrong.

Shadows moved near the drawbridge. Yemaya recognized Simtire amongst the pack and called to her.

"Simtire. Wait!" she ordered. She changed quickly into hiking clothes and boots and ran out the door, almost colliding with Maria and Andrei.

"We heard them, too," Andrei said.

"Follow me with some of the men. Something is terribly wrong. Simtire will show me the way. One of the others will wait for you. Marie, call me when Dakota gets in. I have my cell phone."

Grabbing the small backpack Marie was holding, she trotted toward the young wolf waiting by the drawbridge. The two disappeared into the woods.

"I don't like this," Marie muttered, turning to Andrei.

Shaking his head, Andrei picked up his own pack.

"Neither do I. Call Bruneo and Cheznic. Tell them to get Romano and let him know the mistress may be in trouble. One of the wolves will meet them at their campsite." Looking into the darkness, he sighed. "She's a brave woman, but whatever can upset the wolves this badly may be more than even she can handle. I don't like her going off alone like this."

"She knows what she's doing. Yemaya was raised in these woods and Simtire is with her."

"Maybe, but Simtire is young and inexperienced. Youth and caution rarely travel the same paths. I'll call you when I find out what's happening."

Several young wolves crouched on the far side of the moat. Seeing Andrei, they wagged their tails enthusiastically before jumping up to run to him. Laughing, he petted each one before motioning them to move out.

Regina was the first to catch the smell of death. Turning her nose to the wind, she inhaled deeply and whined. Clovn's scent was strong. Anxious to make sure her youngest pup was well, she loped in the direction of the smells. Voinic caught up and charged ahead to ensure the safety of his mate, as well as his offspring.

In the shadows of the forest, well beyond the town lights lay the body of a young wolf. Beside him lay Voinic's daughter, Clovn. He stopped and tested the air. The stench of another animal filled his nostrils. Growling, hackles raised, he crouched, unwilling to approach the two wolves without ensuring it was safe to do so.

Seeing her mate's agitation, Regina circled the area but found no visible signs of an enemy. Both wolves slowly moved forward. Voinic sniffed at the body of the young male. Although not a member of his pack, he recognized him as kin to the wolves in the next valley. After nudging the body several times, he lay down and rested his chin on the cooling body.

Cautiously, Regina nudged Clovn, hoping for some sign that she had survived whatever attacked them. Rubbing her cheek against her daughter's, she whined softly. When that failed, she licked Clovn's face tenderly. In her heart, she knew her youngest pup was dead. Raising her nose to the sky, Regina howled, voicing the age-old anguish of a mother who had lost a child.

The wind carried her cries through the forest, across the high ridges, and into the mountains beyond. Voinic joined in, their mournful howls announcing to the world their losses. Within seconds, they were answered by the other packs. The howls traveled quickly from clan to clan until the dead male wolf's family received the news. For nearly an hour, the countryside was filled with the sound of sorrow. The forest remained unnaturally silent.

In their grief, the two wolves failed to notice the human form standing in the shadows until it stepped into the moonlight. Raising her head to watch the approaching figure, Regina whined but didn't move other than again lowering her chin protectively across Clovn's face.

The woman knelt and stroked the graying fur of the old wolf's forehead. "I feel your loss, Queen Regina," she murmured softly, her voice low and soothing. "No mother should lose a child."

Regina kept her eyes closed, comforted by the warm hand stroking her forehead. The woman stood and moved to Voinic, who watched the exchange between his mate and her. Growling slightly, he warned her that he was less accepting of her presence.

"I understand," she said, acknowledging his objection. "I'll respect your privacy. I only wish to see the cause of their deaths."

Voinic stared unblinkingly into her eyes before finally lowering his head.

"Thank you."

Again the woman knelt, running her hand over the soft fur of the dead male. When it passed over the neck, she stopped to probe the muscles and spine. The neck was broken but in such a way as to keep the animal alive for a short period. Frowning, she returned to Clovn's body and found the same injury. She leaned down and peered closely at the throat. Sighing, she stood to leave.

"Your mistress comes. She'll take care of your child and her playmate. Remember well the smells you first noticed here, queen. That is the scent of both death and the killer. You must warn the packs to avoid this one. You can't defeat him. Only your mistress can, if she's wise and lucky."

The woman walked away and disappeared into the shadows. Regina reluctantly left Clovn to nudge her mate, sending him on his way to find the mistress. She would guard the bodies. Unhappy about leaving Regina alone, Voinic grudgingly conceded, loping quickly away into the darkness.

Twenty minutes later, he located Yemaya trotting in his direction with Simtire in the lead. Whining softly, he sank to his belly and crawled toward her. Yemaya knelt beside the old wolf, resting her head against his. Wrapping her arms around his neck, she held him against her breast, sensing his need. His pain was unbearable, but for his sake, she endured the waves of grief hoping to give him some comfort.

"I am so sorry, Voinic," she whispered, her voice husky from unshed tears. "We must go now. Regina needs us."

Rising tiredly, Voinic growled, looking in the direction Yemaya had come. Within minutes, Andrei and the rest of the pack appeared. Several of the younger males ran to Voinic, sniffing to make sure their sire was okay.

"I thought I told you to bring the men," Yemaya grumbled, reluctant to show her relief at having his company.

"They're on the way. I've telephoned our location to Cheznic. He and Bruneo are meeting Romano's men by the river and will be coming up from that direction. They should be here in about twenty minutes. The wolves will show them the way."

"Very good. Clovn and another wolf have been killed. Regina is guarding the bodies, so we need to make sure she is still safe."

"It's a sad day for all, mistress," Andrei said, his voice breaking slightly.

"Yes" was all Yemaya said, motioning for Voinic to take the lead.

Yemaya would never forget the scene before her—the bodies of the two young wolves, cold and stiff, Regina lying next to them, her head resting wearily on Clovn's.

Eyes closed, the old female acknowledged Yemaya's arrival with only the faint flick of her tail. Andrei quickly brushed a tear away as he knelt next to the three wolves. Yemaya sat by the old queen and her daughter. Placing her hand on Clovn's forehead, she closed her eyes and concentrated.

Overwhelmed by a sense of freedom, Yemaya could feel Clovn's youthful exuberance bouncing around the young male, teasing him mercilessly as she flirted. Eager to impress her, the wolf nipped playfully at her shoulder before dashing off, only to stop a few feet away, a wide wolfish grin spread across his face. Their playful enthusiasm prevailed over caution, leaving both vulnerable to the stranger watching from the shadows.

Clovn was the first to smell him. Hackles raised, she growled, baring long fangs. The male wolf reacted quickly, stepping in front of Clovn to protect her from the intruder.

Yemaya shivered at the sinister laughter coming from the tall, humanlike figure who stepped from the shadows. She could feel Clovn's confusion. Nothing about his smell was human. Nudging the male, she whined, wanting to retreat. Unfortunately, the young male wanted to impress her with his bravery and shouldered her aside. Crouching slightly, he slowly approached the stranger, growling ominously. Had the man been more human, both wolves would have loped off into the darkness.

It was the taunting laughter that was the wolf's undoing. Inexperienced, the wolf sensed the mockery and lunged. With unnatural speed, the man grabbed the wolf by the throat and held him high above the ground. Clovn reacted by launching herself at the man's face, but he turned, placing the body of the struggling male between them. His laughter mocked her.

"Try again, young one," he taunted, shaking the helpless animal in his grasp. "Here, let me give you some incentive." With a sharp twist, he snapped the wolf's neck, flinging the limp body to the side. Holding his hands out, he motioned her forward. "Come! You can do it. He was weak, but you're strong. I smell it in your blood. You know you want me," he coaxed.

Growling, Clovn looked at the limp body of her friend, then back at him, unsure of what she should do. Her decision was made when she saw him pick up the dead wolf and bite into its neck, blood running from the wound and down the silver fur. Fury replaced common sense and training. Clovn snarled and attacked. When the hands closed around her throat, she struggled, kicking and snarling at the creature holding her captive. His laughter only increased her fury and her fear.

"Your mistress will be proud of you. Such a shame you have to die so young, but alas, life is filled with inequities. Your death is sure to get her attention. If not, there's always the journalist."

Clovn growled and snapped at the hands around her throat

desperate to free herself. Ramus laughed, amused at the wolf's feeble attempts, and tightened his grip.

"Now, now. Is that any way to act? You should consider this an honor. Your death will ensure a meeting between your mistress and me, something I'm very much looking forward to. She seems to have very unusual skills that I find rather *interesting*. So you see, you're the messenger and unfortunately, in this case, I am killing the messenger."

With a flick of his wrist, Clovn felt a slight twinge. The image of Regina passed swiftly through her mind and she whimpered.

Yemaya jerked her hand away as if burnt. Shaking uncontrollably, she rocked back on her heels, trying to distance herself from the lifeless body. The image of the young wolf's last cry for her mother and the blackness rushing in to steal her soul was unsettling.

Her own darkness stirred restlessly, sensing a weakness in the defenses she had built against it. Recognizing the time wasn't right, the *beast* settled back into its cave. It was learning patience.

Yemaya took a deep breath. Tears streamed down her cheeks. She shifted Regina's head onto her lap, stroking it tenderly. Words eluded her. Silence was the only comfort she could offer her lifelong companion and friend.

A wolf mother's love was as great as any human's, perhaps greater since their lives were often shortened by the harshness of their environment. She would deal with the killer later when the time was right.

Andrei clutched the thick fur around Voinic's neck, massaging the tense muscles. From across the clearing, several men approached quietly, making sure not to disturb Yemaya and the aging female wolf.

"Ola, Romano," Andrei said in a low voice. "It's late and this is a hard climb for you. You should have just sent the younger men to handle this."

"Andrei. It's good to see you. You know I would never disgrace my people by remaining behind. I'm their leader. I don't *stay behind* on matters this grave."

"The mistress and the queen would understand. If something happened to you on the way here, they'd be devastated."

"I'm old, not decrepit. Don't bury me before my time."

Chuckling, Andrei slapped his friend on the back. "Forgive me. You're right."

The men stood quietly watching Yemaya and Regina.

"This is a sad day for all of us," Romano said, his brown eyes watering from unshed tears.

"Yes. The old queen has lost her youngest and possibly the last she will ever bear."

"Regina has lived a long life. I fear she has only a few years left. Tonight's sorrow will be nothing compared to the day her spirit moves on. She and Yemaya have been together almost eighteen years."

Nodding, Andrei didn't want to dwell on that inevitability. "We must take the bodies to the burial grounds and perform the ritual to send their souls to the afterlife. Can you send your men ahead to make the preparations?"

"It's already done. They await our arrival. Vyushir won't be disappointed."

"Thank you."

After a few minutes, the men heard Yemaya whispering, her voice tinged with sorrow.

"It is time, Regina. My people will take care of Clovn and her young friend."

Regina refused to move, whimpering softly. Yemaya pressed her cheek against the graying forehead, feeling suddenly very old and tired. Realizing she had tuned in on the wolf's emotions, she ruffled her fur gently.

"I know you want to be near her, but I need your help if we are to find this killer. Others are in danger. I can't do this without you."

Regina raised her head to stare into the eyes of her mistress, offering everything she had to give. Yemaya felt herself being drawn into the world of the wolf's mind. Coffee brown irises gleamed silver, reflecting the light from the moon. Images wavered and danced elusively as she saw and felt the pain. Had she not been invited into this merging, she would have felt like an intruder.

Both understood the importance of the connection, so she continued watching the events prior to her arrival. It was the shadowy figure of a woman that temporarily pushed away the sorrow. Not only had she offered the wolves comfort, but neither

Regina nor Voinic had objected to the stranger's presence. Regina had even accepted her comforting touch and words as if she were an old acquaintance.

"Who is this woman?"

Regina had no answer. Time was irrelevant in a wolf's life. Although stories and information were passed down from one generation to the next, the origins of them held no significance other than for learning and keeping the alliances.

"Have you met her before?" Yemaya continued, trying to fathom the connection between the stranger and the wolves. The negative response made her frown. "But you trust her. Why?"

Regina couldn't explain why. At best, Yemaya caught a fleeting vision of Corona, Regina's mother, Silva, her grandmother, then shadowy images of wolves beyond them. This usually signified a past well beyond the memories of their lifetimes. To refer to such a period meant the wolves were honor bound by a pact made in the distant past.

Yemaya found the thought unsettling. To her knowledge, only her family held such an alliance. Regina nuzzled her mistress's hand to reassure her. One had nothing to do with the other. The images of the mountain wolves flashed through her mind, along with the stranger's, Yemaya's, and curiously Dakota's. Smiling, Yemaya felt comforted.

"Thank you, Regina. I am neither mistress nor keeper of the wolves. You owe me no explanation. I only wish to understand who is friend and who is enemy. Is there anything else that might help?"

The feeling of the stranger's touch stroking Regina's head was disconcerting. The touch was warm and soothing, like the blue flames in Lia's dreams.

"We must leave now. Your daughter is in good hands. Vyushir will guide her spirit to a place free of pain and hunger. You will see her again."

Motioning for Andrei and Romano to take over, Yemaya stood and walked away. It would take her and Regina a couple of hours to get home.

"You know what to do," she said, turning to Andrei.

"Yes. They'll be honored in the old way."

"Thank you again, Andrei. We have had too many of these

funerals lately. Hopefully, this is the last for many years."

Andrei nodded his agreement.

"Romano, you should not have come here. It is too long a hike from your camp."

"It's my duty and my wish. Would you expect me to do otherwise?"

Giving the old gypsy a quick hug, she shook her head. "No, but I still worry about you. Would you have *me* any different?"

Romano smiled and motioned for two of his men to pick up the wolves' bodies.

"Preparations are made, Yemaya. Go home!" he ordered brusquely, then followed his gypsies into the forest.

Andrei pulled gently on Voinic's fur, a sign for the old male to accompany him. Voinic looked to Regina for permission before walking slowly away with the stocky human.

Stroking Regina's head, Yemaya leaned down and whispered. "Tonight, when all is quiet and you are resting, Vyushir will come for you so that you may run with your daughter's spirit. She is only gone in body. I promise you this."

Regina again nuzzled Yemaya's hand gratefully. The mistress never made promises she couldn't keep. It would give her comfort to see Clovn one more time.

CHAPTER FOURTEEN

Dakota lay on the couch, thumbing through the manuscript Constance had entrusted her with. It was obvious it spanned thousands of years of culture. Much of the content was transcribed from personal diaries of Gebian women.

"Listen to this," Dakota said, stopping at one of the entries. "It's dated almost seven thousand years ago. I didn't even know there was a written language that old."

Yemaya looked up from her notes, having returned an hour earlier from her rendezvous with the wolves. She had given Dakota a brief sketch of events but didn't go into a lot of details. Aware of her lover's need to come to terms with the loss, Dakota didn't question her. She suggested they relax in the den and asked Maria to make them warm chocolate.

"If those transcripts are real, it would turn historians on their heads," Yemaya replied. "I find it curious this is the first time we've heard about these people. What does it say?"

"Let's see. Okay. Here goes."

Day 7 Cycle 3 of Queen Pherena's 13th year
I weep for my children. All of them! The gods have cursed me. I am unable to bear a live child. Carliff swears it makes no difference. He says he will always love me, but I fear his love will fade if our next one dies. Today a friend told me of a secret society of women who can help me. I promised not to reveal their existence to anyone. I do not like deceiving Carliff, but I will do anything to have the child in my belly. Tonight I meet one of these women. She will take me to meet the others. —Eleesa

"It ends there, but another entry two days later picks up on it."

Leaning back in her chair, Yemaya listened as Dakota continued reading.

Day 9 Cycle 3 of Queen Pherena's 13th year
I am so excited. Constancia gives me hope. She says my child
will live if I follow her instructions. She is wise. I do not understand
why the secrecy. The lives they could save would ensure the survival
of our people. Tomorrow I take the vows and drink the sacred blood.
It is a small price for the life of my child. —Eleesa

"Hmm...There seems to be some pages missing or she didn't
write for a while."
"Probably the latter. Where does it go from there?"
"About three weeks later. Let's see."

Day 21 Cycle 9 of Queen Pherena's 13th year
We are doing well. My faith in the society grows each day. I
cannot believe it. Soon I will be a mother. I am hoping for a son.
Carliff is happy. He has been so good to me. I wish I could tell him
about the ceremony. —Eleesa

"Does she say what this ceremony is, what she means by the
sacred blood?"
"No. At least nothing so far. Wait, here's something. It's several
years later." Thumbing through the pages, Dakota frowned. "The
first part of the manuscript appears to be copies of personal diaries.
Okay, here goes."

Day 12 Cycle 9 of Queen Pherena's 28th year
It is time. My daughter must learn the truth if she is to save her
unborn child. I tried to tell her when she carried her first, but she
thought me old and witless. Her daughter was born dead. Now my
daughter will listen. I will tell her of the ritual and its history. If she
agrees to take the sacred oath and drinks the blood, she will save
the child growing in her womb. In time, she will pass the truth on to
her own daughters. It is not something we are proud of, but it gives
us hope. Every life has become precious to our existence. My people
are dying. We thought ourselves doomed until the coming of the
wise one. She showed us the way. The solution seems so simple now.
Why did we not see what was before our very eyes? The cravings.

106

Our savior was the life force flowing within all life—blood. We tried the raw meat of animals, and it helped but was not enough. While carrying the child, we needed more, so we drank the blood of wild beasts, hoping the precious liquid would satisfy our needs. It did not. Ours was the only blood that guaranteed our children's survival, and we offered our own to protect our unborn...until we discovered the primitives. Their blood fulfilled our needs. Isis has blessed our people. Our children live and thrive. Is that not proof enough? —Eleesa

"This sounds more like a Stephen King story than a history book," Dakota said, flipping a few more pages.

"Truth can be that way. Is there any reference to actual dates other than mentioning the reigning queens?"

"Not really. They talk a little about Isis, but that doesn't help. I wonder if there's a way to find out when she was supposed to have existed."

"Well, you *are* the Internet expert. You tell me."

"Very funny! Seriously, though, I don't see where this has anythi—" Dakota frowned, turning the manuscript into the light to get a better view.

"What?"

"Listen to this! It was written several centuries later."

Did we really think we could keep the secret forever? That our men would not notice how we kept our youth and our beauty while they grew old and feeble? Or that one of us would not betray the society for love? Did Ma'at really believe when she told her beloved Anubis of our rituals that he would keep the knowledge to himself and not want his own family and friends to live as long as him? Could anyone be so innocent or trusting as she to betray herself and the society by breaking the vow? Was her love so great she threw away her honor to be with her husband? Who's to say? And who am I to judge? All these questions and no answers. Alas, the deed is done. Men know the secret of our longevity and choose to partake of the elixir of the primitives to increase their own lives. What once was a sacred act of survival for our people has become a lust for longer lives. Some think we may even achieve immortality now. Who is to say? Constancia believes we will only be long lived...but how long, no one knows. I know of no female Gebian who has died of age or illness since the taking began. We seem immune to sickness. Death only comes at the hands of the gods and they pay little attention to mortals. May Isis forgive us for what we have become.

"Let me see that!"

Dakota handed Yemaya the manuscript and watched her scan the pages.

"This really does cover thousands and thousands of years," she said in amazement.

"I know. That's why I think this is more like folklore. It's a great story, though, don't you think?"

"If it is a story. Something about this feels real, though."

Yemaya read another excerpt.

Our people are mad and so the elders have ordered new laws to be enacted to bring the sanity back. As the historian of my people, I am to present them to our queen by the next full moon. If she approves, her chosen will enforce these laws and all must obey. It is a great honor and a great burden to be granted this privilege. The primary decree must forbid future killings. Some of our men have succumbed to the bloodlust in the belief it would make them immortal. Our women only take small amounts of the sacred fluid and live equally long lives. I believe it will work the same for males. This must be the primary and most important rule. We must take only enough to sustain our needs. Next, it will be forbidden to disclose our existence to the primitives. Their ability to reason has evolved greatly. Our survival depends on our anonymity. In time, they will fear us and hunt us to extinction. Third, there must be only one historian. She will be the guardian of our history ensuring its purity. Since power and wealth pass from mother to daughter, as ordained by Isis and Geb, the guardian will also be a woman. Once approved by our Queen, Antianna, the 123rd descendent of Isis, these laws will remain forever unchanged.

Yemaya put the manuscript down and leaned back in her chair.

"Wow! That's rather intense," Dakota said. "What do you think?"

"I am not sure yet. There are a lot of details for it to be fiction. It is either a great story or possibly a potential nightmare."

"Yeah. Makes me want to believe in vampires now."

"I would not go that far. Nothing could compare to such a horror," Yemaya warned. "Did Ms. Lorraine say anything in particular about this manuscript?"

"No, she wanted me to read it and return it to her as quickly as possible," Dakota said. "Did you notice the references to Constancia?"

"Not really, why?"

"Maybe it's just coincidence, but Ms. Lorraine's first name is Constance."

"It is an old and very common name."

"Maybe. Still...."

"I am not sure if any of this has to do with what is happening in Teraclia, but it definitely gives us something to think about." She handed the manuscript back to Dakota.

Before Dakota could reply, Yemaya's cell phone rang.

"Yemaya here...Good evening, Dr. Lichy...No, I have time to talk...What can I do for you?"

Dakota watched her lover's face as she listened to the one-sided conversation while she continued to flip through several more pages.

"When did they find him?" Yemaya asked, giving Dakota a strange glance. "I see...The same symptoms? I will come by tomorrow. Perhaps the rest of the tests will be in by then."

Hanging up the phone, she turned to Dakota. "Another victim has turned up. This time, a young man. Hopefully, Dr. Lichy will have more news by tomorrow."

"Maybe I can do some more research, too," Dakota said. "I can't see how these people, even if they exist, have anything to do with what's happening here. I must admit, though, I'm anxious to finish reading this. I can accept a few coincidences, but there's a limit."

"Did you find something else?"

"Well, this is a little spooky." Dakota read a small excerpt.

What has become of our people? The men wander the planet lusting for immortality. The women pretend not to notice. The queen has ordered all to obey the laws as set forth by Isis and Geb or face the wrath of both the gods and her chosen. I pray our people will listen, but I fear many will not. Already Ramus has denounced Inanna and Elil as weaklings, unfit to rule. I believe his hatred for our queen and her chosen has affected his mind. He will need watching for he fears nothing and no one.

"That's the name of the man in the elevator." She looked up at Yemaya. "Do you think he's related to this guy?"

"I honestly am not sure. It is a possibility. You did say your historian commented on these people being long lived."

"But that would make him several thousand years old. That isn't possible."

"Nothing is impossible, but I agree. Still, I like to keep an open mind. There are fewer surprises that way."

"I suppose." Dakota yawned. "I don't know about you, but I'm exhausted. Let's get a few hours of sleep and maybe things will make more sense in the morning." She laid the manuscript on the table.

Grinning, Yemaya jumped up and reached down to pull Dakota to her feet.

"Great idea! The last one in bed gets a back rub," she challenged, grinning broadly.

"Oh, like that's supposed to make me hurry or something?"

"I hope not. It just makes me want to be first." Yemaya laughed. "Then I get the top."

"Damn! I didn't think of that." Pushing Yemaya backward onto the couch, Dakota dashed to the door, slamming it loudly behind her. Shaking her head, Yemaya grinned to herself.

"Looks like I get the back rub," she chuckled. "I do so hate to lose," she added, casually strolling from the room and up the stairs.

CHAPTER FIFTEEN

S arpe could do nothing to save the wolves. The species was not hers to protect. Still, she felt a deep sorrow over the death of the two youngsters. She would make sure that Vyushir knew of their bravery, even if the foolish bravado of youth had cost them their lives.

For several hours, the serpent spirit had wandered deep into the forest, her thoughts continually returning to Ekimmu. Something about the woman unnerved her. She had never felt that before. Sarpe rarely assumed human form. The effort was exhausting, requiring a lot of concentration and energy.

Lying quietly amongst the leaves in her natural form, she watched the wolves romping playfully in the meadow, oblivious to the world around them.

When the tall man appeared, Sarpe immediately sensed a powerful darkness. It reeked of an evil she had touched upon only a few times in her long existence, although never in human form. She didn't know its origin but was very much aware of the destruction that usually followed its coming.

Watching him kill and feed from the wolves was painful for her. Although their deaths didn't involve her species, Sarpe felt an obligation to Vyushir to at least let her know how they died. The wolf spirit would seek her own justice.

Ekimmu's arrival had surprised Sarpe but not as much as Regina and Voinic's acceptance of her. Wolves rarely allowed outsiders into their world; that Ekimmu could actually touch the alpha mother or her dead offspring confirmed a bond between the two species.

Shifting into human form, Sarpe followed Ekimmu until they arrived at the outskirts of Teraclia. Only then did she make her presence known.

"A nisse night for a walk," she said, startling Ekimmu.

"Where'd you come from?" Ekimmu demanded, uncomfortable at not having noticed the woman sooner.

"Oh, I dessided to take a sstroll and notissed you sstanding here."

"You must have good vision then."

The sarcasm didn't escape the spirit. "Yess, as a matter of fact, I have exssellent vision," Sarpe said, smiling.

Since Ekimmu's vision was also exceptional, she noticed the smile and chuckled. Stepping close to Sarpe, she leaned toward her and whispered, "I think there's more to you than excellent vision."

"And what would that be?" Sarpe asked, amused at the woman's audacity.

"At the moment, I'm not sure. But I'll know shortly," Ekimmu promised.

Neither knew who made the first move when their bodies merged. Sarpe felt the heat pulsating through her as Ekimmu wrapped her arms around her in a gentle embrace. Orange flames danced mysteriously within the pale blue eyes, making it impossible for Sarpe to break eye contact.

They swayed slowly back and forth, Ekimmu's eyes drawing her into a world of hot, lustful sensuality, a feeling unfamiliar to the spirit. Waves of heat pulsed though her like rays from a warm summer sun lulling her into a sense of serenity. Her body, pressed tightly to Ekimmu's, savored its soothing warmth, robbing her of all thought except the desire to become one with her captor. Leaning her head against Ekimmu's shoulder, she relaxed and for the first time in her long existence, felt at peace.

Ekimmu burned inside. Desire overwhelmed her. An uncontrollable need to touch and taste her mysterious captive confused her. She had experienced lust many times in her life, but never anything so powerful. Sarpe's body was cool and refreshing, a soothing balm to the fierce fire raging through Ekimmu. Pressing her lips against Sarpe's neck, she flicked it with her tongue, surprised at the musky, honey sweet flavor. Craving more, she gently took the skin between her teeth, wanting to taste.

Sarpe shivered as the tongue caressed her neck, the sensation both chilling and exciting. It was the teeth that brought her to her senses, causing her to jerk away, startling Ekimmu. The spirit quickly stepped away, confusion evident in her expression as she reached up to rub her neck.

"Thiss isn't ssuch a good idea," she said softly.

"I wouldn't have hurt you."

"It's not me I'm thinking of."

Ekimmu frowned. "I don't understand."

"I know. Let'ss ssay I'm not what you think I am." Sarpe sighed. "I can't let you sseek what you want from me."

"I want you," Ekimmu said. "I need to touch and taste you."

Sarpe stared at the woman. She too felt a need to experience the sensations Ekimmu had just described. "I wish it could be sso, but I could never allow you to feed from me, although I don't find the thought at all repulssive."

"You know!" Ekimmu exclaimed, surprised.

"I ssaw you with the human female. I watched your dansse."

Ekimmu frowned, remembering back to the night she and Lia had met. Other than the girl and her, the area had been devoid of any life form except for the strange snake. Shaking her head, she rejected the absurdity that Sarpe and the snake were somehow connected.

Sarpe smiled but said nothing, giving Ekimmu time to think.

Perhaps it was the moonlight reflecting off the golden brown eyes, perhaps the musky scent of the woman, or just the inevitable conclusion.

"Who or what are you?"

"I could assk you the ssame questions," Sarpe said, stepping away. Ekimmu inhaled slowly, not wanting to believe what her mind told her was true.

"You know who I am," Ekimmu said evasively.

"I know what name you call yourssself and that you appear human, but you aren't. Sso, the quesstion is, who or what are you?"

"This is ridiculous. Of course I'm human. What else is there?"

"A good quesstion."

"You haven't answered my question."

"It would sseem that what you ssee is what you get, according to you. As you ssaid, what elsse is there?" Sarpe smirked.

"Touché." Ekimmu chuckled. "So we apparently have a standoff unless one of us takes the initiative, right?"

Nodding, Sarpe remained silent. It would be up to Ekimmu to take that step. Sensing the moment of truth, Ekimmu wasn't sure what to do. She wanted to know Sarpe better. Sighing, she took Sarpe's hand and pulled her toward a grassy moonlit area. Lying down on her back, she rested on her elbows and stared up at the stars.

"Come on! Lie down." Ekimmu patted the grass. "Somehow I think you'll find it familiar ground. No pun intended."

Smiling, Sarpe lay on her side, her head resting on one hand.

"Where to begin?" Ekimmu mused.

"A wisse persson onsse ssaid the beginning is always a good place," Sarpe teased.

"Of course. I suppose I should preface this by saying you'll probably think I'm nuts. What I'm about to tell you will sound strange."

"I've sseen sso many sstrange things in my time that life has sseased to be sstrange. In fact, I became very bored with my exisstence, until now."

"I know the feeling. The beginning, huh? Okay. That would be a few thousands years ago, as impossible as that might sound."

"A mere drop in the bucket," Sarpe said.

"Umm. Sure," Ekimmu agreed, not sure if the woman was being sarcastic. "Anyway, my people go back a long ways. Our records date to a time before the most ancient of civilizations existed, to the time of the gods, if you believe in gods, that is."

Sarpe smiled. "I do."

"I'm glad. My people believe we are the chosen people of the gods Geb and Isis. Supposedly, I'm the direct descendent of Isis. If we lived in a community, I would be their queen, but we're a solitary people. A few have been lucky enough to find one of our own to bond with."

"Why one of your own? There are billions of people on thiss planet. Are you incapable of mating with humans?"

"I don't think so. It's just that, well, we are rather long lived. I've had many lovers in my life. It's depressing watching them grow old and die. Eventually, I came to realize it's easier to stay away from relationships."

Sarpe remained silent.

"Sorry, I'm digressing. As I was saying, we're long lived. Our best chance at happiness and the survival of my people is staying with our own kind. The sad thing is that will also be our doom. There are only about a thousand of us left. In a few thousand years, we'll be gone, but then, that's the way all things go, isn't it?" Ekimmu asked.

"Sso it would sseem," Sarpe agreed. "Jusst how long do your people live?"

"I could tell you stories of my childhood. My earliest recollection is Babylon," Ekimmu said hesitantly, waiting for the outburst of disbelief.

"Babylon. Ssuch a long time ago," Sarpe said. "For ssome," she amended.

Ekimmu gave her a strange look. "You sound unimpressed."

"Ssorry. I'm very much impressed. I've never heard of a sspecies sso long lived. It gives me hope."

"Hope?"

Sarpe's eyes twinkled with amusement. "Thiss is your story, remember?"

"I get the feeling you aren't surprised by any of this," Ekimmu said, reaching over to stroke Sarpe's cheek. "Perhaps you're used to the ramblings of crazy women."

"Like I ssaid, I've sseen a lot of sstrange things in my life." Sarpe leaned into the caress, her skin tingling at the touch.

"I guess I might as well expose my entire sordid history," Ekimmu threatened. "Don't say I didn't warn you."

Shifting closer to the warm body, Sarpe wrapped one arm around the woman's waist while resting her head on Ekimmu's bicep. "I'm all earss," she replied.

For hours, the spirit listened to Ekimmu describe her childhood, her parents, and her experiences. Only when Ramus was mentioned did she interrupt.

"Ramuss. A rather unssavory creature, I would ssay."

"Yes. Unfortunately, he still lives. I fear he's found his way here. In fact, that's why I was out so late tonight. Well, actually, you started it," she accused.

"Me? What have I to do with thiss?"

"I was restless after our meeting and decided to go for a walk. I heard the wolves crying and decided to check it out. When I found them, they were dead, the work of Ramus, I believe."

"Sso that was Ramuss!"

"You saw him?"

"If he's the one who killed the wolves, then yess. Tall, sslender, very sstrong. At first, I thought he was a vampire."

"Vampire?"

"He drinkss the blood of his victims, but I realized he was of the living unlike those who musst hide from the light."

"It's true we need blood, but we are no different than other living creatures. It provides certain elements essential to our health. All living things must eat."

"Yess, that is the way of life, but thiss Ramus enjoyss the kill more than mosst."

"I know. Stay away from him. He's dangerous."

Sarpe shrugged, snuggling closer to enjoy the warmth. "He'ss no threat to me."

"He's a threat to anything living," Ekimmu countered angrily.

"Perhapss, but not to me," Sarpe reiterated. "Trusst me on thiss. I've been around a long time, and very few things can harm me."

"You sound like an immortal," Ekimmu joked.

"Not really. That'ss a *human* concept."

"*Human*! You make them sound like a disease."

"No. Jusst different."

"Let's stop this verbal charade. I've told you about me. Now it's time to tell me about you."

Sarpe laughed. The more she was around Ekimmu, the more she liked the woman, human or not. Then again, since she was the serpent spirit, human or not didn't mean much to her.

"I ssuppose you have a point. You remember assking me if I believe in gods?"

"Yes."

"Do you?"

"I'm not sure. Are you going to tell me you're a goddess? Of course with your looks and body, I'd willingly believe it." Ekimmu grinned and wiggled her eyebrows up and down.

"No. I'm definitely no goddesss." Sarpe smirked. "But closse."

"Damn! A woman can only hope. So how close is close?"

"Would you ssettle for a sspirit?"

"Spirit? Like in spirit spirit?"

"I don't know of any other kind."

"You mean *the not real but a ghostly spirit type*?" Ekimmu asked, reaching over and poking at the warm body pressed against hers. "You feel real."

"Of coursse I'm real. Sspirits aren't imaginary. We're very much alive, jusst different."

"How come you look like us? Wait, that *was* you the other night! You were the snake. Are you a shapeshifter?"

"No, not in the way you mean. I can take on many formss. The oness like my kin are the easiesst. I haven't ussed this one in over a thousand yearss."

"You're a snake?"

"Sserpent. More correctly, sserpent sspirit. Ssnakes are part of my kin. Does that bother you?"

"I haven't even had time to absorb this, let alone be bothered," Ekimmu said. "But if this is your human form, I have no complaints. Umm...you said they were 'part' of your kin. What else are you related to? Please don't tell me frogs and toads and turtles." Ekimmu looked uncomfortable.

"Unfortunately, yess. They are what you would call *disstant relatives*."

Rolling her eyes, Ekimmu sighed. "Okay. I guess I can live with that, as long as I don't have to attend any family reunions," she teased. "So there is some truth to the fairy tale."

Sarpe frowned. "Fairy tale?"

"You know, the frog turning into a prince. In my case, it's a snake into a princess."

"I'm no frog...and definitely not a prinssess. As for family reunions, I gave those up long ago."

"Good. Cold-blooded creatures give me the willies."

"Like me?" Sarpe asked, leaning away from Ekimmu to look into her eyes.

"I wouldn't say you're cold-blooded. In fact, I'd say you were rather hot and you definitely give me the shivers."

Sarpe smiled, pleased. "Good and I'd ssay you're probably right."

"So, tell me, do spirits feel emotions?"

"We feel everything," Sarpe said. "After all, life ssprang from our essensse. It's rare for uss to bond, although it does happen occasionally."

"I take it spirits are mostly solitary by nature. It appears we have much in common."

"Ssadly sso. I'm happy to ssee the Earth Mother has found one to fulfill her needs and dessires. They're holding their union sseremony in a few days."

"Earth Mother?"

"Mari. We believe she created your world. Yemaya is her desscendant."

"Now that explains a lot. Ms. Lysanne is a powerful woman and very beautiful."

"True, but don't underesstimate her mate. Dakota is the key that keepss Yemaya's darkness in check. Her anssesstor will be Mari's chosen."

"So history repeats itself."

Leaning toward Sarpe, Ekimmu pressed her lips against the spirit's cheek. "Have you ever felt lust, Sarpe?" she whispered, her voice purring slightly.

"No. At leasst not until ressently," Sarpe murmured, turning her face so their lips were almost touching. "But I'm ssertainly willing to experiensse it."

"Good. I'm willing to help, if you want," Ekimmu said softly.

Inhaling deeply to slow her breathing, Sarpe felt slightly disoriented. These feelings were so alien to her. She was unsure of what to do next. Sensing her confusion, Ekimmu wrapped her arms around the spirit, drawing her tightly against her body.

"It's okay. Let me show you," she said tenderly.

Acquiescing, Sarpe relaxed slightly. "You can't feed," she ordered, almost brusquely. "You musst promisse me no matter what, you won't ever sseek nourishment from me without my permission."

"Tonight you have nothing to fear. I promise I won't do anything you don't want me to."

Releasing her hold, Ekimmu rolled Sarpe onto her back while she stretched out next to her, her head resting on a palm. Reaching over, she began unbuttoning the silk blouse and pushed the edges aside. In the moonlight, she noticed the skin beneath the clothing had an unusual pattern covering the stomach and ribs. Irregular light and dark brown patches crisscrossed Sarpe's torso.

"Interesting tattoo," she observed, running her finger along the darker areas.

"It'ss not a tattoo. That'ss my natural coloring. Does it bother you?" Sarpe asked, her skin rippling from the tickly sensation. "I can change it."

"No, I like it," Ekimmu whispered, pushing the blouse apart to expose two small, well-rounded breasts. "No bra," she commented, then frowned slightly.

"I don't need one. Iss that a problem?"

"Oh. No. But, well."

"Ssomething's wrong, isn't it?"

"Oh, no, no. It's just...well...you don't have... nipples."

"Nippless? I don't need nippless," Sarpe said indignantly. "It'ss not like sserpents have need of those things or anyone is going to ssee me unclothed."

"Well, I am and nipples are an important part of lovemaking."

"Really?" Reaching down, Sarpe ran her hand over her own breasts. "They mean that much?"

"Absolutely! You have no idea how much a nice set of nipples contributes to the mood and the pleasure in lovemaking. I'd rank them somewhere between the second and third most important body part."

"Ah! Nippless it is then if they are sso important."

Ekimmu's eyes widened as a nipple formed on each breast. Laughing, she poked Sarpe in the ribs, causing the spirit to jump.

"That's a great skill you have, dear, but could you make them slightly smaller, maybe the size of acorns? They kind of remind me of walnuts, which *is* a little intimidating."

"Ssooo ssize does matter. All right. How's thiss?"

"Perfect," Ekimmu purred, reaching out to stroke one with her thumb. "Can you feel this?"

"Yess. It'ss pleasant."

"That's a relief. Now I'm wondering what else you might be missing."

"There's more?" Sarpe wondered, her golden-brown eyes widening. "Does thiss have ssomething to do with numbers one and two?"

Rolling her eyes, Ekimmu couldn't stop the laughter bubbling up from deep inside. "You don't know much about a woman's body, do you?" she teased.

"I'm the *sserpent* sspirit. Sserpents don't need the extras humans sseem to need." Sarpe looked somewhat indignant as she arched her right eyebrow.

"This is going to be so much fun for the both of us." Ekimmu grinned and stroked the spirit's cheek. "Perhaps a quick lesson in female human anatomy might be a good start before we continue. I suspect you've left out a few small *things* that make a huge difference in how this is going to turn out."

Sarpe shook her head in frustration. "I hope it'ss worth it," she mumbled.

"Oh, I promise you, it most definitely is." Ekimmu tried not to laugh at the dejected look on the spirit's face. "Now the next big question is, do you know what a *clitoris* is?"

Shaking her head, Sarpe sighed. "I'm beginning to feel like your legendary Frankensstein."

Laughing loudly, Ekimmu leaned down and kissed Sarpe hard on the lips. "Not to worry, dear. I'll make sure you have the correct body parts in all the right places before we're finished."

The next several hours were spent describing *and creating* the various essentials of womanhood. Finally satisfied the spirit understood everything perfectly, Ekimmu decided it was time to call it a night. "It looks like we'll have to continue this another time."

"Yess. I have to admit, thiss one was rather exhausting. I can't believe I came here to resst. I never knew human women were sso complicated."

"Trust me. You'll find it's worth the effort. Once I show you the rest, I think you'll be quite pleased with your efforts." Kissing Sarpe soundly, she took her hand and pulled her to her feet. "For now, though, I need to get back to the hotel. I'll be leaving later today. When will I see you again?"

Sarpe smiled tenderly. "You forget. I'm a sspirit. Thiss world holds no boundaries for me. When you're ready, I'll be there," she promised.

"Then I'll see you tonight. No use wasting time." Ekimmu sighed with relief.

After a quick hug, the two separated and went their own ways, each excited over the possibilities the future held. The streets were almost abandoned as Ekimmu strolled toward her hotel. About to enter, she was startled by a hand on her shoulder.

"We have business to attend to. Please come with me."

"Of course," Ekimmu replied dutifully. "I am yours to command."

The two women disappeared into the darkness.

CHAPTER SIXTEEN

Dakota wasn't sure what had disturbed her. She had only managed to fall asleep a few hours before after giving Yemaya a good back massage. The night seemed to beckon to her. Slipping quietly from the bed, she pulled on her T-shirt and jeans.

The bedroom window was open. A gentle breeze disturbed the curtains, carrying the fresh scent of the outdoors into the room along with faint flickers of moonlight. Shadows danced across the walls giving life to the quietness of the room. Feeling restless, Dakota debated whether to wake Yemaya but decided against it, knowing how exhausted her lover was from the stress of having to deal with the death of Regina's pup.

Pushing the curtains aside, she leaned out the window, her elbows on the sill, and stared into the darkness. It would be nice to take a short walk and relax, she thought. Walking to the bed, she kissed Yemaya lightly on the lips.

"Be back in a jiff," she promised softly, then slipped quietly from the bedroom and house.

The crisp air made her shiver. The full moon provided plenty of light, so she tucked the flashlight in her hip pocket. Walking across the drawbridge, she turned upstream, knowing the trip back would be easier. An owl hooted loudly from a nearby tree before launching itself into the air, its silhouette passing eerily across the moon.

"How typical!" Dakota chuckled. "So cliché!" she muttered, thinking back to the Halloween drawings of her childhood. Looking around, she was a little surprised Simtire wasn't bouncing around her. Normally, she appeared instantly whenever Dakota stepped outside. The young wolf rarely left her side during her walks.

Guess she's with Regina, Dakota thought, remembering the detailed description Yemaya had given her of the earlier events. *I hope they're okay.*

A rustling noise to her left startled her. When a rabbit hopped across her path, she giggled nervously. "Maybe this isn't such a good idea," she said, suddenly feeling uneasy.

"Oh, I think it's an excellent one," a low, raspy voice said behind her.

Heart pounding, Dakota spun around and bumped into the tall figure of a man. Instinctively, she pushed away, only to be caught and steadied by two strong hands.

"Did I frighten you? I do apologize, Ms. Devereaux," Ramus said.

"Mr. Falthama. You startled me. What are you doing out here? You're trespassing, you know." She tried to regain her composure.

"One cannot trespass on the land. The Earth belongs to everyone," he said. "Humans delude themselves into thinking they have certain rights. You're an arrogant people."

"I'm not going to debate it with you at this time of the night. Now if you'll excuse me, I have to get back. Yemaya is waiting for me."

"Please don't treat me like a fool. We both know your lover is sleeping soundly. It's been a stressful day for her," he chided. "With the loss of the wolves and everything else. Such a tragedy."

"How do you know about them? It only happened a few hours ago. And take your hands off me."

Shrugging, Ramus released his grip. "I know many things. Did you find Om Loh Rehn's stories amusing?" he asked, changing the subject.

"Amusing? I wouldn't say that. Interesting, yes."

Smiling, Ramus stared at Dakota thoughtfully. "Do you believe what you've read?"

"I don't know what to believe. Right now, I just want to go home and get some sleep, so if you'll excuse me."

"No."

"No? No what?" Dakota asked, frowning.

"No, I won't excuse you. I have use of you. Afterward, perhaps I'll excuse you."

Ramus suddenly jerked Dakota toward him. Holding her by the throat, he bent his head and inhaled, intentionally making the gesture obscene.

"Mmm...not as sweet as Carpi blood but not bad for a mongrel,"

124

he said, grinning with satisfaction when Dakota shuddered.

Struggling against the grip on her neck and the arm that was wrapped tightly around her waist, Dakota realized she was helpless.

"Now, now! This will only hurt a little, so there is no use fighting me. Just a small nip should bring your lover here."

Leaning down, he ran his tongue along her neck. Dakota shivered, repulsed by the contact. His soft chuckle frightened her even more. He was a creature without a soul.

"I disagree," Ramus whispered in her ear, flicking his tongue against the lobe. "I very much have one, otherwise I wouldn't be able to appreciate the wonderful taste of your skin or smell the essence of your blood and fear. Adrenaline! Did you know it makes the blood slightly tart?" He tilted his head slightly, fascinated at her ability to control her fear so well. "You're very beautiful in spite of your impurities."

Dakota tried to scream, but the hand around her throat tightened mercilessly, cutting off the air and the blood supply. Feeling faint, she slumped against his chest. "Yemaya," she cried out silently.

"Yes. Call her, my dear. Bring her to me," Ramus encouraged, his breath brushing her neck, causing the hairs to rise. "She'll come if you call her. She can't resist the cry of her lover. Here, let me give her an incentive."

Forcing Dakota's head back, he nipped the skin above the jugular vein, causing a small rivulet of blood to run down her neck.

"She doesn't have a lot of time, I'm afraid. I grow hungry from your scent," he murmured, licking his teeth suggestively. "Perhaps I should just savor the moment instead of being reasonable."

"Yemaya! Please..." Dakota silently begged. "Don't come. Don't try and rescue me. Don't give in to him."

"Ah, such courage. Sacrificing yourself for her. I'm touched." He smirked and stroked her cheek with his fingertips. "She *will* come, you know. How could she not? Such love," he mused, tracing a droplet of blood with his finger as it slid down her neck. Putting the finger in his mouth, he tasted the warm, rich fluid. "Sweet! I stand corrected. It would seem in your case, the adrenaline only enhances the sweetness."

So entranced was he by his musings, Ramus didn't notice the body launching itself at him until sharp fangs gripped his arm, penetrating the flesh. Surprised, he threw Dakota aside. Simtire immediately released her grip and backed away, aware that this was the creature who had murdered her sister. Still, she was more than willing to sacrifice herself for her beloved mistress.

"So...your savior isn't who I was hoping for, Ms. Devereaux," Ramus sneered, glancing at the puncture wounds in his forearm. "No matter, this impudent young pup is a merely a nuisance."

Wiping the blood away with his hand, he watched the wolf circle him, her lips curled exposing long white teeth. Hackles raised, she crouched slightly, ready to jump if the *thing* moved toward Dakota. Although Ramus knew the wolf wasn't a serious threat to him, she could inflict enough pain to be uncomfortable for a few days. His dilemma now was whether to retrieve Dakota or catch the wolf.

Taking advantage of his distraction, Dakota scrambled farther away from him, looking for an opportunity to assist the young wolf. Escape wasn't an alternative as long as Simtire was in danger.

Sensing her mistress's intentions, Simtire flashed a quick look in her direction before refocusing on Ramus. Dakota felt the wolf warning her not to interfere. *Not on your life*, she thought. *We do this together.*

Ramus knew his best chance to catch the wolf was to go for Dakota. He knew she would automatically try to protect her mistress. Turning slightly, he walked toward Dakota, pretending to ignore the wolf.

"Well, my dear. This has been interesting, but time is growing short. Say good-bye to this one," he advised, reaching for Dakota. As predicted, Simtire launched herself at the outstretched hand. Ramus quickly spun and grabbed the wolf by the neck, holding her struggling body high in the air. Simtire snarled, snapping and kicking furiously.

"Nice try. Such bravery should be rewarded. I'll give you a quick death."

"No!" Dakota yelled, springing to her feet and grabbing Ramus's arm.

"Promise me you won't resist and I'll make her death painless," Ramus said, holding the struggling animal effortlessly, his gaze locked on Dakota.

Before she could answer, another object hurled past her, striking Ramus in the chest, causing him to stumble backward and loosen his grip. Simtire twisted away, falling to the ground. Regina lunged, snapping at Ramus's face, causing him to throw his hands up in self-defense. Realizing a second wolf had arrived, Ramus swore angrily. This wasn't part of his plan. Before he could react, a sharp pain in his right calf caused his knee to buckle. Looking down, he saw an old gray male had sunk its fangs deep into his leg.

Dakota watched, mesmerized by the coordinated attack of the wolves, each springing forward, then backing away before Ramus could react. Ramus was continually kept off-guard, turning left, then right as they nipped at his legs or hands. Howling his own rage, he decided it was time to leave. Unfortunately, his path was blocked by several more wolves sitting a few meters away, snarling angrily.

"Call them off," he yelled at Dakota, feeling fear for the first time in his life.

"They aren't mine to call off," Dakota said, rubbing the small wound on her neck.

"No, they are mine!" a low, extremely angry voice growled from the darkness. "It would seem they know you, Ramus. I believe they wish to collect on a debt," Yemaya said coldly, crossing her arms as she stepped from the shadows. "But I think I will claim mine first. They can have the leftovers. Regina, Voinic, enough!" she ordered calmly. Too calmly, Dakota thought as she jumped to her feet.

"Yemaya," she cried, hugging the taller woman. When Yemaya ignored the embrace and brusquely pushed Dakota away, Dakota's greatest fear was realized. Eyes the color of the darkest coal looked beyond her to Ramus, who was rubbing his right arm.

"I have decided to grant you your wish, Ramus," Yemaya said, her upper lip curled slightly, reminding him of the wolves standing silently a few meters away. "But first, I want to know why you killed my wolves. They were never a threat to you."

Ramus smiled smugly and shrugged, deriving pleasure from the knowledge that their deaths had affected this woman deeply.

"Because I could," he boasted, making eye contact with Yemaya. "And because they reminded me of a woman I knew a long time ago. She was quite fond of wolves, much like you, I'd say."

"You must have hated her very much."

"Quite the contrary, Ms. Lysanne, I loved her. Unfortunately, she didn't return my affections."

"So she spurned you. Smart woman!"

Ramus laughed, amused by her bravado. "If you say so. I'd say she made a poor decision. Sadly, she and her lover died rather suddenly. An unfortunate accident."

"Accident? You call murder an accident? A lot of people die when you're around. I think maybe it is about time someone put a stop to these *accidents*."

"And just how will you do that?" Ramus asked, enjoying their game of cat and mouse.

"I have many skills, as you well know. That *is* why you are here, why you abducted Dakota."

"Partly." He saw no reason to deny her accusation. "You *interest* me. There's a darkness about you, an aura, you might say. I saw two of your shows. You're more than you pretend to be. Even your lover here doesn't know the real you."

"And you do?"

"Perhaps. We're the same, you and I. We share the same darkness, the same desires, the same need for power. Only you suppress yours while I live mine."

"We are nothing alike," Yemaya hissed, taking a step forward. "You are a killer. You kill for the joy of killing with no thought, no remorse, no feeling."

Ramus laughed loudly. "Please. Are you telling me you have never killed anyone?"

"There is a first time for everything. I think tonight you will be my first," Yemaya said coldly. "We have talked enough."

"We even have a common acquaintance, as you would say." He suddenly changed the subject.

Yemaya frowned, caught momentarily off-guard.

"Now I've piqued your interest. Let's just say I paid a visit to your dream girl earlier today. I found our little chat very interesting," he taunted.

"What did you do to Lia?" Yemaya's black eyes blazed with barely controlled rage.

"Why nothing," he replied innocently. "I simply needed to experience what you have. It was quite enlightening. That's how I know we're the same. As for Lia, I have no need for her now. She's damaged and besides, it would make the authorities too suspicious, don't you think? At the moment, they think bacteria caused her troubles. We don't want to disillusion them now, do we?"

"And the dead women?"

"Ah, sadly some unfortunate dog has been discovered to be very sick. Poor thing! The authorities destroyed him," he smirked.

"You arrogant bastard!" Dakota yelled.

"Be quiet!" Yemaya snarled, glancing at Dakota momentarily. Dakota flinched as if struck.

"So you went to all this trouble just to meet me?" Yemaya demanded, once again focusing on Ramus. "You laid your filthy hands on my lover, threatened her, assaulted her. All so you could get to know me?"

Ramus nodded, smiling mockingly, but said nothing, taunting her with his smugness.

Yemaya wasn't amused. "Well then, you have your wish," she said, her voice cool, emotionless. "The very least I can do is reward your efforts."

Surprised at her easy acquiescence, Ramus frowned, looking first at her, then the wolves surrounding them.

"Just like that? You surprise me. And what happens while collecting my *reward*?" he asked sarcastically. "Will the wolves attack while I'm distracted by your *charms*?" He eyed the three animals.

"Why, Ramus. I am hurt. You do not trust me. And here you claim we are so much alike," she sneered, her black eyes gleaming hotly. "Why would I let them have all the fun?"

Ramus hesitated, momentarily unsure. Finally deciding she was trying to intimidate him, he chuckled. "You have a wicked sense of humor."

"Oh, if you only knew! So do we stand here all night or will you accept my offer?"

"I'm glad you've come to your senses."

Yemaya smiled and Dakota shivered. This wasn't her lover. It was the *beast* inside of her. The darkness had taken control.

"Yemaya! Don't do this!" Dakota whispered, grabbing her arm. "This isn't you!"

Yemaya looked at Dakota for a few seconds before reaching down and removing the hand clamped around her arm.

"I...said...be quiet! This is *exactly* me. When will you learn? Now if you are unable to do as I say, I suggest you leave. This is between Ramus and me. No one touches you except me," she hissed. "I intend to teach him that lesson before he dies."

"Please," Dakota begged. "You don't know what you're doing. Let's just get out of here." Tears streamed down her cheeks.

"You go! I have plans. Now run along like a good girl. I will have use of you once I finish here." The look she gave sent a shiver through Dakota's body. Noticing the reaction, Yemaya smiled, satisfied Dakota had caught her meaning. Then turning away, she stared at Ramus. "Shall we?"

"Of course, my dear. I look forward to our union."

Feeling helpless, Dakota looked from Yemaya to Ramus. She knew Yemaya intended on killing Ramus; at least the *beast* wanted to. Her Yemaya was trapped somewhere inside, a prisoner of her own darkness.

"Regina!" Dakota turned to the old female wolf. "We have to stop her. This will destroy her even if she succeeds in killing Ramus."

Regina looked from Dakota to her mistress. She sensed the change in Yemaya. Never had she challenged Yemaya's authority, but something unnatural controlled her human companion. Whining, she looked to Voinic. Rising to their feet simultaneously, the wolves stepped between Ramus and Yemaya, lips curled exposing elongated fangs. Confused, Simtire hesitated but moved closer, offering her support.

"Regina, go away!" Yemaya ordered, angered by their interference.

Ramus remained silent, fascinated at the odd exchange.

The three wolves stood still, unmoved by their mistress's tone.

"Regina, I said leave us," Yemaya hissed through gritted teeth.

Regina wavered. Yemaya had never talked to them like that. Whining softly, she stared unblinkingly into her mistress's eyes. Yemaya stepped forward but stopped when the old female wolf raised her lips and growled a warning.

"You dare to disobey me? I am your mistress. Leave before you anger me further." She glared angrily at the wolves.

Regina bristled, a deep growl rumbling in her throat. Crouching, she prepared to lunge if the thing inside her mistress tried to enter her mind.

"Stay!" a voice commanded from the shadows.

Everyone turned, startled by the interruption. Constance

emerged from the darkness, leaning heavily on Ekimmu's arm.

"What now?" Ramus asked, throwing up his hands in frustration. "A circus?"

"Be quiet, Ramus!" Constance said, staring at him coolly. "You've done enough damage this night. I'll deal with you later. Are you okay, Dakota?"

"Constance, we have to stop her," Dakota cried, running to the older woman. "She means to kill Ramus!"

"She means to try, but she will fail. Yemaya lacks the knowledge to destroy the likes of him. There is a way, though, if you have the courage. You need only join with her and the two of you might be able to defeat him." Constance watched for Dakota's reaction.

"Very good, Constance," Yemaya interrupted sarcastically. "I had not thought of using Dakota against Ramus. It is so *logical*! How about it, Dakota? Join me! You and I will rid the world of this creature." Her voice was gentle and persuasive. "Think of it. No more killing. No more fear of the dark. Help me and it will happen."

Confused, Dakota stared at the black eyes, looking for confirmation that this was her lover. She wanted to believe the woman standing before her was Yemaya and not the *beast*. It was true getting rid of Ramus would end his killing spree and perhaps save hundreds of lives, maybe thousands, if her suspicions were right.

Ekimmu stood by quietly listening. Constance was giving Dakota the opportunity to choose her and Yemaya's fate. No one would interfere once Dakota made her decision.

"I'm sorry, Yemaya. I can't." Dakota sobbed. "And I can't let you do this!"

Stepping closer, she faced Yemaya, her back to Ramus. He remained still, amused by the battle of wills. The young woman had an inner strength even he hadn't imagined. Ekimmu glanced at Ramus, sensing his thoughts.

"I *will* do this, Dakota! You must choose between him and me. Decide now!"

"*No!* I can't let you do this. You'll have to come through me to get him, my love. You've never killed before and I won't let you start now."

"You are such a fool! Did you really think Eddy Jones blew his

131

brains out because he wanted to or that Dalnos hung himself out of remorse? You cannot imagine how easy it is to get people to do what I want or see what I want. I am an Illusionist," she bragged. "I can do anything I want when I want, even to you...especially to you. You were my easiest conquest."

Flinching, Dakota didn't miss the meaning behind Yemaya's words, nor the attempts to place doubts in her mind about their relationship. Straightening to her full height, she returned the black gaze of her lover, her emerald green eyes challenging Yemaya.

"I don't believe you! *It* is making you say that. I know you, Yemaya. You may have done something to those people but never that. You would never force me to do anything I didn't want."

"You are naïve," Yemaya sneered, then decided to change tactics. "Look around. No one here is going to help you. Certainly not Ramus! And the old woman? She will not interfere. Meddling in the affairs of mere humans is beneath her. Now the other one..." She gestured at Ekimmu. "She may be a different matter. She has a conscience, but are you willing to bet on her coming to your aid?"

"I don't need them. I have Regina and Voinic and Simtire. Are you so sure of the others? After all, they came here for a reason."

"Ask them! Prove me wrong." Yemaya smirked, crossing her arms.

"No! Not this time, my love. Before, I didn't have the confidence to help you by myself. Now I do. This is my battle, win or lose," she said. "I know you're in there somewhere listening and fighting. You would never give up without a struggle. I know you love me. I'm here ready to give all of me if that's what it takes to get you back. I'll die if need be. You'd do the same."

Dakota watched Yemaya's face for some sign of her lover. No one else would have noticed the slight movement of the throat, but Dakota recognized the first crack in the *beast's* armor.

"Get out of my way, Dakota!" Yemaya hissed angrily, raising her hand to shove her aside. "Or I will move you myself."

"Then do it," Dakota challenged, pressing her shoulder against the outstretched hand. "But you'll have to kill me first."

Yemaya frowned. This wasn't going the way she wanted. Looking beyond Dakota, she stared at Ramus. "Do you want this or not, Ramus?"

Raising his arms slightly and shrugging, Ramus grimaced. "As you can see, I'm at a disadvantage here." He looked at the wolf blocking his path, then at the two Gebian women. "I'm sure you're more than capable of handling your woman."

Yemaya cursed and frowned. Reaching up, she rubbed her right temple.

Dakota placed her fingers near the spot Yemaya was massaging. Yemaya caught the hand and squeezed hard, watching Dakota's face for signs of pain. Remaining still, Dakota stared into dark gray eyes, refusing to give in.

"That's it, my love. We've beat it before. We can do it again."

As the pressure on her hand decreased, the pain on her lover's face increased. Dakota gently disengaged her hand from Yemaya's grasp and placed her palm against her lover's cheek.

"I know it's hard, but come to me. I'm waiting here for you."

"Do you wish my help, Little One?" a deep voice from within Dakota's mind whispered, temporarily distracting her. Constance, Ekimmu, and Ramus frowned almost simultaneously, looking sharply at Dakota.

"Not this time, Intunecat." Dakota never took her eyes off her lover. "But thank you."

"As you wish, but you need only call and I will come," the Dark One said before disappearing. "At no cost," he added, his chuckle resonating through her mind.

Casting all thoughts of Intunecat aside, Dakota focused her full attention on her lover. "Yemaya, we can do this. Try, sweetie."

Everyone watched the silent struggle. Even Ramus was intrigued. In the thousands of years of his existence, he had seen real love only a few times. Yemaya and Dakota reminded him of Inanna and her chosen. Looking at their daughter, he found her watching him and realized she was thinking the same thought. Constance remained still, ignoring everyone but the two women.

Yemaya closed her eyes and groaned. The *beast* could feel itself being pushed back into its cave. Raging, it resisted, struggling for domination, but slowly gave ground. Somehow, the mistress was gathering strength from Dakota's voice. Howling in anger, it lashed out, slashing at everything within reach of its dark tentacles. Falling to her knees from the white hot pain searing her brain, sweat ran in rivulets down Yemaya's cheeks and dripped onto her breasts as she battled relentlessly against the blackness. In the depths of her agony, she continued to follow the gentle voice guiding her home, gaining strength from its soothing warmth. Finally in one giant burst, she lunged forward, shoving the *beast* deep into the caves of her mind and slammed the door.

Dakota knew the moment Yemaya regained control and grabbed the taller woman as she collapsed. Sinking to the ground, she shifted to a sitting position and pulled Yemaya's head onto her lap, stroking the sweat-soaked hair. For a moment, pale blue eyes opened to stare at her before closing tiredly.

"Take your time."

Looking at Constance, she nodded.

"You've done well, Dakota," Constance said.

Turning to Ramus, Constance frowned. "Come with me!" she ordered. "Ekimmu?"

Ekimmu stepped forward, giving Constance an arm for support. The two women disappeared into the night. Sighing, Ramus shook his head.

"I'm impressed, Ms. Devereaux," he said, his voice holding the faintest hint of admiration. "Rest well. This isn't over yet."

"On the contrary," a voice spoke from the darkness. "Say good-bye, Ramus. Dakota and Yemaya won't be seeing you again."

Grimacing comically, Ramus shrugged and disappeared in the same direction as the voice. One never argued with the Om, even him.

Dakota wasn't sure what had just happened but decided to pursue it later. Yemaya was her only interest now. "Sweetie, can you stand?" she asked softly.

"I...I think so." Dakota helped her to sit up, supporting her back until she was sure Yemaya was stable. Heaving herself off the ground, Yemaya grabbed Dakota's hand and pulled her up to her feet and into her arms.

"I would have never made it without you," she admitted tiredly.

"You'd have come back to me. Our love is too strong for you to fail. I just gave you a slight nudge," Dakota teased, poking the taller woman with her elbow.

"More like a shove."

Smiling, Dakota wrapped her arm around Yemaya's waist, offering her support if she needed it.

"I am fine. Really." Yemaya tried to reassure her lover, but appreciated having a warm, strong body to lean on.

Seeing their mistress was back to normal, Regina and Voinic loped toward her enthusiastically. Simtire ran to Dakota, nuzzling her hand.

"Thank you, Regina, Voinic. And you too, Simtire."

"Yes, thank all of you," Dakota agreed. "I'm in your debt."

After frolicking with the humans for a few minutes, the wolves left to romp in the woods. Loping away, their howls grew faint as they disappeared into the distance.

Yemaya and Dakota made their way home and collapsed on the bed exhausted. Wrapped in each other's arms, they quickly fell asleep.

CHAPTER SEVENTEEN

So, Ramus, I see you're still up to your old ways," Constance chastised.

"And I see you still like to champion the humans," he countered.

"Who else is there since you've done your best to wipe out the species?" she said coldly.

"You exaggerate, Om Loh Rehn. There are over six billion of them now. That's hardly on the verge of extinction."

"For the present, but thanks to you, one of the viruses has reached a pandemic stage. Unless they come up with something soon, there's a good chance this one will destroy them in a few hundred years."

"Bah! They'll find something. Besides, the planet would benefit from a few less humans."

"Perhaps. For the sake of our own race, let's hope they discover a cure for this disease."

Ramus frowned. "Why our race?" he asked. "What does the virus have to do with us?"

Constance glanced at Ekimmu, who had been quietly listening to the conversation. Nodding, she signaled the younger woman to take over.

"Did you think your little creations only affected humans, Ramus?" Ekimmu asked, stepping forward. "That we were immune to them?"

"Of course we are. We don't have the same immune systems. It doesn't jump species easily. I made sure of that," Ramus declared smugly.

"You're an arrogant fool!" she hissed. "You can't really believe viruses remain the same forever. Haven't you learned yet that they adapt according to their needs?"

"Not that fast. It's only been a few decades now. It'll take hundreds of years for it to mutate enough to threaten us. By then, we'll have evolved also, developing our own immunity. We adapt quickly. Besides, our people only feed on the healthiest humans. That alone gives us protection."

"You've misjudged both the virus and our people. Three have already died from it in the past ten years. Several more are infected and don't have much time left."

"I don't believe you. If they died, it was because of something else. I won't be blamed for the death of any Gebian," he declared angrily.

"What you mean is you never personally killed one of us, right?" Constance asked scathingly.

"Of course! It's the same thing."

"Is it?" she demanded, her black eyes challenging him to deny the truth.

Ekimmu listened, sensing something else was going on behind the conversation.

"With respect, Om Loh Rehn..." Ramus countered, glancing at Ekimmu nervously. "I don't think now is the time to debate semantics. What is past is past."

Constance acknowledged the wisdom of his words. Ekimmu suspected Ramus was involved in her parents' deaths, but she wasn't sure. After all this time, learning the truth served no purpose.

"Perhaps you're right, Ramus," she admitted grudgingly.

Surprised, Ramus nodded once. The last thing he needed was for Ekimmu to come after him.

"At least there's one thing we agree on," he said respectfully. "So where do we go from here? No doubt you have something in mind."

"We go our separate ways as we have always done and hope time heals the damage you've done. I pray you've learned something this night."

Ramus chuckled. "Oh, no doubt! I've learned much this night. Tell me something. If Ms. Devereaux had chosen to assist Ms. Lysanne in trying to kill me, would you have intervened?"

Constance thought about the question. "Probably not," she said honestly. "I created those decrees for Queen Antianna. I will not dishonor her memory by putting them aside so easily...even for the likes of you." Her disgust wasn't lost on Ramus.

"I see…and if I had decided to kill one or both of them? Would you have stopped me?" He tilted his head sideways to watch her expression. "You seem fond of them."

"I don't believe I would have stopped you even then," she answered truthfully.

"But I would have," Ekimmu growled, wanting to make sure Ramus understood she wasn't so committed to the ancient decrees. "Om Loh Rehn may follow the old ways, but I don't. I'd kill you now if we were alone and never look back. Unlike others of our race, I never believed we should have let you continue your maniacal atrocities. If mother and father had listened to me, you'd be long dead and gone."

"And they wouldn't be," Ramus added, unable to resist the barb.

Ekimmu frowned. "What do you know about their deaths?"

"Why, Ekimmu…" he taunted.

"Enough!" Constance bellowed. "Ramus, I warn you. Cease this now, or I promise you, I will break my oath this one time and destroy you myself. Don't push your luck too far."

Surprised, Ramus couldn't think of any retort.

"Leave us!" she ordered. "I've grown weary of this. Leave Teraclia by tomorrow and make sure you stay away from Ms. Lysanne and Ms. Devereaux…and me."

"As you wish, Om Loh Rehn," he said somewhat sullenly before turning to Ekimmu. "It's so good to see you again, Ekimmu. I look forward to our next meeting." He smiled broadly.

"If we ever meet again, Ramus, it will be your last. Only my respect for the Om keeps me from ridding this world of your filth," she sneered, blue eyes blazing.

Shrugging, Ramus chuckled and walked into the night.

"I don't understand, Om Loh Rehn. Why do you continue to allow him to live? He is worse than a plague."

"Because it's our way," Constance said. "Your parents understood and respected that."

"My parents are dead. Their beliefs couldn't save them, and I suspect Ramus had something to do with that. If I ever find out for sure, nothing will stand between him and me avenging their deaths."

The old woman sighed and took Ekimmu's arm, shaking it

firmly. "Listen, child, revenge is never sweet. There's a heavy price to pay for the taking of a life, and although there are times it may be necessary, it's the last act of desperation and can never be undone. Ramus has done much to warrant his death, but he has served a purpose in a strange way. The diseases he helped perpetuate were not his creations, only his tools. At some point, they would have evolved, with or without his interference, and millions would still be dead. Fortunately, humans are resilient and resourceful. Besides, Ramus in all his arrogance may have brought about his own destruction. His time in this world is very short."

"How so?"

"Ramus gambled on his genes to protect him from the future. It was a foolish wager."

"I don't understand."

"He thought he was immune to the viruses he toyed with. Up until the last one, he was right. As you so wisely pointed out, however, viruses adapt. He's carried this particular one in his blood for decades, unaware it was continually changing and evolving, adapting to his own immune system, the way it did with the humans."

Ekimmu smiled. "Perhaps there's a god after all."

"Perhaps, or perhaps nature just likes to have the last laugh. Now I'm tired. Walk me to my room. I leave for home in the morning."

"What about Ms. Devereaux and Ms. Lysanne? They're going to have a lot of questions."

"I leave all of that to your good judgment. Tell them what you must and give Dakota my best. She has a manuscript that belongs to our people. Please retrieve it for me."

"As you wish. Should I ship it to your home?"

"No, keep it. I think you'll find it most interesting and perhaps it'll bring you some peace."

Ekimmu stood quietly for a few minutes deep in thought.

"Something bothers you, child."

"Not really. I was just wondering. Why did you give Ms. Devereaux that manuscript? It's strictly forbidden for anyone but you to have them. You've always been so adamant about obeying the edicts of Isis."

"Desperate times, my dear. She is an important part of our future."

"How so?"

Constance sighed. "You're the last direct descendant of Isis and Geb. You've chosen not to take your rightful place as ruler of our people, and I suspect your chosen will not be capable of making you pregnant. With your passing, so goes our people."

"I don't understand. I'm just one of almost a thousand. Many are still capable of bearing children. Surely, there's hope."

"I didn't say we're destined to extinction."

"Then why give the manuscript to an outsider?"

"If we do become extinct, no one will know we ever existed. Dakota is a journalist. At the right time, she'll let the world know about us, but only after we are long gone."

"Om, I think you're growing forgetful. Ms. Devereaux will be dead long before we are. The knowledge will disappear with her."

"Dakota will become the keeper of our history in time, and she'll make sure we aren't forgotten. Trust me. So what else is bothering you?"

Ekimmu couldn't help but laugh at the all-knowing Om.

"No wonder you are the Om." She smirked. "How did you know I was in Teraclia? I should have sensed your presence."

"Like you knew Ramus was here?"

"Point taken. Apparently, time has dulled some of our senses."

"Not time, life. You, like many of our people, have reduced your need for human blood. I believe eventually, if our race survives, we will revert back to our original state."

"Meaning shorter lives. We really are a doomed species, aren't we?" Ekimmu said sadly.

"I fear it may be so, child, or at least a changing one, but then the world is a different place. Who can really predict the future? I guess we can only hope."

"Hope has never been one of my strong points, but I will try."

Constance chuckled and nudged Ekimmu in the ribs. "You've never been one to believe in spirits, either," she teased. "Funny how life has a way of changing us."

"Spirits? Umm..."

Laughing, the elderly woman patted Ekimmu's arm. "Not to worry. I saw you and the strange woman at the restaurant. Maybe you didn't believe in them, but I'm a lot older than you, dear. I've met a few in my life, although I'm not so sure they knew what I was.

I gave up the bloodlust a long time ago. I'm still alive, but I'm aging more quickly now. Soon, I'll be with the one true love of my life."

Constance grew quiet. Ekimmu knew she was thinking about the person she had just mentioned.

"You still miss him?"

"Her. And she was very beautiful," Constance mused, almost to herself. "It's been a long time." She sighed, remembering the precious moments spent with her tall, red-haired warrior. Unfortunately, Lynara had been both human and a lieutenant in the army of Queen Boudicea. She died in battle defending her queen. A part of Constance had died with her.

Shaking her head slightly, she took Ekimmu's arm and walked toward the hotel. Neither spoke, each lost in her own thoughts. Once back at the hotel, Ekimmu gave Constance a gentle hug and bid her farewell. Wearily, the older woman said her good-byes and disappeared into the elevator.

Feeling restless, Ekimmu wandered the streets for several hours before returning to her hotel room. The events of the night had given her a lot to think about, especially since meeting Sarpe. Her combination of innocence and disillusionment intrigued Ekimmu. For the first time in Ekimmu's life, she felt something more than just the hunger. The loneliness had lessened some.

Once back at the estate, Yemaya and Dakota barely had the energy to take their clothes off before slipping into bed and falling asleep.

"Well, now. 'Bout time yah bez a joinin' the festivities."

Groaning, Dakota tried to ignore her grandmother.

"Don't yah go on thinkin' I ain't knowed of what yah bez a doin' thar, chile. Now wakes up that thar woman of yourn. We've been awaitin' on yah but kent holds out much longer."

"Oh, Grandma!" Dakota grumbled. "I don't have the energy and Yemaya is exhausted. Can't this wait a few hours?"

"This here bez the spirit world, chile. Yah kin gets yer strength from us'ens. Ain't that right, dahlin'?"

Opening one eye, Dakota looked to see who Grandma Dakota was calling darling. Mari stood next to the spirit, smiling warmly at the younger Dakota.

"Sorry, Dakota, but if we don't get started soon, the rest of the guests are going to rebel. We've been waiting for you two. Do you think you and Yemaya could join us for a little while? Then you can quietly disappear. Once the festivities get in full swing, no one will see you leaving."

Dakota could never resist Mari. She reminded her too much of Yemaya. "Sure. Let me get Yemaya. We'll be here shortly."

"You already are here." Mari laughed. "But thank you. I know you've been through a lot already."

"Did someone call?" a low husky voice whispered in Dakota's ear.

"Hey, you're awake!" Dakota exclaimed, hugging Yemaya.

"I am not so sure about that, but here I am. Shall we join the party and get these two spirits *heetched*?"

Everyone laughed at Yemaya's poor imitation of Maopa.

"I suppose so. Otherwise no one's going to get any rest. All right, Grandma, Mari, let's get you two joined so the others can party and do all the things spirits normally do when they want to have fun. Then Yemaya and I can sleep."

Ursa let out with a growlish "whup" when Mari called to their guests.

"My friends, my daughter, Yemaya, and my soon-to-be-daughter Dakota, thank you for attending this joining. Tonight, I pledge my soul and my energies to Maopa and she to me. It is the happiest moment of my existence," she declared proudly, leaning down to place a kiss on the elder Dakota's cheek.

"As it be mine," Maopa agreed, grinning broadly.

Everyone cheered with the exception of Intunecat. He stepped from amongst the crowd and raised his hands to silence the group. "Quiet!" he ordered. The spirits immediately obeyed.

"As the eldest, it is my honor and duty to perform the ritual binding these two together. Mari, Maopa, step forward and join hands."

The Earth Mother took Maopa's hand and approached the Dark One. Kneeling, they bowed their heads.

"From the blackest darkness to the birth of light, I have seen many changes in our world. We have had only a few joinings, but none so significant as this. Mari, you are the Earth Mother, born of the light, but you have lived in partial darkness for thousands of years because of your loneliness. Maopa, you are but an infant in this world and so you bring to it the vitality of youth. In this bonding, you will become the strength to each other's weakness, but you will also become a weakness to the other's strength. Your pain will be shared, but your joy will grow tenfold. Are you willing to accept those conditions?"

Mari and Maopa nodded. Yemaya and Dakota stared into each other's eyes as if the words were meant for them. Intunecat noticed the lovers' locked gaze and smiled.

"Yemaya, as daughter and only girlchild of the Earth Mother, do you approve of this union?"

Mari and Maopa looked up, surprised that Intunecat had veered from the ancient ceremony.

"Yes," Yemaya whispered, her eyes never leaving Dakota's.

"And you, Dakota, daughter of Maopa and representative of her kin, do you give your approval of this union?"

"With all my heart," Dakota said.

"Then from this moment forward, you, Mari, and you, Maopa, are one. All who are present now bear witness to this joining. Let the celebration begin."

Joyously, the spirits sprang forward, lifting the couple high in the air. "Now bez your time to get goin'," Grandma Dakota yelled to the two humans. "Thank yah for comin'."

Mari smiled at Yemaya and Dakota. "Daughters. We are all blessed this day. I know you would like to sleep now, but before you go, I have a surprise and a thank you gift waiting at the foot of the falls. Please humor me on this," she begged, her voice low and husky.

Even Yemaya blinked from its effect as the words brushed across her skin like a warm spring breeze sending a pleasant chill through her tired body.

"Now you know how I feel when you do that to me," Dakota whispered. "You can thank your ancestor for that skill."

Laughing, Yemaya picked Dakota up and carried her toward the falls. "I'm glad that you didn't get Granny Dakota's accent," she teased. "Although I would love you anyway."

"Gee thanks."

Maopa gently touched Mari's arm, temporarily distracting her from a conversation she was having with Ladyhawk and Arbora.

"Sarpe bez a bit under the weather, I thank," she said, nodding toward the serpent spirit coiled up near one of the many bonfires burning near the lake. "I'm a thankin' she may be needin' someone ta lend her an ear."

Mari glanced at Sarpe, her brow wrinkling as she pondered her oldest friend's distracted expression.

"You may be right, love. Perhaps I should see what's bothering her."

Putting her hand on the tall spirit's arm, Maopa squeezed it for a second. "Yah needs ta take care of the guests, dahlin'. Sometimes it be easier jawin' with a stranger than friend. Hows about I jest wander on over and see if'n she needs company?"

"Thanks! I think you may be right."

Smiling, Maopa walked over to the serpent spirit and sat next to the coiled figure.

"Say thar, I heerd yah been keepin' right busy, Sarpe."

"Sssoo it would ssseem," Sarpe hissed, rearranging her coil to get more comfortable.

"Well now, yah gonna lay thar broodin' or yah gonna go ahed an tells me all about it?"

Sighing, Sarpe knew Maopa could be quite persistent if she wanted to be; not to mention she showed no deference to the elder's position.

"I sssuppose you'll be pesstering me all night if I don't," Sarpe grumbled.

"Now, now. Whatcha mean pesterin'? Is that any way ta be talkin' 'bout someone who's jest tryin' ta be neighborly?"

Shaking her head, Sarpe yawned, feigning boredom.

"Ssorry, Maopa," she said, looking somewhat contrite. "I guesss I'm a little confused at the moment. I met sssomeone who brings out feelings I've never experienssed before."

"Now that I understands. Mari does that ta me. So who be this here person? Does I knowed her?"

Maopa looked around at the spirits gathered near the bonfires, wondering which one had caught the serpent's fancy.

"No, she's not a ssspirit."

"Ya means ta tell me she be human?"

"Not quite."

"Not quite? What kind of answer be that? How ken someone be not quite human?"

145

"Becausse she isn't quite human," Sarpe said, enjoying the other spirit's confusion. "She's closse, though."

"All right. Now bez a good time ta jest let loose and tells me what ya be a jawin' about and quit pullin' my leg."

"Well, she looksss human, but she's not. It'sss hard to explain. Let'sss jussst sssay when I'm around her, I feel ssstrange. All coiled up insside. Her touch is exciting," Sarpe admitted. "That'ss the only way I can explain it."

"Well, dang, girl! Ya has a hankerin' for her. What be the problem, other than maybe the few yars yah might be a havin'?"

"That'sss jusst it. Her people have very long lives. We could have many yearss together."

"I dun knowed why yah be a churnin' yer guts over this then," Maopa said, confused by the other spirit's dilemma.

Sarpe sighed heavily and briefly outlined what she had learned about Ekimmu—her need for small quantities of human blood and how she obtained it. Her greatest fear was that she might give into her feelings for the mortal and permit Ekimmu to drink her essence, hoping it would either give her immortality or at least lengthen her life span.

"Yeah. I ken see that might be playin' with fahr. Does yah loves her?"

"I don't know. I've never known love like thisss before. She makesss me feel different, but I don't want uss to become clossse, only to lose her when she passsesss to the Great Beyond. How could I not share all of me with her if it meant prolonging her exisstensse?"

"That definitely be a hard one. I doesn't have an answer fer yah. I knowed I'd do almost anythin' ta keep Mari with me. I loves her that much. But she already be a spirit, so I doesn't have ta make that choice. I suppose yah has ta makes that decision sometime, but does it hafta be now?"

Sarpe thought about the question. "No. I guesss not," she said. "After all, thisss may jusst be…how do you humans sssay it? A fling?"

"Umm…in my day, we calls it rompin' in the hay and I must say, they ken be more fun than tarrin' and featherin' two-legged polecats." Maopa chuckled.

Arbora was passing by just as Sarpe rolled her eyes. Laughing, she called out to Maopa. "You go, girl. I've only seen her do that twice."

Uncoiling, Sarpe shook her head in disgust. "Great! She'ss not going to let me forget thisss," the spirit hissed. "I guesss we should join the party. Thanksss for your help. I'll work thisss out later."

"Good. Mari's been a watchin' us like we be the last meal of a starvin' dog. I thinks I better head on over yonder and help her chat up the others, doesn't yah thinks?"

"If'n yah wantsss ta get sssome later," Sarpe said, mimicking the human spirit's accent.

"Sarpe, you rascal, behaves yohrself. Now get yohrself out thar and gives Mari a hand, figuratively, of course." She smirked.

"Of coursss," Sarpe said sarcastically, uncoiling her large body and gliding away.

Shaking her head, Maopa walked back to Mari.

Near the Great Falls, Yemaya found a small grove of fruit trees. Beneath one of the trees lay a blanket, a small basket of fruits, and a flask of golden wine.

"Wow."

Yemaya lowered Dakota onto the blanket.

"Wow is right." She stretched out next to Dakota. Picking up some grapes, Yemaya offered her one, rubbing it across her lips. Dakota responded by placing a strawberry between Yemaya's lips, then leaned over to bite half of it.

"Mmm. Fruit never tasted this good back home."

Yemaya smiled mischievously. Sliding her body over her lover's, she felt pulses racing. "This is a dreamworld, so nothing here is like home."

"I wouldn't say that." Dakota grinned, running her fingers lightly up Yemaya's sides. "Maybe we should test the theory."

"Hmm," Yemaya murmured, lowering her voice to sound like Mari. "Would you care to experiment with me?"

Dakota shivered. "You do that on purpose," she grumbled.

"What?" Yemaya's voice grew deep and husky.

"That...that voice. You know how your voice affects people and especially me."

"I need all the help I can get," Yemaya whispered, running her tongue along the ridge of Dakota's left ear. "You taste sweet."

Dakota groaned. "You don't need help," she murmured, capturing Yemaya's lips with her own.

Yemaya gathered Dakota in her arms and pulled her tightly against her chest. Tongues lightly touching, they felt the blood surging through their veins as hearts pounded.

"You so take my breath away," Yemaya growled, looking at Dakota's breasts. "Umm. Dakota?"

"Yes?" she answered distractedly.

"Have you noticed that we happen to be very naked?"

Blinking, Dakota looked at her chest, then at Yemaya's.

"That's a definite plus for the spirit world," she said, grinning. "I wonder what others we'll find."

Smiling, Yemaya ran her finger across Dakota's nipples, watching in fascination as they hardened. "I have to say I am not the least tired now."

"Me…Me neither."

"And I definitely know my hormones are raging."

"Mmm...me…too."

"Perhaps we should do something about that. What do you think?"

"I'm...n...no…not. I mean yes..."

Yemaya chuckled. Obviously, Dakota was experiencing the same intense needs she was. Sliding her lips down Dakota's neck to her shoulder, she nipped the skin lightly. Feeling her lover arch her back slightly, she smiled. She loved the way Dakota reacted to her touches. Leaning slightly away, she traced her fingers along Dakota's ribs and down her left hip to her thigh. Dakota felt the goose bumps pebble up on her arms and squirmed. Grinning, Yemaya walked her fingers back up Dakota's body and cupped a breast, rubbing the nipple lightly with her thumb.

"Do you think our bodies are feeling anything in the real world?" she asked, kissing the other breast tenderly.

"Oh. I think so. Our sheets are going to be drenched."

"Good" was all Yemaya said, once again capturing Dakota's lips. Locked in a heated kiss, Dakota's senses were on overload when she felt a hand stroking her inner thigh. Arching upward, she moved her leg slightly, inviting Yemaya's hand to take her. Feeling the movement, Yemaya ran the tip of her finger across the lower lips but then slid her hand back up to Dakota's stomach, massaging it gently. Dakota groaned.

"You're going to make me beg, aren't you?"

"Never that," Yemaya whispered softly. "But I am going to make this last all night, like I promised earlier."

"Promises, promises."

"One I intend on keeping." Yemaya's breath brushed warmly across Dakota's skin. Feeling her own excitement growing, she rose to her knees and slowly ran her hands down Dakota's body until they rested on her hips. Dakota closed her eyes, enjoying the caress and contact with her lover. Anticipation grew as Yemaya moved her thumbs in a circular motion. With a quick tug, Yemaya brought their bodies closer together as she knelt between Dakota's thighs.

"This is where you are meant to be. It is what you were made for. To be loved by me."

Dakota opened her eyes to stare into Yemaya's. Blue flames flared brilliantly, making her gasp. Although they had made love many times, this was their moment of truth, the total surrender of their souls to each other as they exposed their innermost feelings. Overwhelmed at such love, Yemaya wasn't aware of the tears sliding down her cheek until Dakota reached up and gently brushed them away.

"I didn't know," she whispered, for some reason feeling the need to apologize.

"I know," Yemaya said, leaning her forehead against Dakota's. "It is not easy letting someone past the walls, letting them see the real me, the good and the bad."

"Oh, Yemaya. I've loved you such a short time, but it seems like forever. How could you not know how I feel? I want all of you. What little bad there is doesn't compare to the goodness in you. All I've ever wanted was for you to love me."

"With my heart and soul, my love." Yemaya leaned down for a kiss. Unable to hold herself back, she lowered her head and placed her cheek on Dakota's stomach, nuzzling the golden pubic hair. Inhaling, she was surprised at how quickly her mind remembered Dakota's taste. Twirling her fingers through the curls, she tugged gently on one.

Dakota groaned, growing impatient.

"Please, Yemaya."

Unable to resist her pleas, Yemaya slipped her fingers between the warm wet lips and stroked the soft skin buried beneath the golden hairs. Raising her head to watch her lover's face, she found herself barely able to breath. This is what it means to be loved, she thought, awed and equally humbled by the knowledge.

"I love you so much, Dakota," she whispered. "It scares me."

"I know," Dakota said, her voice heavy with arousal. "Please, Yemaya..."

Nodding, Yemaya gently separated the lips, lowered her head, and gave her lover a kiss before running her tongue along the tender skin. She vowed to herself she would do everything in her power to protect the gift bestowed on her.

They made love well into the night, both insatiable in their desire to please the other. Neither Yemaya nor Dakota remembered falling asleep. When they awoke, they were in their own bed back at the estate.

"Was it real?" Dakota wondered aloud.

"Yes," Yemaya answered, looking at Dakota. "I think it was Mari and Grandma Dakota's way of thanking us."

"We should attend their festivities more often then." Dakota grinned. "Although I don't think I could take many nights like that and still hold down a job." She smirked.

"Me neither," Yemaya agreed, laughing. "I think I would give up my day job for nights like that," she added, wiggling her eyebrows.

"Yeah, me too!"

A knock on the door interrupted their musings.

"This is getting to be a regular habit," Dakota grumbled.

"So it would seem. Come in, Maria."

The door opened slowly.

"Sorry, mistress, but there's a Ms. Ekimmu Elil downstairs. She said she needed to talk to you and Ms. Devereaux before she leaves town."

"We will be right down. Thanks."

"That's the woman with Constance last night."

"Yes."

"I wonder what she wants."

Ekimmu listened to the crackling of the fire while she stared into the flames. They reminded her of her own inner struggles. Perhaps she would never find the answers she sought. Did anyone ever, she thought. Turning toward the door before it opened, she watched the tall Carpi and her mate walk into the room.

"Good morning, Ms. Elil. Can we offer you something to eat or drink?"

"No, thank you, Ms. Lysanne. I don't have much time. I have to leave soon, but I thought you might have a few questions left unanswered."

"That's thoughtful of you. Where's Ramus?" Dakota asked.

"Gone."

"Gone? Gone where?" Yemaya asked, not liking the answer.

Shrugging, Ekimmu turned back to the fire. "It's strange," she said. "When I watch a fire, I see life, a living organism struggling to survive. It needs oxygen to breathe, fuel for nourishment, and in a way must reproduce to stay alive just like us. Have you ever thought about it?"

Not sure who she was talking to, Yemaya and Dakota looked at each other.

"Not really," Yemaya replied. "But you may be right. What does that have to do with Ramus?"

"Nothing. Everything. We're all flames in a way, searching for anything to prolong our existence. Ramus is no different."

"Ramus is a cold-blooded killer who has ruined an unimaginable number of lives. He's a parasite…a plague!" Dakota said angrily. "And you say he's 'gone,' as if that's all there is to it. Do you expect us to just accept that?"

"No, but you really have no choice, and before you start thinking about looking for him, remember that he has traveled this planet for a very long time. He knows of places you have never even dreamed of."

"We will find him," Yemaya said coolly.

Ekimmu smiled. "I almost believe you could. I'd advise against it, Ms. Lysanne. You and Ms. Devereaux might get lucky and destroy him, but at what price? Are you willing to sacrifice each other for the likes of him? Besides, I wouldn't worry too much about him now. His days are numbered."

"Numbered? We don't understand," Dakota said.

Ekimmu debated how much to reveal. Deciding now wasn't the right moment to tell everything, she kept the explanation simple.

"Ramus is dying. Apparently, he hasn't been *discreet* in his lifestyle. He's contracted a virus that will destroy his immune system in a matter of a few years."

"That gives him plenty of time to ruin more lives," Dakota said. "And you expect us to do nothing?"

"No, I imagine you'll try to find him. Your search will be long and fruitless, but it's not in your nature to do nothing, Ms. Devereaux. I envy you that tenacity," Ekimmu said, smiling gently. "I've spent most of my life doing nothing about him. Do what you feel you must. In the end, he *will* be long dead and you will have wasted precious years on the hunt. At least think about what I've said. Time is everyone's enemy, but especially his. Now I really need to go," she added, looking at her watch.

"Thank you for coming, Ms. Elil. Perhaps my driver can take you to the airport in Cahul," Yemaya offered, placing her hand on Dakota's arm to silence her.

"Thanks, but a cab is waiting outside. One more thing, though. Ms. Lorraine asked me to retrieve the manuscript she gave you a few days ago."

"Of course!" Dakota said, walking to the desk and picking it up. "I'm surprised she mentioned it to you. It seems to be a very valuable historical record."

"It is and I'll protect it until it's returned to her."

Tucking it under her arm, she nodded her thanks. Walking to the door, Ekimmu stopped and looked at the two women. "I envy you your love," she admitted. "And, Ms. Lysanne, I look forward to seeing one of your performances someday. I have no doubt it will be a flaming success." Winking, she quietly opened the door and left.

"How strange!"

"Yes." Yemaya's brows wrinkled in thought. "Would you mind if I worked a little while on my new show? I just had an idea I would like to develop."

"Nah, I have a few articles to turn in. My old boss is still bugging me about freelancing with him."

Standing on her toes, she gave Yemaya a kiss on the cheek. Already, she could tell her lover's thoughts were miles away.

CHAPTER EIGHTEEN

The sweat tickled as it trickled between her breasts before continuing its path down her stomach to her navel. Reaching down to wipe it away, she stared at the moisture on her fingertips and realized she was almost naked. Confusion and a sense of loss brought tears to her eyes, and she closed them momentarily in an effort to regain some sense of being.

Falling to her knees, she looked up, her arms spread apart, begging to be saved. The flames danced magically around her, holding her captive. Jumping to her feet, she ran in circles hoping to escape the prison, only to have her path blocked by the orange, red, and blue fiery tentacles of the flames flaring upward. Swaying back and forth, in and out, they beckoned her closer. Occasionally, one would snake out to caress her body. Scrambling backward, she looked left, then right, searching for help, but there was no one.

She withdrew into a corner in an attempt to escape her tormentors' searing touch. Relentlessly, they moved closer. She dropped to her knees, and her hands pressed against her chest in fear. Terror made her scream, but no sounds were heard. Clutching her throat in pain, she swayed dramatically back and forth. Finally exhausted and accepting her fate, she sank to the floor, curled in a fetal position, and covered her head with her arms.

A silver blue flame sprang up behind her. Moving gracefully, it danced seductively around the prone figure forcing the orange flames to move away as brilliant silvery blue tentacles lashed out. Angry hisses could be heard but were ignored. Returning to the woman, the blue flame touched her shoulder tentatively. Opening her eyes, the young woman looked around. The orange fires still danced mockingly around her. It took her a few moments to realize something was different. Then she saw the blue flame. Its second touch was bolder, a warm caress that brought her to her feet. Slowly, she stretched out her hand.

The flame flickered momentarily, then stretched toward her, touching her fingertip hesitantly before running up and down her palm; then it receded, dancing seductively across the floor. The orange flames retreated farther. Curiosity overcame the woman's fear. Moving toward the flame, she held out her hand. The flame moved forward, dancing slowly, its tentacles swaying like a snake. Gaining confidence, the woman stepped into the fiery embrace. Silver blue arms tenderly enveloped her body. As the two merged into one, like lovers, they danced slowly in a circle seemingly unaware of the danger around them.

Jealous and angry, the orange flames closed in on their captive. Suddenly, the blue flame flickered brightly and exploded, sending thousands of sparks into the air, followed by a large puff of smoke. When they finally settled to the floor, both the woman and her fiery lover had vanished. The other flames screamed their frustration and died out, the performers sinking slowly to their knees.

Complete silence followed.

The crowd roared, jumping to their feet. Applause thundered through the arena. Spectators turned to their neighbors asking if they had seen where the Illusionist and her companion had disappeared. Because the stage was in the center of the audience, there was no avenue of escape without being noticed.

"It's an illusion," the young man seated next to Dakota said.

"Obviously," she agreed sarcastically, trying to ignore him.

"I've studied these magicians, and they all use mirrors to pull off most of their tricks," he said, wanting to impress her.

"I see! So where exactly are these mirrors?" Raising an eyebrow, she gave him a skeptical look.

"That's the really cool part! They've placed them all around and have mirrors to conceal the mirrors. Each mirror picks up a reflection of something and transmits it to another. Pretty soon, there are so many reflections, the mind gets confused and can't see what's directly in front of it. It's quite ingenious, you know."

Sighing, Dakota decided she had tolerated the young man's ignorance enough. "Uh-huh! Look, why don't you go find one of those mirrors for me while I write down a few notes? Now if you'll excuse me, I don't have time to talk right now."

"Oh, sorry," he said, blushing.

Dakota shook her head. *Idiot,* she thought. Reaching into her purse, she pulled out her pen and paper and made notes about the show. After a few words, the pen skipped.

"Oh, no, you don't!" She stuck the pen in her mouth and sucked hard, oblivious to the shouts and applause of the crowd. "I don't care who gave you to me. You do this again and I'm tossing you in the trash."

It was then she noticed the crowd had quieted. Looking up, she saw Yemaya standing onstage looking at her. Several members of the audience had turned in their seats to see who the Illusionist was staring at.

"I give up!" Dakota muttered, taking the pen from between her lips and throwing it in her purse. Smiling sweetly at her lover, she shrugged nonchalantly.

Yemaya laughed softly and winked before turning her attention to the audience and bowing.

"Ladies and gentlemen, thank you for your generosity. The proceeds from tonight's show will go to HIV and AIDS research. Hopefully, with your contributions and the help of several scientists, we'll win this battle soon. Be safe on your way home and remember to tell those you love how you feel. You may not get another chance."

Yemaya waved, walking toward the nearest exit. At the door, she stopped and peered at the back of the arena on the far side. A figure moved stealthily along the aisle and disappeared behind a partition near a service entry door. When Dakota saw Yemaya stop, she followed the woman's gaze, curious.

"Ramus," she muttered angrily, looking back at Yemaya, who acknowledged her thought before leaning down to listen to one of her staff who was whispering something. Motioning for Dakota to meet her in back, she left.

"That was Ramus," she declared, hugging Yemaya tightly.

"Yes, but calm down. Ekimmu was right. He's dying."

"Serves him right! What did he want?"

"Apparently, he is interested in our *cause.*" Handing Dakota a piece of paper, she waited for her reaction.

"It's a check for a million dollars!"

"So it would seem. I guess he thinks he has something to gain if a cure is discovered."

"I hope he's long dead and gone by then," Dakota growled, tossing the check on the table.

"I could not care less if he is," Yemaya said. "It is the cure that matters. Where the money comes from is not important as long as it moves us forward."

"Yeah, I guess, but I can still fantasize."

"Only about me, love. What did you think of the show?"

"I think the next time I attend one, you need to make sure I don't sit next to some idiot," Dakota grumbled. "And get me a damn ink pen that works. Do you have some type of power over those things?" She eyed her lover suspiciously.

Laughing, Yemaya hugged her. "No, I think you just like attracting my attention," she said. "How about we go back to the hotel? Those flames made me hot."

"I think it was your attendant. Where'd you find her? She's quite attractive and a very good actress."

"That is Lia. This was a form of therapy."

"Lia? She's recovered?"

"Pretty much. Dr. Lichy thinks the bacteria have a very short life span. She fit the role for this act, so I thought I would give her a chance. Who better to play the captive?"

"Good point. By the way, are you ever going to tell me how you do that flame impersonation? It looks so real!"

"Would you believe me if I said it was?"

Dakota eyed Yemaya suspiciously. "Actually, I wouldn't put it past you."

"There you go." Yemaya smirked.

"That's okay. Keep your secrets. I happen to know exactly how you do it," Dakota declared, strolling away with a slight swagger.

"Oh? Do tell."

"Mirrors. Lots of mirrors," Dakota said smugly.

Rolling her eyes, Yemaya was about to make a smart remark but decided discretion was wiser. "Umm. Right. Mirrors."

Grabbing Dakota's arm, she pulled her into her own and kissed her. Dakota groaned as the heat from her lover's body inflamed her passions. "Or not!" Yemaya whispered, feeling very warm. "I think we need a nice long vacation away from all of this."

"Our bags are packed. How soon can you finish up here?"

"Sonny can take care of that. We have more important matters to attend to. Care for a little romp in the hay, as Grandma Dakota would say?"

"Shore 'nuff. Last one to the plane gets the back rub, and I'm talking about a *very* long rub," Dakota purred as she ran toward the exit where a limousine waited outside.

"Damn. I hate losing like this," Yemaya muttered, strolling slowly after Dakota.

In the alleyway across the street, shiny black eyes peered stoically at the two women as they climbed into the limousine. Watching it drive off, his lips twitched slightly before he turned and walked into the darkness.

CHAPTER NINETEEN

Lydia glanced nervously at the man sitting in the darkened corner of the bar. Every night for the past three weeks, he arrived at the same time and occupied the same spot. At first, she paid him little attention, but soon found it eerie how the occupants of that particular table would always get up and move away when he approached them. Perhaps they felt the same unease she did whenever she waited on him. Even the customers sitting at nearby tables would glance in his direction nervously, only to find him stoically returning their gazes. Immediately, they turned away and whispered amongst themselves or moved to another part of the bar.

Turning to the bartender, she asked for the usual bottle of water and a glass of ice, knowing the stranger drank nothing else.

"This guy gives me the creeps," Lydia said, putting everything on a tray. "He keeps watching me."

"That's because you're easy to look at," Germaine teased. "But I agree. He certainly isn't good for business. He makes everyone around him uncomfortable."

"Can't you get the boss to ask him to leave? Something about him scares me."

"Nope. I already asked. He said the guy's not doing anything wrong. There's no law against watching people, and since he pays for his water, the boss said we treat him like the rest. Besides, I think he's harmless enough, probably just lonely. He never seems to stay long anyway."

Lydia shook her head in disgust. "Maybe not, but I don't like it. Have you noticed some of our regulars haven't come back since he started coming in? Even Joey's been gone for over a week and he hasn't missed his Tuesday and Thursday nights here in over two years. Maybe the guy's a serial killer or something."

Germaine laughed. "Lydia, you have a great imagination. You ought to take up writing."

"Laugh all you want," she said, disgusted by the bartender's lack of concern. She picked up the tray, walked over to the stranger and put the water and glass on the table. When he handed her a ten-dollar bill, she started to give him the change.

"Please keep it," he said, his voice deep and formal.

Glancing at his face, she noticed the black eyes. The color of polished coal, there was no distinction between the pupils and the irises.

Sort of alien looking, she thought. Shivering slightly, she mumbled a quick thanks and hurried away.

"I tell you there's something not right about him," she muttered to no one in particular, glancing back in his direction nervously. The stranger smiled and nodded. Catching her breath, Lydia rubbed her arms, trying to erase the goose bumps that had suddenly appeared. She couldn't shake the feeling he knew what she was thinking.

Deciding to take a break, she signaled to Germaine that she was going outside for a quick smoke. She hoped the cool air would steady her nerves. Leaning against the side of the building, she drew deeply on the cigarette and relaxed as the warm smoke filled her lungs, giving her a quick fix. Slowly exhaling, she glanced down the street, hoping her boyfriend would show up soon.

Two men stood several feet away. Apparently unaware of her presence or not caring, they argued loudly, their voices carrying clearly across the short distance.

"Listen, Aiden. I tell you, she'll pay a hundred grand for him, no questions asked."

"But we don't know that's him," the other man replied, flicking his cigarette onto the street and crushing it with his foot.

"Mambo Lucretia said he was tall, thin, and had eyes the color of coal. Have you looked at this guy? He fits her description perfectly. It's him. All we got to do is nab him when he comes out and call the old witch. It's easy money."

"Maybe. But if it was so easy, how come he's still sitting in the bar and no one has caught him yet? It doesn't make any sense."

"Shit, man. It's not like the woman put an ad in the paper. The only reason I know about him is through my cousin Peety. He knows her bodyguard, a big bruiser named Boudreau, and the guy told Peety his boss was looking for this man."

"Peety's an idiot! He's always coming up with some crazy bullshit stuff. I'll think about it. The guy comes here every night, so I'm not going to decide anything until I sleep off the booze and check this out."

"Damn it, he might be gone tomorrow!"

"Then he's gone! The last time you talked me into one of your wildass schemes, it cost me big-time. I'm not going to jump just because your cousin tells you something that might not even be true."

"But, Aid..."

"You heard me! I said tomorrow."

Shaking his head, the other man walked away mumbling, his hands tucked in his pockets.

Throwing her cigarette on the sidewalk, Lydia stepped on it and turned to go back into the bar. Suddenly, she was grabbed from behind and spun around. Ready to strike her attacker with her fists, she was pulled unceremoniously against a solid chest, hugged, and kissed hard.

"Hey, baby."

"Billy!" Lydia yelled, slapping his arm. "You scared the shit out of me."

"Aw, come on. You know how I am," he said with a boyish grin.

"Yeah, and you know how nervous I've been with this creep coming into the place."

"He's still here, I take it."

"Yeah, the boss says since he's not causing problems, we can't kick him out. I think he's interested in me. He watches me all the time. It's like he knows what I'm thinking or something. He just sits there and smiles this scary little smile."

"He just likes your looks, baby," Billy said, taking her arm to guide her inside. "Can't blame him for that."

"Damn it, I wish you'd take me seriously."

"I do. Honest. I just think you're overreacting. Look, you buy me a beer and I'll check the guy out. How's that? Besides, I bet all your admirers are wondering where you are."

Lydia quickly glanced toward the dark corner and noticed the seat was empty. Looking around, it was obvious he had left.

"Thought you said he was here."

"He was. Just a few minutes ago, I gave him some water. Maybe he left through the back."

"Looks like I can indulge in a few beers then." Billy grinned.

"I'll get you one."

Pulling him by the arm to the bar, she grabbed a beer and motioned toward a table.

"Thanks, baby. I need this. So what time you getting off tonight? I may go shoot some pool with the guys from the dock."

"Same time. It's been pretty slow tonight…umm…I just heard two guys outside talking about this creep. At least it sounded like him. I think he may be wanted or something. One said there's a reward out for him."

"What kind of reward?" Billy asked, taking a swig of the beer.

"A hundred grand."

"Jesus, Lydia!" Billy exclaimed, wiping beer from his chin. Looking around, he lowered his voice. "By who?"

"That old voodoo woman, Lucretia. One of them said she was offering a hundred grand for someone like him. They said he fits her description."

"Wait here. I need to make a call."

Handing her the bottle, he pulled out his cell phone from his shirt pocket and hurried out the door.

"Hey, Lydia, you gonna sit there all night or wait on the customers?" the bartender yelled.

"Oh, shut up, Germaine! You aren't the boss!" she shouted back. Germaine smirked and went back to pouring drinks.

"Hey, baby!" Billy whispered, walking up behind her. "You heard right. Mambo Lucretia put the word out on a guy a few months ago, and apparently, she wants him bad. I'm surprised no one's caught him by now."

"I'm not. I think he's dangerous. Everyone avoids him."

"He doesn't scare me. Tomorrow, you and I are going to nab him. I need to check out a few things. I'll be back later to pick you up."

Nodding, Lydia gave him a quick kiss and left to wait on her customers.

Billy returned shortly after closing time. Lydia finished clearing the tables and grabbed her sweater.

"Hey, Germaine, I'm out of here," she yelled, then waved goodbye. "I'll see you tonight."

"Later. Hey, Billy…you take good care of my girl now. She's the best barmaid we've got," Germaine yelled back.

"No problem!" He grabbed Lydia's arm and pulled her toward the exit. "I think we can do this." Billy said enthusiastically. "Tonight when you come in, if the guy's here, tell the boss you're not feeling well. Leave about forty-five minutes before closing and head toward the apartment, okay?"

"Where are you going to be?"

"I'll be nearby. You just do what I say. If this works and he's really interested in you, we're gonna be rich and you can leave this dump."

"Okay, but how is my leaving early going to help you get him?"

Billy looked at his shoes and scuffed one toe back and forth. "I know you're not going to like this, but you have to trust me, baby."

Lydia suspected what Billy was alluding to and immediately balked at the thought. "No," she said, stepping away from him. "You can just forget everything you're thinking about."

"It's not like I'm asking you to sleep with him. Hell, you probably won't even have to flirt. The guy obviously has a thing for you already, and a little extra attention should do. You're hot! You just be real nice, chat him up some, and pretend you feel sick. I bet he offers to walk you home."

"No, I'm not encouraging him."

"Aw, baby, I'll be nearby. Don't you trust me?"

"That's not it and you know it. He's too weird. What if something happens and you aren't out there?"

"Okay, look. I'll call you first. Then you'll know I'm here. Nothing's going to happen. Let him take you home, and I'll do the rest." Wrapping his arms around her, he leaned down and gave her a kiss. "Please, for me?" he begged. "It's our ticket out of here. We'll go to New York like you've always wanted. Hell, I bet we can even find a small bar somewhere. A hundred grand can be a pretty good down payment."

"I'll think about it," she said reluctantly.

"That's my girl." Billy hugged her tightly. He knew when she

163

said she'd think about, he had won.

That evening, Lydia made an effort to pay a little extra attention to the stranger. His failure to react, however, left her confused, feeling she may have been wrong. Perhaps he wasn't attracted to her after all. The few times she tried to initiate conversations with him, he seemed distracted. His only response to her advances was a small smile but no reply.

Eventually, she gave up and left him alone. When Billy called, she told him what had happened.

"Don't worry about it. He's probably playing it cool. Just take him his last drink and do like I said. If he doesn't offer to take you home, I'll go to my backup plan."

Hanging up, Lydia grabbed another bottle of water and carried it to the table.

"Last call, mister," she said weakly. "Germaine will help you if you need anything else. I'm not feeling well, so I'm going home."

Cool ebony eyes stared at her. She wasn't sure if he was smiling or smirking, but his expression made her stomach jittery. Now she really did feel sick.

"I'm sorry to hear that, Ms. Lydia," he said quietly.

"Oh, I'm sure it's just a stomach bug. I should be back tomorrow."

"You're probably right."

When he didn't say anything more, Lydia shrugged and left to tell Germaine she was leaving. Stepping into the cool night air, she looked around for signs of Billy. Not seeing him, she flipped her jacket collar up around her neck and headed home.

"You should not walk the streets at night by yourself."

Startled, Lydia spun around. She could feel her heart pounding furiously. Behind her stood the man from the bar, his hat pulled low to shade his eyes.

"Oh. It's okay. I go the same way all the time," she said, her voice shaking.

"I see I've frightened you. Please forgive me."

Lydia noticed he had an Old World formality, which gave him a certain charm. The faint accent and softly spoken words soothed her frayed nerves.

"That's okay. Nights just spook me sometimes."

"The nights are quite beautiful, especially here. They remind me of my homeland."

Lydia noticed the sadness in his voice. "I guess I'm just jaded. I was raised here, so it's all I know. When you're brought up in New Orleans, all you hear about is spirits and voodoo and ghost stories. Not that I believe in any of that stuff, but I suppose we all have our weak moments. Anyway, I guess I should get moving."

"May I walk you home, Ms. Lydia? I would feel better knowing you arrived safe."

"Thanks. That's sweet, but I don't think it's a good idea. Besides, I don't even know you."

"You're right, of course," he apologized. "It's obvious I've forgotten my manners. My name is Ramus. Ramus Falthama. It would be my honor to walk you home, particularly as your young man isn't here to accompany you."

At the mention of Billy, Lydia again looked around. Not seeing him, she hesitated. Unfortunately, she couldn't think of a reason to refuse. Besides, he genuinely seemed concerned about her welfare. Perhaps she was wrong about him, she thought.

"Well, if you're sure it's not a problem. You never know when a nut is out there lurking in the dark."

"You're very wise to be so careful. There are many undesirable things that travel the night."

Holding out his arm, he offered it to her. Surprised at the courtly gesture, she hesitated, but then slipped her own arm through his. For several minutes, they walked in silence. Finally, she decided she should at least thank him for his kindness.

"I've never met a real gentleman before. I notice you have a slight accent. Sort of foreign."

"Unfortunately, it's something I've never been able to eliminate."

"It's nice. I like the way you talk," Lydia said and realized it was true. "So you're not American."

"No. European actually, but I'm well traveled."

"I envy you. One day, I'd like to travel. I feel like I've been trapped here all my life."

"Perhaps one day you will. You're still very young."

"Yeah, I guess." She sighed. "European, eh? Are you French?"

Ramus smiled. "No, but I speak the language."

"That's cool. I wish I did. You'd think living here, I'd at least know Creole, but my folks never let me associate with Cajuns. They said they were too crude and superstitious. How many languages do you know?"

"I'm not really sure after all these years. I would imagine at least two dozen fluently and a handful more conversationally."

"Two dozen! I didn't know there were that many on the planet."

Ramus laughed, amused by her teasing. Lydia was pleased. She suspected he was not a man who laughed easily.

Mysterious black eyes shadowed by immeasurable pain and sadness moved restlessly, searching the darkness for possible threats. Pale skin was stretched tightly over high cheeks and the straight nose. His lips were thin, but when he smiled, he had perfect white teeth, although his canine teeth seemed unusually long. It was impossible for her to guess his age. She imagined he was probably in his seventies. Lydia realized that Ramus was quite handsome in spite of his strangeness.

"Do you mind if I ask you a question?"

"You may ask. I'm not sure I'll answer it."

"It's not exactly a question, but you don't look well. Are you sick?"

Ramus glanced down at her, one eyebrow arching. "You're very forward."

"Oh, I hope I didn't offend you."

"Not at all. I find it quite refreshing. To answer your question, though, I do have health issues. Nothing that you need fear."

"Gosh, I wasn't even thinking that. I was just concerned. You seem like a nice man."

Bowing his head slightly, he accepted the compliment graciously.

"I believe you're the first person who has ever said that about me or showed concern," he said, smiling broadly.

Lydia was stunned at the transformation. Ramus Falthama was more than just handsome. He was actually quite beautiful. As a young man, she imagined he would have devastated the women with his looks and charm.

"Thank you," Ramus said, grinning.

"For what?"

"For the compliment and for worrying."

"Oh, no problem."

For a few blocks, neither spoke. Lydia was hoping Billy had gotten sidetracked by something else. During her brief interaction with Ramus, she realized her fears had been unwarranted. He was just a lonely old man looking for company.

Aware of her thoughts, Ramus was amused. She had no clue as to his real age. The irony was that she was more right than she could ever imagine; not about his years, of course, but that he was old. So many centuries had come and gone, he had lost track of the number.

"I believe we are only a few blocks from your..."

Before either could react, an object whizzed by Lydia's head, striking Ramus in the shoulder near his neck. Without thinking, he shoved her away in an attempt to protect her and turned to face the assailant. Unfortunately, his illness had slowed his reflexes and he couldn't react fast enough to stop the bat from crashing down on his skull. The pain was excruciating but fleeting. Sinking to his knees, he felt the darkness rushing in and tumbled onto his side, unconscious.

Billy stepped from the shadows, looking as if he had just won the lottery. "Hey, baby, you did swell!" He glanced up and down the street to make sure no one had seen the attack. At the moment, the area was empty.

"Did you have to hit him so hard?" Lydia cried, leaning down to feel for a pulse. "I think you killed him," she said, genuinely concerned for the man lying by her feet.

"Nah, he's fine. I barely hit him. Now help me get him in the car before someone sees us."

Dragging the limp body to the car, Billy and Lydia pushed it in the backseat and drove to a secluded warehouse near the waterfront. Inside, they lifted Ramus onto an old table and tied his hands and feet. Billy searched the stranger's pockets, removing his wallet. Rifling through it, he pulled out several bills and some credit cards.

"Damn it, Billy! This isn't right! He's just a nice old man."

"Make up your mind, baby. First you don't like him, and now all of a sudden, he's a nice guy. Besides, he won't need the money or the cards, so stop worrying."

Ramus slowly became aware of his surroundings and the pain

in his head. Instinctively, he tried to massage the area that hurt but found his hands had been bound together and tied to the ropes around his ankles.

For the first time in his life, he knew how it felt to be helpless and he was afraid. He hated feeling vulnerable. With that came the realization that he was mortal after all. Sweat streamed down his cheeks and dripped onto the cream-colored silk shirt clinging damply to his emaciated chest.

Although blindfolded, he could sense two people standing several meters away. It was apparent they didn't want him to hear what they were saying. Fortunately, or unfortunately, depending on whose point of view, he had excellent hearing.

"I tell you it isn't right," Lydia argued, sounding nervous.

"Get real! He's worth a lot of money. The old woman said she'd pay us a hundred big ones for this guy," the male replied in exasperation. "You want to throw away that much money because of scruples?"

"It's got nothing to do with that and you know it. I just don't think we should get involved with that old witch and her people. She's creepy."

Glancing nervously at their prisoner, Billy tried to appear confident. "She's just an old woman. Mambo Lucretia makes her living terrorizing her followers and anyone else who believes that mumbo jumbo. You don't really believe in this voodoo crap, do you?"

"That's not the point. People are afraid of her. She can get any one of them to do anything she wants. I heard two tourists disappeared last year after refusing to pay her for a reading. Then they called her an old fraud and threatened to expose her as a scam artist. No one's seen them since."

"People disappear all the time in this town. All that hocus pocus is for the tourists. They love this voodoo shit. Besides, who's to say they didn't just go home?"

"And leave all their clothes and personal things behind like that? Give me a break. Let's just let him go. He hasn't seen your face. I'll tell him it was a mistake. He's a nice man. We can head up to New York for a while. Please," she pleaded, clutching his arm tightly.

Looking down at her hand, Billy shook his head. "With what? We don't have any money. Once the old witch has this guy, we're home free. We grab our money and get out of town. Trust me, baby. I know what I'm doing."

Sighing, Lydia looked doubtful. Nothing about this felt right.

"Okay. But I'm scared and I still say I don't like it. You didn't have to hit him so hard. I thought you killed him."

"Nah, I went easy on him. He's just sickly. Who knows, maybe we're doing him a favor."

Lydia ignored the comment. Sometimes, she thought Billy could be such an idiot.

"So what's next?" she asked hesitantly.

"I make the call and tell her we have him," he said, giving her a quick kiss. Picking up his cell, Billy dialed a number.

"Hello. Mambo Lucretia?…Yeah, I'll wait…Mambo Lucretia?…It's Billy. I have him...yeah, he's alive, just like you wanted...well, I had to give him a good knock on the head, so I imagine he has a headache, but he'll live...no, no one saw me... okay...you have the money, right?…No, I'm not questioning your word....I'm at the old warehouse near the Café du Monde...the one we talked about earlier...okay...thirty minutes."

Snapping the phone shut, Billy gave Lydia the thumbs-up.

"Thirty minutes and we're rich. Then we're out of here."

Lydia gave him a weak smile and walked over to where Ramus lay tied and blindfolded. She wanted to say something to him but couldn't think of any words to excuse her role in the abduction. Placing her hand on his shoulder, she squeezed it gently.

"I'm so sorry," she whispered, her eyes watering from unshed tears.

Receiving no response, she turned and walked away. Leaning against the far wall, Lydia deliberately avoided looking at their captive.

"Women," Billy muttered, shrugging. Walking over to the man, he nudged him on the shoulder and frowned.

"You sure don't look important enough for a hundred grand. I wonder why the old witch wants you so badly."

When the man didn't answer, Billy thumped him with the back of his hand.

"Hey! Nothing to say? If I were you, I'd be worried. I hear this woman's crazy and uses human sacrifices in her rituals. Oh, well, none of my business. As long as we get our money, we don't give a damn why she wants you. Right, baby?" he asked, looking at Lydia. When she ignored him, he cursed under his breath and left the room.

Ramus lay still. He had felt a genuine attraction to Lydia. From the moment he noticed her in the bar, he was drawn to her but sensed her aversion to him. Still, every night, he felt compelled to go back hoping to see her again.

The few times they talked, he felt a strange peacefulness. Those were the nights he left the bar early and returned to his hotel room without satisfying his need for blood.

After several weeks, the weakness set in. He knew he needed to leave town. To stay in New Orleans would mean dying…or worse. If he stayed, he would eventually kill Lydia as he had done to all his lovers. It was his nature.

Knowing he would never see her again was physically painful. His chest had ached at the thought. That night, he had gone to the restaurant for one last look before moving on. The decision had cost him dearly.

CHAPTER TWENTY

L ucretia Mordeau hung up the phone and motioned for her servant to go, leaving her alone with her young apprentice.

"Claudine, get Boudreau. Mission accomplie! Nous devons partir immediatement."

Nodding, the petite black woman picked up the phone and dialed a number. "Boudreau, Ms. Lucretia say you come quickly. Bring the coffin. We have cargo."

Fifteen minutes later, a large black man arrived, driving an old black hearse. Bowing respectfully to the tall dark-skinned woman emerging from behind a rusty wrought iron gate, he held open the car door, making sure not to come in contact with her or her clothing. Eyes lowered, he mumbled a respectful greeting and waited for her orders.

"To the warehouse, Boudreau, and be deescreet," she commanded before leaning back in the seat.

Twenty minutes later, the hearse pulled quietly into a small alley between two buildings. Opening the passenger door, Boudreau again lowered his eyes as his mistress climbed from the car and looked around. From the shadows stepped a young man in his twenties. Short and stocky with mousy brown hair, he nervously sucked on a cigarette before throwing it on the pavement and crushing it with his foot.

"Ms. Mordeau?"

"Oui. Billee?"

"Umm. Yes. I'm Billy, but I don't speak French," he said, shrugging. "Do you have the money?"

"But of course, et une petite surprise aussi. Um, how you say? And a leetle sometheeng extra."

Billy grinned, pleased. He could always use a few more bucks.

Glancing at Boudreau, Lucretia walked toward Billy while the large black man moved to the back of the car and opened the trunk. Reaching inside, he pulled out a small leather case and respectfully stood several feet away.

"You weel show me my mershandise now, oui?"

Billy's gaze wandered slowly up and down the woman's body, admiring the tall slender figure beneath the colorful scarves and midcalf-length black dress. Her skin was smooth, milk chocolate brown. Braided locks pulled back from her face emphasized the high cheeks. Coffee brown eyes stared back at him in amusement as she waited patiently for him to finish his perusal. After staring into her eyes for a few seconds, he glanced away, embarrassed at having been so obvious.

"Sorry, Ms. Mordeau. I've never seen a voodoo priestess before. You're not exactly what I expected."

"Mais what did you expect?" she asked.

Billy coughed and blushed. "Well, you know how the movies are."

"Certainment, I do. You do not like what you see?"

"Oh, no! I mean yes. That's not what I meant. You're very beautiful. I just thought you'd be a lot older is all."

"How old do you theenk I am?" Lucretia asked curiously, tilting her head.

"Gosh, I don't know, mid-forties maybe," he stammered.

Lucretia laughed and hooked her arm through his, turning him toward the shadowed entrance of the warehouse. "Merci, Billee," she said, chuckling softly. "My forties left me long ago, but eez nice to hear from such a handsome young man. Maintenant, where eez my mershandise?"

"Inside."

Lydia heard the two talking a few seconds before they walked into the room. Beside her boyfriend walked a middle-aged woman of striking beauty. Although obviously of African descent, the refined features and bone structure left no doubt about her mixed ancestry.

Seeing Lydia leaning against the wall in a dark corner, Lucretia turned to Billy.

"You breeng your young madame to such a place as thees?" She arched one eyebrow and frowned. "Thees eez no way to treat your petite copine, cher," she reprimanded. "Such a pretty jeune fille should never see such theengs. Where are your manners?"

Blushing again, Billy remained silent.

"Never mind. I theenk you learn your lesson, oui? Now to business, eh?"

"Umm...sure. He's over there." Billy pointed to a door and handed her his captive's wallet. Glancing at a credit card, Lucretia tucked it back into its slot and gave it to Boudreau.

"Merci! *Boudreau, donnes l'argent à ce jeune homme et accompagne-les à leur a voiture. Tu sais quoi faire.*

"Oui. Pardon mais si je peux suggerer. La jeune femme vous serais utile pour le kanzo de Claudine."

"Excellente idée. Surveille la fille. Dis à Verell de l'emmener et de la placer avec les autres. Le garçon servira de repas aux gators. Les loas seront contents. Allez!"

Bowing, Boudreau backed away and motioned for Billy and Lydia to follow him. Outside of the warehouse, several of Lucretia's followers waited in the shadows.

"Au revoir, Billee. Enjoy your reward."

Lucretia disappeared into the other room, leaving Billy and Lydia no option but to follow the large man from the building.

Ramus knew immediately when she entered the room. Her scent was a mixture of spices and herbs. Her blood smelled rich and coppery, causing his stomach to cramp in rebellion. He hadn't eaten in a long time. Silently, he cursed the disease raging through his body. Were it not for the virus, he would have crushed this woman like the vermin she was.

"Bonjour, Monsieur Falthama. Comment ça va?"

"What do you want with me?" he demanded, turning his head in the direction of the voice.

"C'est toi que je veux. Parles-tu Creole ou Français?"

"No!" Ramus lied, realizing he might have an advantage if she thought he didn't understand her mother tongue.

"Dommage. I am deezappointed. I would have thought deefferently. Are you not well traveled, monsieur?"

"Travel doesn't make one a linguist, madame. Now perhaps you will answer my questions."

"Ah, mais oui. Where are my manners? Let me say, you have sometheeng I weesh very much."

"And what is that?"

"Why, the same theeng you would weesh, Monsieur Falthama."
She laughed.

The sound of the door opening interrupted their conversation.

"Pardon!" Boudreau interrupted. "J'ai fait ce que vous m'avez dit."

"Très bien. Please take Monsieur Falthama to the estate, et, Boudreau, he eez very valuable, tu comprends? You must handle him gently. Like un petit bébé," she warned.

Bowing, Boudreau strolled over to the table and lifted the man as if he were a child. Carrying him to the hearse where several men stood near an open coffin, he gently lowered him inside and signaled for them to place the lid on it. Then the coffin was lifted and slipped into the vehicle.

Lucretia slid into the passenger seat and motioned for her servant to take them home.

CHAPTER TWENTY-ONE

Sarpe lay brooding by the Eternal Flames. It had been several weeks since she had seen Ekimmu, and she was beginning to have doubts about their relationship, not to mention being confused about her own feelings. Human emotions were difficult to analyze, although she had to admit that she enjoyed every minute she spent with Ekimmu.

"Am I disturbing you, Sarpe?"

The serpent spirit looked up at her oldest friend. Even she wasn't immune to the warm huskiness of the Earth Mother's voice. Of all the spirits, Mari was the one who came closest to arousing feelings similar to those by Ekimmu, but only close. Their friendship had lasted an eternity without the complication of lust.

"No, I was jusst thinking," Sarpe replied somberly.

"About Ekimmu?"

"Yess, I'm not ssso sure thiss is ssuch a good thing."

"This. You mean your relationship with the mortal? Why?"

"I don't know. We are ssso different. These feelings. They are sstrange. When we are together, I feel alive. When we're apart, it's like I'm losst. The loneliness I onsse accepted willingly now ssuffocatess me."

"I understand completely, old friend. I'm like that with Maopa. To be so in tune with another living thing can be scary. Still it's a small price to pay for the rewards of love, isn't it?"

"Love? Maybe. But what does a sserpent know of love? It's not an emotion my sspecies feels deeply. It'ss fleeting and lastss only long enough to procreate. Then it vanishes."

"I seriously doubt you're having procreational feelings," Mari teased, laughing softly. "As for Ekimmu, maybe, but then she's made that way."

"Sso, you think thiss is the reasson she enjoys my company?"

Sarpe asked despondently. "She wantss to procreate?"

"No, I don't. That doesn't even make sense. Besides, Ekimmu is ancient in her own right. I doubt that she has thought about bearing children in a very long time. I think it's pretty obvious that she loves you."

Sighing, Sarpe rearranged her coils restlessly, her elliptical eyes narrowing as she thought about Mari's words. "I don't know. Even if it'ss true, what future could we have together?"

"Is the future so important you would sacrifice what you have now? You have today, and hopefully many tomorrows. Enjoy them. If you waste time worrying beyond that, opportunities will pass you by, and sadly, you'll have an eternity of regrets."

"As always, you're right."

"Not always, my friend." Mari laughed. "But most of the time. Now don't you think you should visit that young woman of yours? I'm sure she's wondering what happened to you."

"Perhappsss you have a point," Sarpe agreed, uncoiling her long body.

"Good. Talk to her. She must be having her own fears about you."

Bowing her head slightly, Sarpe vanished.

"You handled that mighty fine, love," Maopa said, wrapping her arms around the tall spirit from behind.

"Of course," Mari agreed smugly, then turned to embrace the smaller spirit. "There's a good reason why I'm the Earth Mother."

"That be so. You was made that way. Not that I be a complainin'." Maopa chuckled. "Now hows about we does some skinny dippin' in the lake? I feels some hot flashes stirrin' in my bones."

"What bones?"

Leaning down to kiss her lover, Mari ran toward the Great Falls. "Last one in gets a full body massage," she yelled.

"Dang! I just hates to lose like this," Maopa grumbled, strolling slowly after her.

CHAPTER TWENTY-TWO

The pain was the first thing Billy felt. Sluggish, with a slight headache, he tried to open his eyes. All he could see were shadows in a dimly lit room made of cinder block walls. A few rays of light peeked through a tiny barred window in a heavy wooden door.

He blinked to clear his blurry vision and rubbed his forehead, trying to massage away the headache. As it eased, he sat up to inspect his cell. In the corner, a large rectangular box lay perched on a large concrete slab.

"Oh, shit!" he exclaimed. The realization that he was locked up with a coffin sent him scrambling to the farthest corner. Back pressed tightly against the wall, he slid down to a squatting position and let his hands fall loosely between his knees. His elbows rested on his thighs. Several minutes passed before the uncomfortable position became too much and he slowly pushed himself up to stand.

"Maybe it's empty," he muttered to himself, but knew he didn't have the guts to find out. Deciding to ignore the casket and hoping it would somehow disappear, he walked to the door to inspect it for signs of weakness. Finding it solidly bolted from the other side, he glanced back at the coffin, almost expecting to see a hand pushing up from beneath the lid.

"Hello! Anyone out there?" he yelled through the bars of the window. "I said, is anyone out there?"

When no one answered, Billy shook the bars angrily, trying to vent his frustration and hoping one of them would pop out. Unfortunately, they were solidly installed in the heavy wooden planking.

"Fuckin' bitch tricked me," he muttered, thinking about Lucretia. "She'll pay big-time for this when I get out of here." The words gave him some comfort. After all, what could she do to him? Keep him for a few days, then tell him they weren't going to pay him? Well, he'd just tell them it was okay, and once free, he'd make them pay. By the time he was done, they'd double what he was owed.

Looking again at the coffin, he decided to take a closer look. If there was a body in it, he thought, the person would be dead anyway. It was probably just another way to scare him. Swallowing, he shuffled toward the coffin, hesitating occasionally to listen.

It was an old-fashioned wooden box made from pine slats. The boards were held tightly together by vertical strips of lumber and copper brackets. Unlike modern coffins, the top was flat instead of curved. The cover had not been nailed down.

"It's got to be empty," he mumbled. "I bet those bastards hid me in it and brought me down here. That's sick."

Dragging his hand across the lid, he noticed the varnished finish. Whoever built it had done a good job. Gathering his courage, he hooked his thumbs and palm on the outer edge and pushed up.

"I would not do that, Billee," a familiar voice said from behind.

"Jesus Christ!" Billy yelped, spinning around. Through the bars, Lucretia stood watching him. "Let me out of here," he demanded angrily.

"Certainment! I apologize for scaring you. Boudreau, ouvre la porte, s'il-te-plaît."

The door swung open and Lucretia stepped back.

"About fuckin' time! How come you kidnapped me...and where's my money?"

Ignoring his questions, Lucretia motioned for Billy to follow her. His lack of interest in the fate of his girlfriend confirmed her opinion that the young man was self-centered. Lydia was better off serving her than servicing him, she thought.

Billy stepped into a dimly lit hall. Two burly men grabbed him by the arms and pushed him against the wall.

"Hey!" he yelled.

A large hand clamped over his mouth, pressing harshly against his lips.

"Please, Billee...no cursing...no yelling. I do not like thees rude side of you. You weel behave, oui?"

Billy nodded, his eyes moving from the woman to the men holding him captive.

"C'est mieux. Now you weel accompany me like the young gentlemen you are."

Again he nodded, wanting the men to release his arms. If the opportunity arose, he'd make a break for it. He had no doubt he could outrun his captors. Unfortunately, neither of the men relinquished their grip, and he was marched forcefully down the hall and through a door leading to the outside. The darkness caught him by surprise. Apparently, he had been held captive for several hours. The moon was just peeking over the horizon.

At least I can hide in the darkness if I have to, he thought, examining the area for an escape route. With Lucretia in front, the two men holding him firmly on each side and Boudreau behind, he realized an escape would be difficult.

"Where are you taking me?"

"We weel be turning you loose very soon. Please do not worree," she said amicably. "You must learn patience, mon juene ami. You young are so impatient, are they not, Boudreau?"

"Oui. C'est vrai."

Laughing, Lucretia continued down a well-worn path but didn't say anything more. Billy wasn't sure how much time passed but soon saw a flicker of light through the trees.

At last, he thought, thinking it a street or house light.

Disappointed, he realized it was moonlight reflecting off the bayou. Uneasy, he slowed his pace, only to be roughly jerked forward by his bodyguards.

"Umm. Hey, look. I really don't need the money. Let me go and I'll just forget this," he pleaded.

Lucretia stopped at the edge of the swamp and turned to look at him. For several minutes, she said nothing, appearing to consider his words. Then as if making a decision, she signaled the men to release him.

Billy sighed in relief and relaxed. Boudreau stepped past him carrying a large bucket filled with raw meat. Throwing several chunks into the water, he stepped back as it boiled with activity. Several large gators lunged greedily at the tidbits. A fight ensued as the largest challenged the others for the meat. Billy realized he would be next when the two servants grabbed his arms again.

"Please! Please! I won't say anything! I'll do anything you want," he begged, pulling unsuccessfully at the hands holding him.

"You don't need to do this!"

"Je me regret, Billee," was all Lucretia said before walking away, not looking back.

A splashing sound made him look back at the water. As Billy pushed backward with his legs, trying to prolong the inevitable, Boudreau threw more meat into the water then signaled for his two companions to throw Billy in.

Terrified, Billy struggled frantically, throwing his guards off-balance. Whatever hope he had disappeared when he was picked up and heaved into the water, arms and legs flailing.

Sinking beneath the surface, he collided with something hard. He pushed away with his feet and propelled himself away, only to bump into something else before reaching the surface. Gasping for breath, he quickly scanned the area looking for his captors and signs of movement in the water near him.

The three men were walking back in the direction they had come from, apparently confident the alligators had finished him off. A few quick kicks brought him to the bank. Scrambling and clawing at the muddy slope, he managed to pull himself partially out of the water. Billy couldn't contain the hysterical laughter bubbling up as he lay face down, half in and half out of the lake.

"I did it! I did it!" he gasped, taking deep breaths to fill his oxygen-starved lungs. Unaware of the fourteen-foot monster gliding silently toward him, his exhilaration was short-lived.

A deep grunt and a sharp pain in his ankle brought him to his senses. Seized by enormously powerful jaws, he was jerked backward. The alligator shook him vigorously, trying to tear off the leg. Kicking and screaming, Billy clawed at the mud desperate to break free of the iron grip on his foot.

When his heel connected with the monster's bony eye ridge, it roared a booming hiss of frustration and released its prey. Lunging at the shore, Billy felt a momentary sense of relief.

Seconds later, massive jaws clamped around his right knee, dragging him beneath the lake's surface. Twisting and spinning, he was pulled to the bottom. Instinctively, he held his breath and fought desperately for his life.

As if playing a game, the alligator released its grip, then just as quickly bit into Billy's thigh and began spinning around, causing the water to churn and boil. Billy opened his mouth to scream. When the water surged in, he gagged and lost consciousness. He never felt his leg ripping from the hip socket, turning the water crimson. Several smaller gators moved in for their share, tearing ferociously at the sinking carcass and gulping down his remains.

Minutes later, a slight breeze gently brushed the surface of the lake, sending small ripples across the water. An owl hooted from a nearby tree and the night continued as if nothing unusual had happened.

The moon was directly overhead when the small gathering of worshippers emerged from the darkness into the clearing. Flames from several bonfires burned brightly, causing shadows to dance eerily back and forth. Dressed in white, the hounsi, a young black woman, walked slowly around the fires, chanting softly to les loas, encouraging their appearance.

Two older black women led a young white female to a stone altar and pushed her to her knees. She appeared dazed and unable to respond to their rough treatment. Others chanted, oblivious to her presence. From the opposite side of the clearing, four men, naked to the waist, entered the circle carrying a long coffin. Carefully placing it by the altar, they removed the lid. The body of a man was lifted out and placed on the altar. His arms and legs were then chained to iron rings. Once secured, they joined the chanters.

The sound of petro drums, the ti-baka and the manman, beat monotonously in the distance. When the chants reached a crescendo, a shrill bloodcurdling scream pierced the air, sending the crowd to their knees. They bowed their heads submissively and trembled in fear.

A small explosion, followed by a large puff of gray smoke appeared by the bonfire near the coffin. Before them stood the bokor, high priestess to the serviteurs who were kneeling in the clearing. A large snake lay draped across her shoulders, its massive head resting between her breasts. One hand held a bowl filled with a dark red fluid. Dipping her fingers into thick liquid, she knelt and drew a veve, the sacred symbol of Bondye, their supreme god.

"Bonne nuit, mes enfants," Mambo Lucretia greeted. "Ce soir nous honorons les loas." She motioned to the white woman and the man tied to the altar. Nodding slightly, two serviteurs stood and lifted the woman to her feet. Leading her to the priestess, they again pushed her to her knees. Lucretia lifted the huge boa from her shoulders and handed it carefully to one of her initiates. Turning back to the woman, she grabbed her by the hair and pulled her head back, forcing her captive to look at her.

Brown eyes stared vacantly at the priestess. The potion she was forced to drink had done its job. Satisfied, she released the hair and took the cup an initiate was holding. The woman's face was grabbed by one of her guards and her mouth forced up. Placing the cup against the captive's lips, the priestess tipped it, allowing the liquid to spill down her throat. Within seconds, she fell to the ground, unconscious.

"Voyez! Elle est morte!" Lucretia cried out. "Y a-t-il quelqu'un parmi vous qui doute de moi?"

No one doubted.

"Très bien."

Motioning for the body to be removed, she lowered her voice and switched to English, making sure no one else heard her words. "Take her! Watch her! She weel rise in three days."

Her servants bowed obediently. Once the woman was carried away, Lucretia walked over to an old woman being supported by two young men. Crippled, arthritic, and weak from a bad heart, she gasped painfully for air.

"Ancelin, très chère, j'ai un cadeau qui vous rendra votre jeunesse."

The worshippers gasped. Mambo Lucretia had promised the old woman her youth again. The high priestess smiled confidently. That night would bring her power and immortality. Moving to stand next to the altar, she leaned down to whisper to the man chained to the slab.

"So, Monsieur Falthama, tonight you fulfeel your destiny and mine, oui?"

"My destiny was written long ago. I've grown weary waiting for it to arrive," he said calmly. Ramus willingly embraced death now but was curious about the priestess's motives. "Tell me, what will you accomplish by killing me?"

"Immortalité, Monsieur Falthama, like you have enjoyed."

Ramus chuckled softly. "I fear you will be greatly disappointed. I am not immortal."

"I know of your kind, monsieur. You are vampire, the undead.

Your blood eez powerful. I believe eet weel cure my nephew. He has been indescrete weeth young men and now suffers the seekness. For me, I theenk eet weel give me immortalité."

Ramus actually laughed at the irony of her words, causing Lucretia to frown. "You both will be greatly disappointed."

"I theenk not. How old are you, monsieur?"

"It's of no consequence now," he said in amusement. "As you can see, even immortality has its limits."

"You evade my question, but eet eez not important."

Knowing the futility of trying to reason with the woman, Ramus remained silent.

Mistaking it for fear, Lucretia patted his arm. "I weel make thees as painless as possible."

"And I am to thank you for that? Do what you will." He sighed, having grown tired of her foolishness. The woman was obviously delusional. "Tonight will bring me peace. I take with me the satisfaction of knowing you will curse the day we met."

Lucretia wasn't sure how to respond. Shrugging, she motioned for Boudreau to step forward. Clutched in his hand was an enormous snake, its mouth forced opened to expose massive fangs. Carefully taking it from her servant, she raised the serpent high above her head, displaying it to her followers.

"Behold! Dambala, the serpent spirit."

The crowd gasped. To hold an evil spirit in her hands was proof that their priestess was a powerful bokor.

"Thees man eez evil. He keels without remorse and feeds on the souls of the helpless. Dambala claims the right to punish him for the evil he has done. Evil must destroy evil, but good weel come from thees. Do you believe?" Lucretia asked.

The crowd mumbled their assent.

"*Do…you…believe?*" she yelled, holding the serpent higher.

Jumping up, the people screamed their faith.

Nodding at Boudreau, the priestess watched as her servant ripped open the captive's shirt, exposing a thin, bony chest. Lowering the snake's head, she pressed the fangs deep into the stomach wall below the ribs and squeezed the glands behind its neck. Ramus flinched slightly but gave no other sign of pain.

Not how I would have chosen my death, he thought, *but it will do.* He would have the final laugh. The priestess had no idea what demons she was about to unleash upon herself, her friends, and her family. He actually felt an urge to enlighten her but realized she wouldn't believe him; besides, she didn't deserve mercy.

"Merci, madame," he whispered, laughing softly, then he closed his eyes and died.

"You must be mad!" she murmured under her breath.

Shaking her head, she picked up the ceremonial knife and showed it to her followers. Cups were placed beneath his arms. With two quick slices, she opened each wrist, almost severing the bones. Blood flowed into the cups filling them completely. Two more cups replaced the first. Only when the last drop was collected did she turn back to her followers.

Taking one of the cups, she poured it into a bowl, added several herbs from small pouches around her waist, and stirred it with her finger. Licking the blood from her finger, she motioned for Ancelin to be brought forward.

"Ancelin, you have leeved weeth the pain of aging for many years. Your body suffers the mange-moun. Tonight I weel cure you. Drink," she commanded.

Hesitantly, the old woman looked at the dark red fluid. Already it was beginning to coagulate.

"Hurry, très chère. The potion weel lose eets power. Ogou balanjo came to me promising you weel be healed."

Taking the cup, the old woman placed it against her lips and swallowed tentatively. The spices and herbs helped to conceal the coppery flavor. Draining the cup, she handed it to the priestess. Immediately, she felt a warmth creeping from her belly to her chest, then flow to her arms and legs.

At first pleasant, it suddenly burned like fire, scorching her insides. Clutching her stomach, she groaned and sank to the ground. Writhing in agony, she moaned pitifully.

"Behold the zanj fight the djab for her soul. Only eef you believe weel the zanj win and Ancelin saved," the priestess beseeched, tears streaming down her cheeks. Chanting loudly, Lucretia's followers danced wildly around the fires praying to les loas to help their sister. Satisfied that she had the complete support of her followers, Lucretia signaled for the drums to stop. Exhausted, the dancers calmed down and awaited her instructions.

"Take her home! Tomorrow we weel know eef the djab have

won." Glancing at the dead man, she shivered. Something terrible was going to happen. Les invisibles, the spirits, had failed to appear to her like she had hoped. It was only because of her followers' faith that she was able to make them believe something special had happened.

"Boudreau, get reed of the body. The gators weel feed well thees night," she added, remembering Billy's screams as he was pulled beneath the dark waters of the bayou earlier that evening.

CHAPTER TWENTY-THREE

Lying in the hot tub, Ekimmu wasn't sure what to think about her encounters with the serpent spirit. Sarpe hadn't made an appearance in several weeks, leaving her with serious doubts about their relationship.

Granted, neither had made any type of commitment, but still she missed the spirit's company. They had spent hours getting to know each other, not to mention the sex was great.

Ekimmu enjoyed teaching Sarpe the advantages of having a human body and the mysteries of the female anatomy. It had been a challenge explaining the specifics that made sex pleasurable, but Sarpe was a quick learner. Too quick, Ekimmu thought, remembering the last time they were together. She had been surprised by the spirit's innovative techniques.

Just the thought of her tongue stroking her clit sent shivers through her body. There definitely was an advantage in being able to change shapes and sizes, she thought. She could feel her stomach muscles twitching from the memory.

Ekimmu decided she had soaked enough. Thinking about Sarpe was making her edgy. She needed to find something else to do. Feeling hungry, she dressed quickly and called the front desk.

"Bonne nuit! May I help you?" the clerk asked.

"Bonne nuit, Serena. Would you call me a cab?"

"Certainment, Mamselle Elil. It will be only a few minutes."

"Merci."

Montréal was always fascinating. Ekimmu had visited the city several times over the past two centuries. She was particularly intrigued by the Village near Mont Royal. The strange mixture of cultures provided a rather unique eclectic atmosphere. During the day, the area literally vibrated with energy; people scurried about chaotically, although everyone usually had a specific goal in mind. She had chosen a hotel near the Village. Usually her evenings were spent at the café Kilo people-watching and wondering why everyone was so eager to get nowhere fast.

That night was different. Ekimmu needed to feed. Not the normal rare meat, broth, or vegetables she ate daily to sustain her, but the warm, rich blood necessary to keep her alive. At least once a week, she had to supplement her diet with the nutritional elements found only in human blood. It was amazing that less than 130 milliliters, about half a cup, was all she required to stay healthy. After hearing Om Loh Rehn confess she had given it up for over a century, Ekimmu wondered if one day she would have the courage to do so. The Gebians most honored historian was aging. The lack of blood was probably contributing to her rapid deterioration.

The Om's age was as much a mystery as the woman herself. It was rumored she was over five thousand years old. Ekimmu suspected she far exceeded the estimate, although it really didn't matter. She may have only a few centuries left if her present symptoms were an indication.

Constance's death would be a tragedy to their people and a personal loss to Ekimmu. Not only did she like and admire the elderly historian, but the woman was the last of her race to know Ekimmu's parents. Of course, that excluded Ramus. She suspected he had either killed them or had been involved in their deaths.

Stepping into the cool night air, she walked to the park instead of taking the cab. The exercise felt good. Although it was well after midnight, several people were moving about the streets.

Occasionally, she caught the faint smell of marijuana or heroin. The scent was strong in the blood of several young people who wandered up and down Rue St. Catherine. On a few corners, scantily dressed women paced back and forth, willing to sell their bodies for a few dollars to buy drugs or pay their rent. It was a hard life. Perhaps one day she would talk to some of them to see what drove them to such desperation. But not tonight. Her stomach grumbled annoyingly.

In Montréal, Le Parc du Mont Royal was Ekimmu's favorite nightspot. With over twenty kilometers of trails, it wasn't difficult to find someone to satisfy her needs. It also brought back memories of a young woman she had met a long time before.

CHAPTER TWENTY-FOUR

It was 1829. Ekimmu had lived in the States for several years exploring the new territories. During her travels, she heard rumors about a Canadian settlement called Montréal, a mecca for European immigrants. As a boomtown, it attracted large numbers of people from around the world, making it the cultural capital of Canada.

After living with farmers and explorers, Ekimmu felt a need to be with people of culture. The frontier folk were wonderful in their simplicity. Their daily struggles for survival made them alive and vibrant. It also made them old before their time.

Walking to the area she had first met Jeannette, Ekimmu looked around searching for something familiar. Sadly, everything had changed. Closing her eyes, she remembered that night long before.

A young woman leaned against a tree. Staring at the sky longingly, her eyes were filled with an unspeakable sadness. Not wishing to disturb her, Ekimmu watched from the darkness. She had intended on taking the woman, but the sadness was so tangible she could taste it.

Turning to leave, Ekimmu heard the faint rustle of leaves. Several feet behind the woman hidden in the shadows, a man crept stealthily toward his unsuspecting victim. The scent of lust was so strong. Ekimmu felt a rage welling up inside. Gliding quietly amongst the trees, she slipped behind him and tapped his shoulder. Startled, he jumped, swinging his arm in her direction. In his hand was a large knife.

"I think not," Ekimmu said, keeping her voice low and controlled as she easily avoided the slicing motion.

Unable to make out her features, he snarled. "Well, now, missy. Ain't you somethin'?"

Ekimmu stepped back, although not from fear. Rotting teeth and foul breath assailed her nostrils, repulsing her. His lack of hygiene made her wonder why she hadn't noticed his smell before she heard him.

Encouraged by her retreat, the man straightened boldly. "Now, now, no need to be actin' like that. I'm just lookin' for a little fun. You'll do nicely. Don't often see darkies like you this fer north. If'n you just lays back and spreads those handsome legs of yours and lets me dip my dick in that wet pussy, I'm sure we'd both enjoy it."

"You overestimate your prowess," Ekimmu said calmly. "I don't do *dicks,* and even if I did, I don't do vermin like you."

"Ah, now why'd you haf to go say that? You insulted me manhood," he grumbled.

"I doubt it," she sneered. "First, you'd have to be a man, which you're not, and second, nothing I say could insult the likes of you."

Ekimmu could sense the flush rushing up his neck to his cheeks and was prepared when he lunged.

"You need teachin' a little respect, missy," he snarled.

Laughing, she stepped aside and kicked him in the butt, sending him crashing into a tree. Furious, he spun around, slicing the empty air behind him. A slap behind the head caused him to stumble forward awkwardly. Again he turned and tried to cut her, and again Ekimmu kicked him.

"Fuckin' bitch!"

"Perhaps, but at least my women enjoy it, and it's something you won't be doing again."

Hesitantly, he backed up. "What's that supposed to mean?"

"It means dead men don't fuck. They're just plain fucked," she said, reaching out to grab him by the throat. "And you're a dead man."

Reluctant to maintain contact with the filth in her grasp, Ekimmu ended the confrontation quickly. Before he could raise his knife, she grabbed his head and snapped it to the left, breaking his neck. For a split second, his eyes widened in horror, then he went limp. Releasing the body, Ekimmu stepped away, allowing it to fall to the ground.

"And feel lucky you died so easily," she growled, rubbing her hands on her coat as if wiping away dirt. Only then was she aware of someone watching.

"Il est mort?"

"Oui," Ekimmu said.

"Bon débarras!" Saying nothing more, the woman walked away.

Frowning, Ekimmu followed. "Mamselle, are you okay?" she asked, unconsciously switching to English because of her years in the States.

The woman stopped but didn't answer. Ekimmu wondered if she understood the question or was just thinking about the answer.

"I will be," she finally said. "I will be."

Ekimmu sensed a hopelessness in her voice.

"Perhaps you would like to talk. I may be able to help."

"No, there's nothing anyone can do. I made my bed a long time ago. Now I must lie in it."

"Beds can be remade," Ekimmu joked, wanting to lighten things up. Glimpsing the faintest hint of a smile, she chuckled. "All right, bad joke, but at least I have your attention. Talk to me. You never know, sometimes the future isn't so dark if you can find someone with a light."

"Ah, a philosopher! And have you a light, madame?"

"How will you know unless you tell me what saddens you?"

Shrugging, the woman leaned against a tree and stared at the stars.

"Do you think there's a god?" she asked somberly. Chilled by the cool night air, she rubbed her arms unconsciously.

"I used to. Now I'm not so sure."

"Neither am I. Would a god make people so cruel? Or create such misery?"

"If he did, he wouldn't be much of a god, would he? He'd be the devil, I think."

"Yes, he would be, but then that would make life hopeless, wouldn't it?"

"Possibly. I believe we control our own destinies. If we think life is hopeless, it is. If we dare to hope, we do everything in our power to succeed."

"And when everything we know, everything we feel tells us it's hopeless?"

"Then we look beyond what we know and feel. There are things in the world we have never seen nor heard, but they're real. Not knowing or believing doesn't make them any less so. What is it that makes life so unbearable for you?"

"I'm with child," she said as if the statement explained everything.

Ekimmu was stunned and confused. "But that's wonderful," she exclaimed. "To give life is what most women hope for."

"To be pregnant and unwed is not. It's a sin here. To kill this child's father is murder and certain death."

"Why would you kill the father of your child?"

"Because he was also my own, and no one would believe me. If the child is a girl, he would have taken my baby and raised her as his, and eventually, she would be forced to endure his filthy touch," she whispered, revealing her shame.

Not sure what to say, Ekimmu stepped close to the woman and wrapped her arms around her. "Then you've done nothing wrong. When did this happen?"

"The rape or killing my father?"

"Killing your father."

"This night! He came to my room while I slept. I told him I was with child, but he wouldn't listen. All he could think of was satisfying his needs. When I fought him, he said he would give me to the church and take my baby as his own. He would tell everyone I was a whore, so I grabbed a knife and stabbed him. He would never get my baby. I would kill me and my child before letting him have her." She sobbed.

"Where is he now?"

"Probably where I left him. We live alone. Someone will find him after the sun rises. He always goes into town to drink with his friends."

"Good. Show me where you live. We must get rid of the body."

"It's too late."

"Remember, madame...what *is* your name? Mine is Ekimmu."

"Jeannette."

"Remember, Jeannette. We make our destinies. Now where do you live?"

Hesitantly, Jeanette told her. Ekimmu took her hand and pulled her in the direction of her house. Once there, she sent Jeanette to get some blankets and told her to leave, giving her the key to her hotel room.

"Wait for me. I'll take care of this."

Jeannette started to argue but changed her mind. She had nothing to lose now.

After she was gone, Ekimmu lifted the body and carried it into the woods. Walking a considerable distance, she dropped it on the ground. If anyone found it, they'd think he was killed there.

After returning to the hotel, she quietly entered her room. Jeannette was sleeping soundly on the bed. Covering her with a blanket, Ekimmu sat in the chair next to the bed observing the woman.

With long blond hair and pale skin, Jeanette looked to be no more than nineteen or twenty. Ekimmu wouldn't have described her as pretty, more like handsome and boyishly so. Soon the sun peeked through the window. Jeannette stirred, stretching slowly. Opening her eyes, she stared at Ekimmu in confusion until the night's events came back.

"You sleep like a baby."

"I haven't slept so soundly in years," Jeannette confessed.

"Good. It's a beginning."

"To what? When they find..."

"I've taken care of him. If they find him, they'll think someone else killed him. The only thing you need to worry about is what you want to do now."

Jeannette remained silent. For some reason, she didn't doubt Ekimmu, but she couldn't think about the future yet. Everything was happening too quickly.

"Stay here," Ekimmu offered. "When the time is right, you'll know what you want."

And stay she did. For three years, they remained together, the bond between them growing stronger each day. Ekimmu would have liked the relationship to be intimate but realized Jeannette needed a friend more than a lover. Aware that time was against them, she stayed only long enough to ensure the safety and security of the woman and her young son, Jean-Pierre. Jeannette had met a young French-Canadian by the name of Lambroux. They had fallen in love and married. Ekimmu moved on.

Several years later, she returned to Montréal for a short visit. Jeannette knew some of Ekimmu's history and didn't question her youthful looks. Pierre Lambroux had been killed in an Indian raid. Her son, Jean-Pierre, had traveled to the States as a trapper and fur trader but had recently returned to Montréal. He had grown into a handsome man, tall with dark brown hair and bright green eyes. When he smiled, dimples appeared, giving him a boyish charm, something he made excellent use of with the ladies.

The night before Ekimmu was to leave for Europe, the three of them dined together.

"You've had quite a life for so young a man, Jean-Pierre," Ekimmu said. "Surely you're ready to settle down now and raise a family."

"Moi? Never," he said. "What would the women say if I settled down? It would break their hearts," he added, placing his right hand over his own heart dramatically.

"Ah, yes. I hadn't thought of that. You certainly can't let that happen, but I'm curious. Hasn't there ever been even one woman who tempted you to the altar?"

Jean-Pierre sat back in his chair and looked longingly into the flames of the fireplace. "Once, a long time ago, but it wasn't to be."

"You sound like you loved her."

"Perhaps I did, Aunty. She was a rather strange woman, you know."

"Strange? In what way?"

Jean-Pierre laughed. "In every way. I met her when I was trapping the mountains in the States. She lived with Indians. They believed her to be a powerful Shaman. Even now I can still picture her. Long blond hair, green eyes, and wild as the mountain streams. The first time I saw her, she was running through the woods half-naked. You can imagine what I thought, Mama," he said, looking at Jeannette.

"I can well imagine." His mother smirked.

"Well, the blood runs hot in my veins. You can't blame me for wanting to bed a pretty young woman who was flaunting her attributes so openly, now can you?"

"I taught you better," Jeannette scolded.

"Yes, you did, but you never told me about this type of woman," he teased. "She was wild and wonderful and everything a man could want. If I didn't know better, I'd say she actually seduced me," he admitted. "But then I *am* quite handsome, am I not?" He struck a dignified pose.

Laughing, the two women looked fondly at the young peacock.

"Quite!" Ekimmu said sarcastically.

"I'm crushed. Have you no pity for my wounded pride?" Jean-Pierre pouted slightly.

"Forgive me. I jest!"

Perking up, he continued with his story. "Of course. Now where was I? Oh, yes. The seduction. As I was saying, I think she seduced me, and once she had her way with me, I was tossed aside like an old rag. Well, not exactly tossed, mind you. Actually, she had a few bucks kidnap me. Next thing I knew, I was drenched in a foul-smelling concoction, tied to my horse, and sent off with warnings not to return. I was damn lucky no one found me, although I have to admit, I smelled so badly, no one would have gotten near me."

Ekimmu and Jeannette couldn't help but laugh at the image of the handsome young man tied to his horse and chased from the village.

"I think you should consider yourself lucky you didn't marry her," his mother said. "I'm not sure I'd have liked her very much."

"Maybe, Mama. It certainly would have been interesting to see you two together. Anyway, that was long ago, and here I am still single and very available to the young ladies of Montréal. So, Aunty, where are you off to now and when are you coming back?"

"Europe, and I don't know. It'll be a few years I imagine." She looked at Jeannette.

Both knew this would be the last time she came to Montréal. There would be too many questions if she returned in Jean-Pierre's lifetime. Already the whispers had started amongst the people she and Jeannette had known. Her youthful appearance after thirty years was raising suspicions.

CHAPTER TWENTY-FIVE

"Am I dissturbing you?"

Startled, Ekimmu glanced around. Sarpe stood a few feet away, dressed in tan slacks and a cream satin shirt, her hands tucked in her front pockets.

"Never," she replied, smiling brightly. "Just remembering the last time I was here."

"Pleassant memories, I hope."

"Bittersweet, but mostly pleasant."

"That'ss good. Sso have you fed?"

"No, I was just looking."

"Then I will meet you at your hotel," Sarpe said, giving her a kiss on the cheek. "Feed well. I've misssed you. Tonight I too am hungry."

Ekimmu grinned as she watched the spirit disappear into the shadows. Thirty minutes later, she finished the hunt and hurried to her room, happily satiated and looking forward to a night with her lover.

Sarpe was stretched out on the bed watching television. A nature series called "Snake Hunter" was premiering.

"These humans are a sstrange sspecies. They live in fear of my kin, yet they are awed and mysstified by us. We are their ssaviour for disease and a demon in their dreams and beliefss."

"I suppose it's because yours is the only species that is identified with the beginnings of their race. There's a mystique about snakes, the way they move, their eyes, their very existence."

"True. We are unique." Sarpe turned off the television. "Sso, what shall we do now?" she asked, flicking her eyebrows, a gesture she had seen others do whenever they were insinuating lewd or lascivious acts.

"Well, now..." Ekimmu winked. "I think we can certainly come up with something to keep us entertained."

Ekimmu took off her blouse to expose bare breasts and tossed it over a chair.

"I have no doubt," Sarpe agreed, her golden eyes glowing.

Sliding her slacks off her hips and down her legs, Ekimmu stepped sideways and placed a knee on the bed, straddling Sarpe with her arms.

"So what would you like?" she whispered, leaning down so her warm breath caressed the spirit's ear.

Before she knew it, Sarpe had grabbed her and flipped her onto her back. Now on top, the spirit grinned mischievously. Sarpe liked the feel of grinning. There was something seductive in the way the lips pulled slightly upward without exposing the teeth.

"I would like you," she murmured. "Hot, naked, writhing beneath me like my kin on the warm ssands of the desert. I want you wet and warm like ssummer rain, the liquid flowing from you like a mountain sstream."

Ekimmu felt her heartbeat increase with every word spoken. Breathing rapidly, she stared into the spirit's eyes. Dark brown pupils turned elliptical, while the irises glowed golden brown. Mesmerized, she understood how prey fell victim to the snake's hypnotic stare. Sarpe lowered her long body onto her captive, moving seductively back and forth, then up and down along the length of Ekimmu's warm body.

"You have shown me much about human ssexuality, Ekimmu. Now I will teach you about the sserpent's sskills."

Flicking her tongue against Ekimmu's cheek, she stroked the jaw, then neck, before sliding it along the ridge of the ear.

"We may not have all the emotions you have, but we are a ssensual sspecies."

Ekimmu could feel the moisture pooling between her thighs. Never before had Sarpe taken control of their lovemaking. The sound of her voice alone would have been enough to make her surrender, but her words were spoken slowly, softly, the tone low and husky. The image of two snakes wound tightly around each other, rubbing their bodies back and forth flashed through her mind.

"Yess, you ssee how it is with us." She imitated the picture in Ekimmu's mind by rubbing her body slowly up and down against Ekimmu. Sarpe let her tongue trail across the exposed breasts, circling the nipples several times before moving downward. Ekimmu was helpless, unable to resist Sarpe's charm. Unsure whether she wanted to be so vulnerable, she groaned.

"I don't control you. You need only wish it and I'll sstop. Tonight, I am the teacher. We sstill have much to learn from each other. Do you wish me to continue?" She pulled back slightly.

Ekimmu nodded, unable to speak.

Smiling, Sarpe kissed her quickly on the lips. "Good" was all she said before lowering her mouth to the small, rounded belly. Again, her tongue traced a path to the navel and downward toward the dark curls. It was then Ekimmu noticed Sarpe's tongue was split at the end, like a serpent. Knowing from their last encounter how skilled she was with it, Ekimmu spread her legs.

Accepting the invitation, Sarpe flicked her tongue several times through the hair, then used the forked tips to separate the lips before working it deeper. Ekimmu gasped as the two tips moved quickly, but separately around her clit without actually touching the sensitive organ.

"Sarpe! Please," she groaned, staring into the spirit's elliptical eyes. Never again would she think snakes had cold lifeless eyes. Sarpe's burned hot from an unquenchable passion.

"Pleasse what?"

"I...don't...know," Ekimmu gasped, confused.

"I do," Sarpe whispered, caressing the clit slowly.

Ekimmu arched her back, trying to push her hips upward. Holding her down, Sarpe increased the tempo of the caresses, her tongue moving rapidly back and forth, the tips circling the hood and flicking it for a few seconds before changing to a slow tease. She intended on rewarding her lover for the patience she had shown during the past several months. It would be an all night affair.

Ekimmu was exhausted. She had never experienced such intense pleasure. Sarpe lay beside her with her head resting on the woman's stomach. As a spirit, she had tremendous energy reserves, but she had expended most of it trying to please her lover. Satisfied that she had succeeded, she now drew strength from Ekimmu.

Looking down at the blond head resting on her belly, Ekimmu ran her fingers gently through the short hair, fascinated at the faint diamond pattern visible on her scalp. Tracing one of the patterns with a fingertip, she smiled tenderly.

"I don't think you need lessons anymore," she teased and laughed softly.

"Oh, I'll alwayss need lessons. Thiss is jusst the beginning," Sarpe promised.

Both women grew silent, each lost in her own thoughts about the future. Neither wanted to dwell too much on it. With luck, they would have centuries to explore their feelings, perhaps even a millennium or two. About to comment, Ekimmu felt Sarpe stiffen.

"What is it?" she asked, pushing up onto her elbows.

"Be sstill!" Sarpe ordered, her voice distant.

Frowning at the tone, Ekimmu reluctantly obeyed.

"One of yourss has died!" Sarpe said matter-of-factly.

"What?"

"One of your people has died. The one called Ramuss."

"How do you know?" Ekimmu asked, sitting up.

"Because one of mine killed him."

The lack of emotion gave Ekimmu an uneasy feeling.

"An accident?"

"No, it wass intentional."

"I don't understand. What happened?"

"There wass a ritual. Often, my kin are part of them. Normally, nothing happens, although occasionally, there are accidentss. Thiss was no accident. Ssomeone forced his fangs into the man's body."

"Still, a snakebite wouldn't kill him. At best he might feel slightly nauseated. Gebians don't die from snakebites."

"Perhaps, but Ramuss had the ssickness. He was weak. The hemotoxins desstroyed his ssystem within minutess. I'm ssorry," Sarpe apologized, feeling guilty.

"It's not your fault. Someone forced this on your kin. The world is a better place with him gone, but I still have to find out what happened. This could mean my people are in danger."

"I'll ssee what I can find out. You musst go to New Orleanss. There you'll find your answsers."

Standing, Sarpe leaned down and gave Ekimmu a hard kiss.

"Be ssafe. Whoever killed him may already know more about your people than you wish. I'll be nearby if you need me. You don't need to whistle," she added, remembering a movie she and Ekimmu had watched together late one night.

Before Ekimmu could say anything, the spirit was gone. Perhaps a better description would be simply faded away. It was the first time Sarpe had actually disappeared within her sight, proof she was disturbed over the situation.

Jumping to her feet, Ekimmu began planning her trip to Louisiana. Her first move was to make a couple of calls. She knew she'd need help once she was there.

CHAPTER TWENTY-SIX

Yemaya sat listening to her brother describe his trip to New Zealand, one of his favorite places. Of course, anyplace was his favorite as long as Reymone was with him. Having just gotten back from a three-month stay with his lover, Raidon was unusually animated.

Reymone sat on the armrest of the oversized chair, his right arm draped casually over his partner's shoulders. Unconsciously, he played with the dark curls resting beneath his hand.

"It was amazing. The mountains were covered in snow. Reymone and I were trapped in a blizzard. If we hadn't found the cabin, I'm sure we'd have frozen to death."

Reymone laughed. "Yeah, but not before I'd had my way with you," he teased. "I can just see it. The rescuers tramping up the mountainside and tripping over our cold, hard bodies. Now who, I wonder, would be on top?"

Slapping Reymone's thigh, Raidon admonished him. "Reymone, apologize! Dakota isn't used to such rudeness."

Laughing, Dakota assured them she had heard worse. "After all, I'm a journalist. You really can't believe I'm that innocent, Raidon."

"That's not the point. There is rarely a good excuse for crude humor when ladies are present."

"Thank you, but I think Dakota and I will agree there are no ladies here." Yemaya smirked. "Besides, I am sure if we were in the same situation, we would definitely warm ourselves the same way or at least in a similar fashion. Would you not agree, sweetie?" she asked, ruffling Dakota's short blond hair.

"Oh, absolutely! What a way to go, too!"

"There you go, Raidon. Two very enlightened young women."

Reymone clapped his hands together happily.

Sighing, Raidon knew he was outnumbered. "So where are you off to now, sister?" he asked, deciding to change the subject.

"Back to the States."

"Didn't you just return from there?"

"Yes, after the AIDS benefit. We had hoped to spend a little more time here, but Dakota has important business to finish. Her ex-boss wants to try to woo her back to the dark side."

Looking somewhat confused, Raidon glanced at Dakota. "Dark side?"

"Yemaya just means he wants to hire me back."

"I would think you'd like a break from that by now," Raidon said. "After all, you've had enough excitement on the *dark side* to last a lifetime."

"And how! Still, I'm a journalist. I can't keep mooching off of Yemaya, you know."

"So while Little Sister here renews her career, what will you be doing for entertainment?" Raidon asked Yemaya. "Are you still thinking of retiring?"

Oh, shit! Reymone thought, noticing the glare directed at his lover. *She hasn't told Dakota yet.*

Realizing that it would be useless to change the subject now, Yemaya sighed faintly. "I will be working on my next show. Danny wants me to do another tour. I think this may be my last, though."

Yemaya glanced toward Dakota. This wasn't the way she had wanted to break the news to her and now felt guilty about Dakota learning in such a manner.

Surprised, Dakota wasn't sure what to say. Deciding the moment wasn't right, she remained silent.

Raidon immediately realized it wasn't a good time to pursue his sister's revelation. Nudging Reymone to move, he stood and took his lover's hand.

"I'm tired. If you will excuse us, I think we'll call it a night. The journey home was long and we're rather tired."

"Good idea, luv," Reymone piped in. "Until tomorrow, ladies. Sweet dreams."

Bowing slightly, both men left, leaving the women alone.

"When did you make that decision?"

Shrugging, Yemaya didn't answer immediately. She had played

with the idea of retiring for almost a year. There was once a time when the adrenaline rush of the illusion gave meaning to her life, but she had eventually grown weary of the lonely nights in her hotel rooms. After meeting Dakota, she wanted more.

"I have been thinking about it for a while," she finally replied.

"How long is a while? Before you met me or after?"

"Does it matter?"

"I think so, especially if it's because of me. Is it?"

"Yes and no. I was considering retiring before we met but had not decided when. I want us to be together."

"We are together."

"I know." Yemaya sighed. "But sometimes I think my work interferes with our lives, even endangers yours. Now you are thinking of going back to work full time, and it would mean long periods apart. Just the thought seems unbearable."

"Listen. My life has had its bad moments long before we met. Meeting you is the best thing that's ever happened to me, but if you give up what you love out of fear or to accommodate me, neither of us will be happy."

"I know."

"Besides, what happened to me becoming your personal assistant?"

"I thought you wanted to pursue your journalistic nature."

"I think I can handle both. I have many skills, you know?"

"Where have I heard that before?" Yemaya asked, rolling her eyes dramatically.

Before Dakota could respond, the phone rang. Looking at the clock on the mantle, Yemaya frowned.

"A little late for calls," she grumbled softly, picking up the receiver. "Lysanne residence."

"Yemaya?"

"Constance?"

"Yes. I'm sorry to disturb you at this hour, but I thought you and Dakota needed to know—Ramus is dead."

Yemaya was surprised at the news but more so at the regret in the woman's voice.

"So soon? I thought his immune system would be able to fight the virus for decades," she replied, placing her hand over the phone and mouthing the information to Dakota.

"It would have. He was killed."

"Killed? Was it an accident?"

"No. Someone got to him. I don't know much more than that, other than Ekimmu just called me with the news. She's concerned it may be an attack on our people."

"When did this happen?"

"An hour or so ago. I'm not sure."

"Did she say how she learned this?"

By now, Dakota had placed her head against Yemaya's and was listening to the conversation.

"No, but I have my suspicions. Anyway, the reason for my call was to ask if you and Dakota had any plans involving a trip to the States. Ekimmu booked a flight for tomorrow, and I'm worried she may get into something more than she can handle. Anyone able to capture Ramus would be a grave threat to her also."

"I agree. We will finish our business here tomorrow and charter a plane. Please give her the details while I make a few calls."

"Thank you. I know this doesn't have anything to do with you two, but Ekimmu is important to our people."

"She is important to all of us. We will talk with you later."

Handing the phone to Dakota, Yemaya left the room to make arrangements for their departure.

"Hey, Constance,"

"Hello, Dakota. How are you?"

"Fine. I'm sorry about Ramus, although I'm not sure why. He wasn't a very nice person."

The chuckle on the other end of the phone made her smile.

"Such tact, child, and no, he wasn't, but he was one of our oldest, and as flawed as he was, he still had a certain charm."

"I'll take your word for it. Personally, I found him creepy."

"With good reason. Anyway, I appreciate the two of you going over to check on Ekimmu."

"Not a problem. I like her. She seems nice, not to mention she is one of yours. That alone would make us want to help."

"Thank you. I'll let you go now. I have a few more calls to make before I book my own flight."

"You're going, too? It might be dangerous. Why not let us see what's happening and we'll call you?" Dakota offered, fearful that the trip would be too stressful for the older woman.

"I may be old, my dear, but not *that* old. Stress is the least of my worries."

"How did you...oh, never mind. Between you and Yemaya, I'm beginning to think everyone but me reads minds."

"Not everyone. Just a few," Constance said. Dakota couldn't tell if she was serious or joking.

"Uh-huh. Look, give me the details and I'll let you know where we'll be staying once we get there. You make sure you don't overdo. I'd be pretty mad if something happened to you and, well, I have connections, you know. I'll have you haunted all through the afterlife."

"Somehow I believe you would. Now here's what Ekimmu said, and where she'll be."

Quickly writing down the details, Dakota motioned to Yemaya, who had returned and was standing quietly next to her. Pointing to the paper, she circled the words New Orleans. Nodding, Yemaya again left. By the time she finished chartering a flight, Dakota had said her farewells to Constance.

"Everything is arranged. We leave the day after tomorrow."

"I don't like this," Dakota confessed. "Ramus may have been sick, but he was a powerful man. For him to have somehow been killed means he was either very weak or his assailant was very cunning."

"I hope he was weak," Yemaya said. "Otherwise, whoever it was is extremely dangerous."

Yemaya and Dakota arrived in the States three days later. The charter jet had made stops in Paris and New York before continuing on to its final destination. During their overnight stay in New York City, Yemaya contacted Sonny Marino, her promotion agent.

"Sonny, I need you to contact the crew and put together a quick program for me for New Orleans."

"How quick are we talking about?"

"Three weeks. Four max."

"Three weeks! Are you crazy?" Sonny sat up in his chair. "I'm not sure I can even get a location, let alone the advertising out in that short a time."

"I will send you the details for the show. Use whatever resources you need no matter what the cost. Just get it done."

"What about rehearsals and the props?"

"Use the props from the last tour. The choreography and music will be easy enough for the crew to perform after a week of practice. Have Suzanne add three or four routines from our past shows as fillers and tell her to call everyone in for refresher courses. I expect them to be in New Orleans within the week. In the meantime, I'll be there tomorrow and do what I can to help."

"You're going to owe me big-time if I pull this off," Sonny vowed.

"If I thought you incapable of this, I would replace you," Yemaya stated cooly.

"You couldn't find anyone better than me and you know it." He laughed. "Now since I have such a gargantuan task ahead of me, let me get to work. I'll call you in a few days with an update."

"Thanks. I know you can do it."

"Yeah, right. When this is over with, I expect an explanation." *Not that that will ever happen,* he thought, shaking his head.

"Bye, Sonny."

Hanging up the phone, Yemaya turned to Dakota, who had been unpacking the overnight bags.

"You think he can do it?" Dakota asked.

"Sonny is a miracle worker," Yemaya said. "If I had any doubts about his abilities, I would find someone else."

"Just like that?"

"Just like that," Yemaya said matter-of-factly.

"Can you really discard someone so quickly?"

"Some I can. I would never get rid of Sonny. I would simply find something else for him to do. He is an old friend, as well as my promoter. Now as to other people, I know of one person I would *never* discard."

Wiggling her eyebrows, Yemaya walked over and nudged Dakota backward until she was lying flat on the bed. Straddling her hips with her legs, she placed her hands on each side of Dakota's face and leaned down, her lips inches from Dakota's.

"And who might that be?"

"Oh, I think you know." Yemaya grinned smugly.

"Prove it."

"Gladly. You know the next few weeks are going to be extremely busy. We may not get much time for this," Yemaya whispered, her warm breath caressing Dakota's cheek.

"I think we can manage to work some playtime into our schedule."

"Well, just in case, I think tonight I should make sure you have something to think about for a while." Yemaya grinned broadly.

Straightening up, she pulled her sweater over her head and tossed it aside. Then reaching down, she pulled Dakota's T-shirt off and threw it on her sweater. Neither was wearing a bra. Dakota tipped her head sideways, admiring the view.

"Mmm. Nice," she murmured, running her fingers gently over the right breast.

Yemaya caught her breath as she felt the light tickle. Stomach muscles rippled as her skin turned pebbly from the goose bumps. Slowly, she lowered herself onto her lover. The heat of her body as she rubbed it against Dakota's brought a groan from Dakota.

Breathing rapidly, Dakota started to say something, but Yemaya stopped her with a hot, searing kiss. Wrapping her arms around Yemaya, Dakota pulled her tightly against her, her hands roaming across the bare skin of Yemaya's back and buttocks.

Reluctantly, they separated as the need for air overcame an unquenchable passion. Gasping for breath, the two could only stare into each other's eyes, unable to speak for fear words would trivialize the depths of their love. Finally, Yemaya lowered her lips to Dakota's ear and whispered, her voice low, husky, seductive. "I need to taste you."

Dakota squirmed as the words flowed through her. Invisible hands caressed her mind and body, making her shudder. Every time they made love, Dakota felt as if it were their first moments together; the wonder and passion overwhelmed her, and she never doubted Yemaya felt the same. Hearing her lover's voice, its deep huskiness describing the most intimate act possible, was almost painful as her heart beat heavily inside her chest.

A slight nod was all that was needed for Yemaya to slide down Dakota's body. Removing her slacks and panties, she pushed them away and ran her hands slowly up Dakota's legs, dragging her nails lightly across the skin. Dakota shifted her right leg, making room for Yemaya to nestle her own body between them. Sliding her arms under Dakota's thighs, Yemaya pulled her forward and slipped her shoulders beneath the bent knees. Lowering her head, she inhaled the warm scent of her lover.

"You make me hungry," she growled.

"Hun..hungry?"

Smiling smugly, Yemaya nodded. "*Verry*," she purred, lowering her head to rest it on Dakota's thighs. Running her finger up the left thigh, she brushed the golden hair with her fingertips. "And a natural blond, too," she teased, her voice lowering to that natural husky, seductive tone that turned Dakota's whole body warm and pliant. It craved her touch, needed it as if its very existence was dependent on Yemaya for sustenance.

Arching her back, Dakota groaned, unable to voice her needs, not that she needed to. Yemaya knew exactly what her lover wanted. Separating the lips, she flicked her tongue across the warm, wet inner skin tasting its salty muskiness.

For several hours, Yemaya worked her magic, taking Dakota on a journey of infinite pleasure and complete exhaustion.

Afterward, she pulled her lover into her arms and closed her eyes. Drifting into a peaceful slumber, she barely caught the faint whisper. "I love you so much, Yemaya." Too tired to realize the words were unspoken, she smiled and nestled under the blankets with Dakota cradled against her chest.

CHAPTER TWENTY-SEVEN

The hotel was on the edge of the French Quarter. While checking in at the front desk, the manager informed Dakota that she had received a personal message for her and had put it in her safe. Retrieving it, she handed it to her and then escorted them to their suite.

"Please let us know if you need anything," the manager offered. "I'm personally looking forward to seeing your show and consider it an honor you've chosen our hotel for your accommodations."

"Thank you, Ms. Bosshart. I hope you won't be disappointed."

"I think that's very unlikely, Ms. Lysanne. I have several friends who attended your Montréal show. They're still talking about it. My staff is so excited you're staying here. I've had to shuffle the schedules just so everyone gets a few days of work with the hope of meeting you. Please let me know if anyone becomes a nuisance."

"I doubt it will be a problem, but if something comes up that we can't handle, you will be the first to know."

"Good. Now I'll leave you to your peace and quiet. Have a good evening."

"You too and thanks again."

After the manager left, Dakota looked at the sealed envelope she had been given earlier. Her name was handwritten in a stylish script unlike anything she had ever seen.

"Fancy, but nice." She showed it to Yemaya.

"Definitely!"

Opening it, Dakota glanced first at the signature. "It's from Ekimmu."

"I suspected as much. Does she have anymore information?"

Scanning the note, Dakota handed it to Yemaya. "At least it's a start. Apparently, she's done her homework. If what she suspects is true, this could be dangerous. I'll do some follow-up research and see what we can find out about this voodoo stuff. It makes sense it was some type of ritual if Ramus was killed by a poisonous snake. From what we know about him, it certainly couldn't have been an accident, considering how long he's been around. There's no way he'd let a wild snake bite him."

"I agree. We will just have to see what else turns up. Tomorrow, I meet with Suzanne and the crew. Unfortunately, I have to get this show put together quickly, so I won't be able to help you with your research, at least not for a few days."

"That's okay, sweetie. It'll mostly be library type stuff and probably pretty boring. The research part of my work usually is. You go do your thing and I'll do mine. If I need you, I'll let you know."

"You had better."

While Yemaya practiced for her upcoming performance, Dakota spent several days at the New Orleans Main Library researching voodoo practices and taking copious notes. Built in 1908, it had a complete wing devoted to voodoo and similar topics. The first thing she noticed was the large section of stories and books written about the town's most famous resident, Marie Laveau. Dakota was intrigued by the history and influence of this particular black woman. During the time of slavery, she had risen to a position of power. Several books gave fairly detailed descriptions of her life. Of particular interest was a short excerpt in an old manuscript written in the early 1900s.

Marie Laveau was a large woman, born in the 1790s. As a hairdresser for the wealthy white women, she overheard the gossip about their personal lives. Eventually, she acquired so much information that she found she could manipulate it to her own advantage by pretending to be a witch.

Dressed in brightly colored clothes, she often paraded around with a large snake named Zombie and held secluded ceremonies in the name of Dambala. Only her initiates could participate or attend them, which added to her mystique.

This would be a great topic for the magazine, Dakota thought, closing the manuscript and putting it back on the shelf. *I'll have to talk to Tony about doing a whole series on this woman.* Picking out another book, she sat back down and continued her research into the dark side of the New Orleans culture.

Except for a few minor mistakes, the performers managed to complete the new routine to Yemaya's satisfaction. Suzanne had done an excellent job of coordinating the stagehands, lighting crew, and electronics technicians in just two weeks.

Several acts were from other shows, so it was only a matter of refreshing everyone's memory, then fine-tuning the routines. Yemaya had told her chief assistant to select a single act from each show in case some of the audience had attended a previous performance.

She had discussed the finale in great detail with Suzanne and instructed her to make sure all performers practiced their parts until they had it right. There was no room for error.

Today was the first time they had performed a complete rehearsal. Afterward, Yemaya pulled Suzanne aside to congratulate her on her accomplishment and to discuss the mistakes.

She was almost finished when her assistant unceremoniously pushed her backward, causing her to lose her balance. At the same time, something collided with Yemaya's left cheek. Flinching at the pain, she reacted by shoving the object away and the person carrying it, sending both flying across the room.

"Jesus, Donnie," Suzanne cursed, bending over Yemaya to see if she was okay. "What the hell's wrong with you?"

"Gosh, Suzanne, Ms. Lysanne, I'm so sorry." He scrambled to his feet. "Are you two okay?"

Touching the bruised area with her fingertips, Yemaya nodded. "What happened?" she asked, smiling her thanks to Suzanne before turning to frown at the technician.

"I...I...got distracted," he stammered, looking first at Suzanne, then at his employer. "Are you sure you're okay?"

"I am fine, but I will not have this type of negligence on my set. We cannot afford distractions in this business, for obvious reasons."

"If I might have a word with you, Ms. Lysanne..." Suzanne interrupted, helping Yemaya to her feet. "I think I should handle this. You need to get that injury checked out."

"It really is fine, but thanks for the concern. You are right, of course. As my right hand, I will leave you to resolve this issue. Whatever you decide to do about it and him is fine with me."

Donnie swallowed nervously. The expression on the women's faces told him he wasn't going to get off lightly.

Smiling at Suzanne, Yemaya winked and walked away. Behind her, she heard Suzanne admonishing Donnie for his clumsiness.

"Just what the hell were you thinking? You could have seriously hurt her."

"I'm sorry. It was an accident. I got distracted and didn't see you two standing there. It won't happen again." He looked like a little boy who had just lost his best friend.

"You better believe it…and just to make sure, I'm taking you off the lighting crew until I think you've learned your lesson. From now on, you're on cleanup. Now get started. This place is a mess."

"But …"

"You heard me, and if I hear another word, you'll be doing litter patrol in the parking lot."

"Yes, ma'am," Donnie muttered, looking around, unsure where he should begin. Sighing, he walked away and kicked at a small plastic water bottle someone had left on the floor.

"I said cleanup, Donnie! Pick it up. Don't kick it," Suzanne yelled after him, then turned away to hide a smile.

Yemaya liked the way her chief assistant handled the situation and made a mental note to give her a bonus. The demotion would give the young man time to reassess his priorities, at least on the job. It was obvious he was infatuated with Suzanne, but negligence wasn't the way to impress her.

Once back in her dressing room, Yemaya grabbed her jacket and headed for the hotel, eager to see Dakota.

After spending almost a week in the library, Dakota had gathered more than enough information about the different types of voodoo and the spirits associated with them. Glancing at the clock, she decided to wander around the French Quarter for a few hours before meeting Yemaya at the hotel. As a tourist, it would give her a chance to ask questions without arousing suspicion.

Wandering the crowded narrow streets, she was intrigued by the party atmosphere of the locals and tourists. Everyone was having a good time. Although it was early afternoon, the nightclubs were noisy. Music blasted from the open doors and windows but not enough to drown out the voices of the people milling around.

Feeling thirsty and a little hungry, she decided to visit the Café du Monde. She had heard about their beignets and wanted to taste them. Lightly sprinkled with powdered sugar, the pastry reminded her of the homemade doughnuts her mom used to make when Dakota was a child.

Sitting at a small wooden table, Dakota sipped her coffee and munched on the pastry. The hustle and bustle of people moving around the veranda didn't distract her from her concentration as she reviewed her notes.

Although born from different cultures, many of the voodoo gods resembled the ancient spirits she had met in her dreams. Followers paid homage to Bondye, the supreme spirit. Dakota couldn't help but feel he (or she) was just another version of Intunecat. Both entities were considered by their followers as the creator of the universe. It would be intriguing to think the two might actually be the same spirit. Then there was Dambala, the serpent spirit, Sarpe's counterpart. Although she had never met Sarpe, Dakota knew the other spirits held her in high esteem.

Perhaps the most intriguing resemblance, though, was Yemanja, the female spirit of the water. Dakota knew her lover was named after the West African goddess, Yemaya. Africans believed she was the creator of the universe and lived in the oceans. The more Dakota thought about it, the more she believed cultures worshipped the same spirits.

Looking at her watch, Dakota gathered up her notes, anxious to get back to the hotel. When she heard the name *Mambo Lucretia*, she hesitated. Mambo was Creole for high priestess. Her instincts told her this was important.

"A hundred grand gone just like that," one of the voices grumbled behind her. "I told you we should have grabbed him that night, but no, you had to think it over."

"Shut up, would you? He probably wasn't the one anyway," another male voice snapped angrily.

"We won't know that now, will we? And it's mighty strange she isn't offering the reward anymore. Why is that, Aiden? Huh? I'll tell you why. Someone else got to him, that's why. They probably heard us talking at the bar. Those black eyes were a giveaway and you didn't have the brains to realize it."

"Damn it, man, would you shut the fuck up? I'm trying to enjoy a meal here and you keep whining. If it was him, he's gone. If he's gone, there's no reward and there's nothing I can do about it. So just shut up and drink your coffee."

Dakota heard the other man mumble something. Picking up her bag of beignets, she hurried from the café and signaled for a cab. Perhaps the conversation had no connection to Ramus's disappearance, but she wanted to run it past Yemaya.

At the hotel, Dakota found Yemaya curled up in a lounge chair, sound asleep. Not wanting to disturb her, she quietly slipped past and entered the bathroom for a quick shower.

She wrapped a large towel around her body, walked over to Yemaya, and knelt to give her a light kiss. Only then did she notice the slight bruise forming on Yemaya's left cheek. Gently, she pushed several locks of hair away from the area and stroked the damaged skin with her fingertips, curious but unwilling to disturb her lover's sleep.

Normally, Yemaya would have awakened immediately upon her arrival. The fact that Dakota was able to enter the suite, take a shower, and get this close confirmed the extent of Yemaya's exhaustion. Pulling her hand away, she was stopped when Yemaya reached up and wrapped her own around the warm palm. Pale blue eyes opened slowly and stared groggily at Dakota.

"Hey," Dakota whispered.

Yemaya smiled, her eyes slightly glazed. "Hey," she whispered back, her tone low and husky from sleep. Dakota shivered, wondering if she would ever be immune to the natural seductiveness of her lover's voice or the unspoken promises of unimaginable pleasures.

"You're hurt."

"A minor mishap. The bruise should be gone by tomorrow."

"What happened?"

Tugging Dakota onto her lap, Yemaya grinned sheepishly.

"One of the techs decided he was more interested in Suzanne than me. I guess I was too distracted thinking about you to react in time."

"I know the feeling. So..."

"So we had finished practicing the final act when he bumped

216

into me carrying some lighting equipment."

Touching the bruise, Dakota frowned again.

"Looks like more than a bump. He must be an idiot," Dakota said, unable to imagine anyone choosing someone else over Yemaya. "This could have been serious, sweetie. I hope you enlightened him."

"I left that to Suzanne. She handles this sort of thing better than I, and she did. He was relegated to the cleanup crew. In this type of work, someone can get hurt if even one person fails to do his or her job properly. Safety is in the details."

Dakota couldn't agree more. Several of Yemaya's acts were extremely dangerous. Any distraction could cause serious injuries or even death. Personally, she thought, she'd have fired the guy for his negligence.

"I doubt that." Yemaya laughed, sensing Dakota's thoughts. "You are too much of a softie."

"In most things, but never when it comes to protecting the people I love."

Hugging her warmly, Yemaya had to agree. Dakota wouldn't hesitate to sacrifice herself if it meant keeping Yemaya safe.

"I have no doubt he is quite repentant. After the final show, I might tell Suzanne to let him have his old job back. All of us make mistakes. I doubt he willl repeat it. Now enough about me. How was your day?"

"Interesting, maybe even productive," Dakota said, launching into a detailed description of her research at the library and finishing with the conversation overheard at Café du Monde.

"Hmm. It does sound as if they were talking about Ramus. Any ideas on how we find out more about this Mambo Lucretia?"

"A few. As a journalist, it certainly wouldn't be unusual for me to do a series of articles on New Orleans and its ties to voodoo and the occult, especially since those who read *Magic and Mysticism* know I've been following you around. I suspect it's a pretty popular magazine in this area."

"As long as you make sure you take no unnecessary chances."

"I won't if you won't."

"Touché!" Yemaya said, lifting Dakota off her lap. "How about we get something to eat and call it a night? I have to be at the theater early. I want one more rehearsal and then give everyone the day off for a much-needed break."

"Not to mention you. Maybe we can have some downtime together and play tourist."

Pretending to think hard about the suggestion, Yemaya didn't immediately respond. "Well, I think I might be able to work you into my schedule, if you are a good girl."

Dakota lightly slapped Yemaya's arm and sauntered off. "One, I'm definitely not a good girl...and two, if you plan on getting any tomorrow, you'd better treat me *real* nice."

Jumping up, Yemaya grabbed Dakota from behind and swung her into her arms. Carrying her into the bedroom, she kicked the door shut with her foot and walked to the bed.

"Who mentioned anything about waiting until tomorrow? I think I should take advantage of you tonight in case you decide to withhold your favors later." She gave Dakota a comically haughty look.

"Oh, Lord." Dakota sighed, placing the back of her hand against her forehead in mock dismay. "Must we again? Don't you ever get enough sex?"

"Me thinks thou dost protest too much, my lady."

"Who said anything about protesting?"

"Hmm. Good point."

Lowering Dakota to the floor, Yemaya grabbed the towel and flamboyantly yanked it away from her body.

"You, young woman, are exceptionally well endowed," she proclaimed, wiggling her eyebrows.

"And you are exceptionally horny," Dakota declared, thoroughly enjoying this side of lover's nature. Normally serious, it was rare that Yemaya let go enough to play such games.

"Please, mamselle," Yemaya begged, falling to one knee. "I am beyond horny. I have not partaken of your sustenance in hours. Take pity on this poor woman, will you not, and let me have my way with you?"

Placing her hands on her bare hips, Dakota looked down at the pitiful expression.

"Well, if you must." She sighed heavily. "But only if you agree to my terms."

"Anything. Name it. I am yours to command." Yemaya jumped to her feet and spread her arms wide.

"Good. Take off your clothes." Flipping her hand up and down, she assumed a regal pose. "Slowly! *If* you please me, you shall have all you desire."

Grinning, Yemaya placed an arm across her waist and bowed.

"That is my only wish," she said as she slowly unbuttoned her blouse. "And may I ask what else mamselle wishes of me?"

"Mamselle wishes for you to get completely naked, lie down on this bed, and let her have her way with you," Dakota whispered, stepping close to Yemaya and running her fingers down the taller woman's left cheek. "Completely," she murmured. "Wholely. You must endure every caress," she continued as she stared unblinkingly into pale blue eyes, "every touch, every stroke of mamselle's hand..."

Yemaya's eyes flared with passion as Dakota slowly enunciated each word, each action.

"My tongue, my lips. Do you agree?" She took a step backward, knowing without a doubt her lover's answer. Dakota was working her own brand of magic on Yemaya.

Heart pounding furiously, Yemaya nodded, finding it impossible to speak. Dakota's seduction was both irresistible and complete.

"Good. Now off with the jeans and get in bed. Tonight, I'm the Illusionist. I'm going to make the whole world disappear. There will be only you and me...and when I'm done, I promise you'll know the depth of my love like never before."

Yemaya sensed the moment the mood had changed from playful to serious. Dakota was staking her claim on Yemaya's soul and offering her own in return. Her statement was not about dominance. She was asking Yemaya to relinquish control of herself, something she had never really done in the past. Now she had to make a choice—trust completely in her lover or admit her doubts and hope Dakota would understand.

Yemaya knew in her heart that Dakota would accept her decision without question even if she didn't fully understand. Perhaps that was the hardest part of choosing, Dakota's total acceptance of who she was and the unconditional love she offered. Humbled, Yemaya looked deep into emerald green eyes, took a deep breath, and nodded, accepting her lover's terms.

CHAPTER TWENTY-EIGHT

Ancelin awoke early. The aches and pains of age that normally accompanied consciousness were gone. Sitting up, she slowly moved her arms, then her legs. Nothing! No burning, no crackling noises accompanied the bending of old joints. Staring at her hands, she flexed the fingers.

Other than the visible evidence of swollen knuckles and the purple veins pulsating beneath the thin transparent skin, there were no signs of the arthritis that had crippled her for years.

"C'est impossible!" she gasped, crossing her chest.

Sliding from the bed, she took a few steps, then a few more, and let out a high, piercing scream.

Moments later, Boudreau barged into his grandmother's room and stopped, stunned at the sight of her dancing across the floor, both arms wrapped around her pillow as if embracing an imaginary partner.

"Grandmère? Comment ça va?"

"Ah mon petit, je vais très bien. Très, très bien!" she cried gleefully, running over to hug him. Boudreau was stunned by her strength. Before she had been given the potion, Ancelin was virtually bedridden. Now she moved with the grace of a young woman.

Picking her up, he swung her around like a small child, wanting to share in her happiness. "Eet's a miracle, grandmère!" he exclaimed. "I was so worried. You've been asleep for over a week. Mambo Lucretia weel be pleased."

Setting her gently on her feet, he pulled out his cell phone and called the high priestess. After telling her about Ancelin and listening to Lucretia's instructions, he hung up.

"The mistress wants to see us now."

An hour later, they arrived at his employer's estate.

Outside the large, wrought iron gates a crowd had gathered. Lucretia's servants had begged their mistress to let them call their friends and family so all could share in Ancelin's happiness and witness the miracle for themselves. Smiling with satisfaction, Lucretia agreed, giving everyone the day off. News traveled rapidly amongst the priestess's followers.

Stepping from the limousine, Ancelin ran to Mambo Lucretia, tears streaming down her cheeks. Falling to her knees, she kissed the priestess's feet.

"Merci, Mambo Lucretia, merci beaucoup! C'est un miracle!"

"Eet eez good to see you again, très chère. I was worried. You slept a long time," Lucretia said, looking closely at the old woman and smiling with satisfaction. Ancelin's skin was smooth and pink. She looked years younger. "Let our people see you! Thees eez the power Bondye geeves me!" she declared, turning toward the crowd. "And the geeft I geeve to you, mes amis. Those who doubt me see I speak the truth. I am bokor to Bondye. I *am* heez chosen."

As one, the crowd shouted their approval. Ancelin had been crippled for years. Now she stood before them pain free.

Signaling for the crowd to leave, Lucretia told Boudreau to escort his grandmother into her living room. The priestess wanted to check her for other signs of improvement.

As she entered the gated garden, a gust of wind blew a flier against her leg, pressing it against her ankle as if held by invisible hands. Reaching down, she pulled it away and started to crumple it. The face on the front caught her attention. Smoothing out the creases, Lucretia stared at the pale blue eyes behind the mask—disturbing eyes, mysterious and compelling.

"Boudreau, vous avez vu ceci?" she asked, handing him the flyer.

"Oui."

"You deed not tell me?" she demanded angrily.

"I only heard of her arrival last night, mistress. Eet eez her last show."

Obviously, this was a sign from Bondye. She had read about the Illusionist and was curious about her.

"Find me more about thees Illusionist. I weel talk to Ancelin later."

Bowing, Boudreau left. After taking his grandmother home,

he drove to the nearest bookstore and thumbed through several magazines. Finding two with detailed information on the Illusionist's performances, he took them to Lucretia.

"Merci, Boudreau. Appel Mayhew, s'il vous plaît. Il doit venire ici ce soir."

Boudreau nodded respectfully and left.

Lucretia spent the rest of the day reading the articles on the Illusionist and researching on the Internet. Although she found thousands of sites, few had anything informative. Most were from fans writing über stories about the Illusionist and her lovers, mostly women. The priestess scoffed. Obviously, they had fantasies about this woman and were simply projecting them on paper.

They attributed her with everything from superhuman powers to being an alien with advanced technology. The one consistent theme in every story was the woman's sexual skills. If the Illusionist was half as talented in lovemaking as they thought, she could turn every woman on the planet into a lesbian. Lucretia snorted at the shallowness of the writers.

A few Web sites, however, did attract her interest, particularly the ones referring to an intimate relationship between the Illusionist and a reporter named Dakota Devereaux, the same person bylined in one of the magazines she had just read. Although there was little in the article about Yemaya Lysanne's background or any great revelations about her stunts, it was obvious the woman was close to the Illusionist. She was the only person who had managed to get personal interviews and exclusive photos of the mystery woman.

A few sites alluded to a relationship between Ms. Devereaux and Ms. Lysanne since they were constantly together. The more she read about the Illusionist, the stronger her feelings that Bondye was grooming Lucretia to be his high priestess. What other explanation was there for the arrival of Ramus, whose blood was proving to be a strong medicine, and the Illusionist, who apparently had great powers? At last, she had earned her spot at the side of Bondye.

Mayhew arrived at his aunt's house as the sun was setting. Tall and slender, he would have been a handsome man if not for the sallow skin and stooped shoulders. At thirty-two, he looked and walked like an old man. Prematurely graying hair hung loosely about his head, braided tightly in long narrow dredlocks. Nothing, however, could hide the natural exuberance he possessed. Mayhew had lived his life fast and hard and regretted little, including his *indiscretions*, a label his aunt put on his sexual activities.

Walking into Lucretia's sitting room, he smiled broadly and gave her a hug.

"Yo, Aunty!" he shouted, knowing how much she detested the greeting. It was bad enough he refused to speak Creole or French, but to stoop to slang was uncalled for.

"You know I hate that you talk like thees. I pay good money for you to speak properly and thees eez what I geet?" she chastised, but kissed his cheek affectionately. "Eet eez no way to show your respect."

"Ah, you know you love me." He grinned impishly.

Patting his cheek, Lucretia smiled. "Such a charmer, mon cher. You look tired. Have you been taking the medicine I geeve you?"

"Every day. I think it's helping, too. I've been feeling better. A lot more energy. The doc says my white count is up a bit."

"C'est un bonne chose! Now I have sometheeng new for you to try. I theenk thees may be better."

"Not something else," he groaned. "The other stuff is so nasty I practically have to gag it down."

"Peut-être. But you weel do as I say, oui? Pour moi?"

"Yes," he agreed reluctantly. "I've been doing better with your concoctions than those the doctor gives me. No reason to doubt you now."

"You are quite deesrespectful." She shook her finger at him.

"You love it when I tease you."

"Pffft!" she exclaimed, but didn't deny it.

Lucretia could never resist her grandnephew's charm. Rascal that he was, his cheery nature brought her much pleasure. Indeed, as his name meant, he was a gift from God. It was a shame one of his greatest assets was also his downfall. Like moths to a flame, he attracted many admirers. Unfortunately, his taste in young men and his carefree attitude toward sex had been his undoing. By the age of nineteen, he was infected with HIV. Although Mayhew took every precaution not to infect anyone else, he still couldn't refrain from a carefree lifestyle or attitude.

Philosophically, he accepted his fate and vowed to enjoy every minute he had left. It was only recently that the signs of the disease's progress began to take a physical toll. The medical cocktails his doctor prescribed did little to slow the virus as it ravaged his immune system. Lucretia had done her best to help him with her own concoctions, but she knew it wasn't enough. Now, however, after seeing Ancelin's miraculous recovery in only a few days, she knew she had found the much-longed-for cure.

"Come!" she ordered, leading him into a room next to the library. Opening a small refrigerator, she pulled out a vial filled with a dark, almost black substance.

"What is it?"

"Never mind," she said, pouring the liquid into a cup. Then picking up a teapot from a nearby stove, she added some warm broth and stirred the concoction. "Maintenant, dreenk it queeckly," she commanded, handing the potion to him.

Mayhew sniffed at the steamy potion and wrinkled his nose. "This smells awful!"

"Eet eez not the smell that cures you. Do as I say before eet cools off."

Shrugging, Mayhew put the cup to his lips and gulped down the thick substance, trying not to gag.

"Ack!" he gasped, sticking his tongue out and wiping it with his hand. "This is worse than the other stuff. I don't even want to know what's in it."

"I would not tell you anyway. You young people don't appreciate the old ways."

"Sure we do. We just happen to like the new ones better," Mayhew countered, winking at her. "Now is that it? Can I go now?" he pleaded, pouting boyishly.

"Oh, be gone weeth you. I don't know why I even bother." She slapped his arm.

"Because you love me. Seriously, though, thanks, Aunty. At this point, I'm willing to try anything if it'll help me feel better, even your voodooey stuff," he teased and ran for the door.

Throwing up her arms, Lucretia could only shake her head. "No respect!" she grumbled.

Taking another two vials from the refrigerator, Lucretia mixed them with the warm broth and carried the steaming cup into the library. Picking up the flier on the Illusionist, she sat by the fire and sipped the drink while she reread the advertisement. After her first sip, she wrinkled her nose slightly.

"He eez right," she muttered. "Thees eez awful."

Circling the date and time of the performance, she called Boudreau and ordered him to get her a ticket to one of the evening shows. If Ms. Lysanne was as good as the articles proclaimed, Lucretia wanted to know why.

Mayhew Porteur loved his aunt, even though she seemed a little over the top sometimes. Still, her strange brews helped him deal with the medicines his doctor was prescribing for his illness. Whether they actually were improving his immune system was another issue, but as long as he felt good, he could at least pretend he was better.

Even his friends commented on the positive changes since taking her potions. After putting up with their continued nagging, he finally confided in a few who suffered from the same disease. They too wanted to try her treatments. Desperation made people willing to do almost anything.

Mayhew had pretty much given up hope on a cure for HIV/AIDS being developed in his lifetime. He still maintained a zest for life and the desire to live as long as possible, if he could enjoy it with his friends.

Although most people thought him carefree and easygoing, he was a practical young man. Arrangements were already made for how he would end his life once the disease ran its course. His closest friends were instructed to throw a big bash and invite everyone they knew.

Mayhew had obtained several prescriptions from a local doctor who was sympathetic to AIDS victims and the stigma attached. The doctor had assured him death would be as easy as falling asleep.

Back at his small apartment, he called his latest conquest, Cornelius, and invited him over. Cornelius was also HIV positive; both felt they could indulge in a carefree relationship without the worries of condoms or passing on the virus. He also liked to keep the young man informed of his aunt's latest antics, especially since her potions made his life easier by easing the symptoms and pains.

Throwing himself on the bed, he groaned when a cramp seized his lower abdomen.

"Damn!" he muttered, reaching down to massage the area. Rolling on his side, he brought his knees up in a fetal position, hoping to ease the pain. Unfortunately, it didn't help much, so he grabbed a bottle of painkillers, poured four tablets into his hand, and swallowed them. Grimacing at the bitter taste, he tossed the bottle aside and rolled on his back, drawing his knees toward his chest.

"This shit is the worst yet," he grumbled, referring to his aunt's brews. Another wave of pain scorched his insides like hot coals searing flesh. Gasping, sweat beaded across his forehead and trickled into his eyes and down his cheeks. Mayhew groaned and stretched his trembling hand toward the phone, deciding he needed to call 911.

Another spasm tore through his insides. Clutching his stomach, he could only lay curled in a tight ball, hoping each attack would be the last. Eventually, pain and exhaustion took its toll and he slipped into a restless sleep. His muscles slowly relaxed.

Several hours later, Mayhew awoke. Slowly, he rolled onto his back, testing each muscle. Feeling no discomfort, he pushed his luck by sitting up. Once perched on the edge of the bed, he was surprised at how well he actually felt.

The achiness that normally accompanied his waking hours was gone, leaving only a pleasant warmth. Perhaps there was something to his aunt's potion this time, he thought. He hadn't felt this good in over a year.

Wanting to share the good news, he dialed Cornelius's cell number and invited him out for dinner.

Already he was formulating a plan to talk his aunt into giving him some of the potion for his lover.

CHAPTER TWENTY-NINE

D rums beat slowly as the dancers circled the fires chanting, their voices low and the words unintelligible. The tempo increased and they moved faster. Their chant grew louder, drowning out the incessant pounding of the drums.

As the voices reached a crescendo, four men emerged from the shadows carrying the body of a woman high in the air. In unison, the crowd turned to stare at the sacrifice being lowered onto the altar between two bonfires. Her hands and arms were bound and chained to large rings imbedded in the altar. Blindfolded, the woman was unable to see her captors. Still, she pulled hard against the bindings, testing their strength. Finally exhausted, she lay quiet.

Dressed in a bright red and black ankle-length gown, another woman entered the circle and walked to the altar. As high priestess, no one dared to challenge her. Tall and dark-skinned with an exquisite body, she exuded power and beauty. Smiling, she reached down to stroke the captive's cheek.

The drums quieted. The chanters milled about nervously, moving first in one direction then turning to move in the opposite. Suddenly, a loud scream erupted from the darkness. A young white woman ran from the shadows and threw herself upon the prone body of the bound woman. Sobbing, she pleaded with the priestess; the futility of her efforts was obvious.

Pulled aside by two chanters, she could only watch as the black woman picked up a large knife and twirled it around in her hands. Dancing wildly amongst her followers, she slashed at several ropes that were displayed by the men, slicing them easily in half. No one doubted the sharpness of the knife.

Next, she jabbed it sharply into a log, demonstrating its strength and then yanked it out. Cries of awe rang out from the crowd as she jumped high into the air and landed lightly on her feet. Twirling rapidly and circling the altar three times, she moved gracefully, swinging the knife hypnotically in various directions. Her own body undulated from side to side, hips swaying seductively like a serpent moving in for the kill.

Nearing her victim, she raised her arm to strike. The young white woman broke free from her own captor and threw herself between the downward thrust of the knife and the intended sacrifice. The chanters fell silent when a large puff of smoke billowed up, concealing the three women. A scream pierced the stillness. The smoke cleared, revealing the knife buried deep in the altar. The priestess stood motionless, partially concealed by the smoke. The captives had vanished.

The audience gasped. Except for the altar having been concealed momentarily by smoke, the entire stage had remained in full view of the spectators. There was no way the chained captive and the young woman could have disappeared without being noticed. Slowly, the priestess turned and walked to the front of the stage. It took several seconds before the front row spectators realized the victim on the altar had morphed into the priestess.

Jumping to their feet, they clapped and cheered. Immediately, the rest of the audience followed suit when they recognized the Illusionist dressed in the priestess's gown. Bowing slightly, Yemaya swung her right hand to the right. Walking on stage, hands clasped, was the original high priestess and the young woman. Both waved enthusiastically to the crowd. Cheers reverberated through the coliseum. Once again, the Illusionist had mystified her audience.

Dakota sat quietly listening to the applause. She always made it a point not to visit Yemaya during rehearsals so she would have an unbiased opinion of the show and the audience's response. Her old boss had agreed to pay her handsomely for any articles she sent pertaining to the Illusionist, her personal life, or her performances.

For Dakota, the personal life of her lover was off-limits, but Yemaya didn't object to Dakota's attempts at exposing her trade secrets. Yemaya realized Dakota's investigative skills were impressive and suspected some of her secrets would eventually be revealed. To have her lover in her life was worth the sacrifice.

This particular show left Dakota drained and somewhat uncomfortable. Perhaps the theme hit too close to home. Every time Yemaya performed, she was putting her life on the line. Except for the time Shezarra, the great white, had crashed through the platform in Charleston, throwing Yemaya into the water, all her shows had been flawless. Of course, the Charleston catastrophe was the result of sabotage, so Dakota really couldn't count it as anything other than that.

The Illusionist strolled around the stage acknowledging the crowd's continued appreciation and waited for the noise to subside. Sensing her lover's unease, she stopped in front of Dakota and winked. Shaking her head, Dakota chuckled softly. Yemaya was irresistible when she flirted. The Illusionist turned back to her audience and held up her hands to silence the crowd.

"Again thank you for attending tonight's performance. I hope my show is all you hoped it would be. If I have given you a few moments of wonder or taken away a few worries these past two hours, this night has been successful for all of us. As always, I leave you with this thought: Whatever you think you have seen tonight, it is merely illusion, but if you believe it to be real, it will be. The same is so in your lives. Look closely at those who seek to influence you. You may find that most of what you are told or shown are illusions, illusions created by others to serve their own purposes. You be the judge of what is real and leave the illusions to me. Good night, everyone!"

She waved farewell to the audience. As she left the stage, Yemaya stopped for a moment and stared toward a darkened corner of the coliseum. It was obvious something or someone had caught her attention. Dakota turned in her seat to see what Yemaya was looking at but was unable to see anything but shadows. By the time her gaze returned to Yemaya, she had disappeared behind the curtains. Dakota slipped from her seat and walked backstage.

"What's up?"

"Just a feeling!"

"Whenever that happens, it usually means something. You have any ideas?"

"No, but I could feel someone watching us. I may have given our relationship away when I looked at you a few minutes ago."

"I think we did that a long time ago, sweetie. I guess we'll just have to wait and see where this leads, though. Knowing our luck, it won't be long before we find out," she joked. "Until then, how about we grab a bite to eat and get some rest? You look like hell."

"Thanks. You sure know how to make a woman feel good."

Dakota grinned impishly. "I most certainly do."

CHAPTER THIRTY

L ucretia sat quietly watching the woman on stage. She had spent several days reading as much as possible about the Illusionist. If the reports were accurate, no one had yet solved the mystery behind the woman or her magic. The fact that she was from an area of the world known for its supernatural connections only added to her mystique.

Her blood combined with Ramus's would ensure a cure for her nephew, and for her, unlimited power and immortality. Of that, she was sure after observing the woman's performance.

Obviously, Bondye wanted her to know about the Illusionist so she could have her powers. Why else would she have appeared so quickly in New Orleans, almost unannounced? What other explanation could there be since the Illusionist normally scheduled her tours well in advance and this one was so spontaneous?

For two weeks, the television and radio stations had been inundated with advertisements about her upcoming show. Fliers were posted throughout the French Quarter. Everywhere she went, pictures of the mysterious Illusionist announced her one-time appearance, and whispers circulated that this was to be her final show before retiring. Yes, it had to be Bondye's intervention that influenced her coming to New Orleans.

Excited by the thought, Lucretia decided she had seen enough. Boudreau was waiting outside with the car and she hated crowds. She was about to stand when she saw Yemaya stop in front of a woman and smile. Obviously, the recipient was special to her. Finding out her identity might prove valuable. As if reading her thoughts, the Illusionist suddenly focused her attention in Lucretia's direction and frowned. The woman seated in the front row turned and looked back toward the high priestess. Not wishing to draw attention to herself, Lucretia remained seated until they both lost interest. Then she quietly left, unaware that two other people had been watching her from several rows away.

"She is the one you are looking for," Sarpe said, nodding in the direction of the high priestess.

"Who is she?"

"She *believes* she is the chosen priesstesss to the high sspirit, Bondye."

"Is she?"

Shrugging, Sarpe didn't answer for a few seconds. "That isn't for me to ssay."

"Meaning Bondye is real?"

"Bondye is very real. Whether thiss sspirit is who they believe it to be is another matter," she said mysteriously. "To these people, Bondye is male. To other cultures, he becomes female."

"Have you ever met Bondye?"

"I meet many sspiritss," Sarpe answered evasively, shrugging again. "Mosst are unimpresssive, but Bondye is not one to take lightly."

"I'll take that as a yes and that you don't wish to discuss this particular spirit at the moment. So from your earlier comment, this woman isn't necessarily in Bondye's good graces."

"I do not presume to know the minds of sspirits nor intervene in their affairs or those of mortals."

"Until recently," Ekimmu teased, patting Sarpe's hand affectionately.

"Until ressently. Don't let what I've ssaid fool you. Thiss woman is very dangerous without Bondye's ssupport. She's powerful amongsst her people and has a very loyal following."

"If that's the case, why did she need Ramus?"

"For the ssame reason she watches thiss one. She craves power."

Frowning, Ekimmu turned to watch the retreating woman. "What has Yemaya or Ramus got to do with power?"

"Nothing and everything. There are those who believe your people possess great powers."

Ekimmu nodded reluctantly.

"That alone makess you a target for the ambitiouss. Yemaya is beautiful and myssteriousss. Many would do anything to possesss those qualities. She has been hunted by ssome already and ssadly will be by others all her life."

"So we have something in common."

"Yess. You have much in common. More than you can imagine. You both are haunted by the hisstory of your anssesstors. She protectss her people, as a mother would her children, but within her lives a great darknesss that could one day desstroy her."

"A darkness?"

"Yess. You ssaw it when she confronted Ramus."

"And what about me?"

"The ssame. You bear the sscars of your anssesstors and your people. Have you not traveled thiss world ssearching for ssomething or ssomeone to bring sstability to your existensse?"

Ekimmu laughed softly. "I'm not so sure of that. I keep on the move from necessity, as do all my people. We can't change our appearances like a certain spirit I know."

"True, but that is not what preventss you from taking lovers."

"No, time does that. We are long lived. It's too painful to be with someone for only a few years, to watch them grow old. Even love can't overcome aging or the jealousy that inevitably comes from seeing oneself growing weak and feeble while the one you love remains young and vibrant."

"It is not nessessarily inevitable. Would you have me believe that you will feel thiss jealoussy in a hundred or a thousand years if we were to remain lovers? I am a sspirit. I will not age, as you musst in time."

Ekimmu switched her gaze from the priestess to Sarpe. She worried about their future together. It was an issue she had deliberately avoided thinking about when possible. Now she had no choice but to face her fears.

"I don't know. I try not to think about my own feelings, only how you would feel once I'm gone."

"And if I ssaid I would ssurvive your death and go on as I was meant to? Would you be hurt or dissappointed?" Sarpe asked, her golden eyes momentarily changing to the elliptical shape of the serpent. It was evident the spirit was experiencing some deep emotion. Ekimmu could only guess at what it was.

"I would hope that you find someone else to share your life. I never want you to be alone again. I know loneliness. Maybe not as long as you have, but even in my short life, by your standards, it was almost unbearable. At least I had family and a few friends."

"Ah! You are misstaken about me. I have a family. They are my friends. Ssome have lassted a lifetime, my lifetime," Sarpe said nonchalantly, as if to minimize the importance of Ekimmu's words.

"Then I'm happy for you," Ekimmu said truthfully, but not in the least fooled by her lover's answer. "It must be wonderful to have a friendship that lasts so long, but I think we both know we're not discussing friends or family. I have no doubt you cherish yours as I do mine, but they do not keep me warm, nor raise my emotions to such heights or depths as you do."

Sarpe stared at Ekimmu for several seconds, then smiled the most beautiful smile Ekimmu had ever seen. Elliptical eyes twinkled, reflecting an inner light far greater than any outside source could create. Lips drawn back exposed shiny white teeth. Two dimples appeared, giving her an impish look.

"I'm glad! I've only jusst begun to know those feelings when we're together and apart. I find them..." Sarpe stopped, searching for the right words, "...dissturbing, but very ssatissfying."

Ekimmu blushed. "Umm, maybe we should discuss this somewhere else," she offered, feeling very warm.

Laughing, Sarpe patted her thigh. "Perhapss you are right. Now is not the time to be having ssuch a converssation. To answser your questions, the priesstess wanted Ramus's essensse and Yemaya's."

"Essence?"

"Yess, that which flowss through all living things."

"You mean blood?"

Sarpe nodded. "Jusst as your people think they need the humans to ssurvive, the priesstess thinks Ramus's would cure her kin of his illnesss and bring her immortality. She believes Yemaya will bring her power."

"Will it?"

"I don't know. Her kin ssuffers the ssame disease as Ramuss, but it is of no consssequensse. She musst be sstopped if your people are to be ssafe. Ssupersstitions die hard. They sspread as quickly as a plague and are jusst as deadly. If others ssusspect she has ssucceeded, they too will want what she has."

"I agree, but if something happens to her and others get

236

suspicious, they'll still go after us. It's a no-win situation."

"True, unlesss her death is natural."

"I won't kill her."

"Don't worry," Sarpe said, stroking her cheek lightly. "You'll figure it out. I wish I could take care of her for you. Unfortunately, she's not mine to deal with. For now, it's enough you know your enemy and theirs," she added, nodding toward Yemaya.

After Lucretia left the coliseum, Sarpe and Ekimmu slipped quietly away.

Ekimmu and Sarpe were relaxing in bed, watching a documentary on the world's most poisonous animals when they were disturbed by a knock on the door.

"I believe that is one of yours," Sarpe said, pushing herself up into a sitting position. Instantly, a tan, silk blouse and cream slacks morphed around her previously nude body. Then leaning back against the headboard, she gave Ekimmu a wicked smirk.

"That's a handy talent," Ekimmu said, shaking her head as she put her own clothes on.

"One of the benefitss of being a sspirit."

"I can imagine."

Opening the door, she saw Constance leaning against her cane.

"Om, what are you doing out so late?" She ushered the older woman into the room. "You should be resting."

"I'm fine, child. I just need to sit for a bit." She gasped, looking around. Immediately, she felt a chair being placed behind her and sat down, trying to catch her breath. "Thank you, deary."

"You are quite welcome, Miss Lorraine," Sarpe replied, backing into a darker corner.

"Ah. You must be Ekimmu's lady spirit. No need to hide in the shadows. Come here and let me look at you."

Sarpe, who had never been ordered to do anything in her entire existence, laughed softly but respectfully obeyed. Stepping into the light, she stood quietly while the older woman pulled a pair of bifocals from her sweater pocket and placed them on her nose. Rubbing each lens with her finger, she finally appeared satisfied and stared at the golden-skinned woman in front of her.

"You certainly are a fine-looking spirit. No wonder she's so taken with you."

Blushing, then realizing she had actually reacted in a human way, Sarpe wasn't sure how to respond.

"Om, I think you just embarrassed her."

"Then I must apologize."

"There's no need for that, and it'ss an honor to meet you, Miss Lorraine. I've heard a lot about you."

"Just call me Constance, child."

"As you wish. I am Ssarpe."

"Sarpe. You are the serpent spirit."

"Yess. You have heard of me?" she asked, surprised since she had been long forgotten amongst most cultures.

"I've been around a long time and have met a few spirits in my time. Your name has come up once or twice. You're highly respected from what I remember."

"I would ssay 'feared' iss more accurate, but thank you."

"If I had meant *feared,* I would have said it. No matter, though. I'm happy to see Ekimmu has found someone worthy of her. She's been alone too long. It's about time she settled down."

"Excuse me, but I'm standing right here, ladies."

"Like we could forget that. Well, the night is getting on, so I should let you two get back to whatever you were doing. I just wanted to see if you had heard anything else about Ramus and to tell you I'm in room 234 if you need me."

Ekimmu updated Constance on the progress she and Sarpe had made and their suspicions about the high priestess. Constance listened quietly without interrupting.

"So you think Yemaya and Dakota may be in danger?"

"I think the priestess covets what she thinks Ms. Lysanne possesses. If that is sso, her mate iss in as much danger as her. Both will need to be watched carefully in casse they need our asssissstansse."

"There are a few Gebians in the area. I can contact them later today," Constance offered.

"I don't think that would be wise. Thiss woman is ssmart. She will have sspies watching for others like Ramus. Your people will be in jeopardy, pluss it may alert ssomeone that we are aware of the priesstess's ambitions. I have many eyes at my dissposal. Should ssomething happen, they will notify me, and I will tell Ekimmu."

"I thought there was some type of rule against spirits getting involved in mortal problems."

"We have no rules in my world, only traditions." Sarpe shrugged. "No one will care if I choose to break a few."

Constance had no doubt Sarpe was a powerful spirit, quite possibly the most powerful if she ever decided to flex her spiritual muscles.

"Good. Then we'll see what happens. Now I'm going to get some sleep. It's been a long day."

Standing, Constance made eye contact with the serpent spirit for the first time. Golden eyes with elliptical pupils stared unblinkingly into her ebony eyes. Feeling disoriented, she blinked a few times, lowered her lids for a few seconds, then reopened her eyes. Sarpe, realizing her snake eyes had startled the older woman, suddenly rounded her pupils, giving them a more human look.

"Ssorry. I forget about them when I'm relaxed."

"Oh, don't worry, child. You just caught me off-guard. I rather like them," she said, patting the cool hand on her arm.

"I'll walk you to your room," Ekimmu said.

"No, no. I'm fine. You two just get back to doing what you were before I barged in. It's been a pleasure meeting you, Sarpe."

"For me too. Be ssafe."

Leaning down, the spirit kissed the old woman's cheek, then whispered into her ear. "I think our world will be much improved when you passs from thiss one. There is much we will learn from each other."

"If that is my destiny." Constance gave her a slight smile and left.

Ekimmu frowned momentarily, not sure she had heard Sarpe correctly. The spirit winked at her lover and laughed as her clothing melted away.

"Want to play?"

CHAPTER THIRTY-ONE

Exhausted, Yemaya threw herself on the bed and sighed. Between the practices and the show, she had pretty much depleted her energy reserves with very little to show for it. Still, she had sensed someone watching her with more than a professional interest. There was a darkness emanating from the person, almost purulent with the stench of evil and the faint scent of Ramus. Unfortunately, she wasn't able to make out the person's face, but she could tell it was a woman, most likely his killer or someone closely associated with her.

"You look done in," Dakota said, strolling into the bedroom wearing only a bath towel.

Eyeing her lover's trim figure, Yemaya smiled, her eyes crinkling slightly at the corners. "That would be putting it mildly." She held out her hand.

Dakota slipped past it and leaned down, placing her own hands on each side of Yemaya's body. Water dripped from her hair onto Yemaya's chest, leaving dark stains on her T-shirt.

"Why don't you take it easy today? I still have some things to check out. I met someone who could give me a little insight into this Lucretia Mordeau."

"I might do that," Yemaya agreed and yawned. "You are not going to do anything reckless, are you?"

"No, dear."

Yemaya shook her head and laughed. "Okay. A few hours of sleep will do me some good. If you are not back in a couple of hours, I will look for you."

"Good. You'll need to rest for when I get back."

"In that case, I definitely will take it easy." Yemaya lowered her voice to that unique huskiness that sent shivers through Dakota's body.

"Damn!"

Yemaya arched her left eyebrow and looked at her questioningly.

"Don't give me that look. You know very well what you're doing and that we don't have time for that now."

"You certainly cannot blame a girl for trying."

"Says who?"

Laughing, Yemaya pulled Dakota close and kissed her. By the time they separated, both women were breathing heavily.

"Says me," Yemaya whispered. "You sure about not having a few minutes?" she asked, wiggling her eyebrows.

Dakota gave an exaggerated sigh. "Well, if I must."

Two hours later, Dakota slipped from beneath the sheets and quietly dressed, making sure not to wake her exhausted lover. Leaning down, she gently kissed Yemaya on the lips and left for the waterfront.

Her inquiries over the previous two weeks had given her a lead, pointing to the Warehouse District as a possible source of information. One of her recent contacts had agreed to meet her with the promise of giving her some important information on Mambo Lucretia, the supposed high priestess with a fairly large following of voodoo initiates. If what he had told her was true, she'd make a great story even if she had nothing to do with Ramus's disappearance.

When Dakota arrived at the rendezvous point, she looked at her watch and realized she was early. It gave her a few extra minutes to look around. Several people shuffled in and out of the various buildings, transporting large boxes and crates while going about what appeared to be routine activities.

Although a few workers glanced at her curiously, no one appeared overly interested in checking her out, giving her an opportunity to snoop around several small back alleys between the buildings. Emerging from a particularly isolated one, she heard footsteps approaching from around the corner. The large figure of a man stepped into the opening, his face shadowed by the bright daylight behind him. Dakota hesitated, then called out to him.

"Mr. Boudreau, is that you?" she asked nervously.

"Oui, Ms. Devereaux. C'est moi."

"Well, umm, I appreciate you meeting me like this. Perhaps we could talk in a little more open place?"

"As you weesh, Ms. Devereaux." He turned away from the entrance and walked toward another building. "I must be discreet, mamselle. Mambo Lucretia, she has many eyes."

"Of course. Anything you tell me is confidential. I certainly don't want to get you in trouble for talking to me."

"Merci. Please follow me. I know where we can talk."

Taking a set of keys from his suit pocket, he opened the side door of a small warehouse office and held it open for her. Dakota peeked inside but was unable to see anything in the darkened room. Glancing at the large black man, she hesitated.

Boudreau shrugged his broad shoulders and reached past her to switch on a light. "Eet eez quiet here."

Shaking off her uneasiness, Dakota stepped into the small room and looked around. Dust covered an old wooden desk and chair. It was obvious no one had been in the place for a long time.

"You might say that," she agreed, noticing the heavy layer of dust covering the floor. "Anyway, thank you for meeting with me."

"Pas de problème. Eet eez nothing," he replied. "What eez it you weesh to know?"

"I'm doing an article for my magazine on voodoo and other mystical practices in America. Some of my sources have recommended I include a woman named Mambo Lucretia. They say she has a following almost as big as Dr. Buzzard."

"An exaggeration, I theenk."

"Maybe, but I'm discovering she's well known in these parts. Hopefully, you can tell me something about her."

"Peut-être."

"Well, anything you can tell me will help. Have you ever met or talked to Mambo Lucretia?"

"Oui, a few times. She eez very private."

"I take it she lives around here, nearby I mean." Dakota took out her pad and pencil.

"Fifteen meenutes maybe."

"Would you be willing to tell me or show me where?"

"If you weesh." He shrugged. "Eez theese sometheeng you weesh to do now, mamselle?"

Looking at her watch, Dakota estimated she had some time to spare before returning to the hotel. "I have the time if you do."

"My car eez parked a few blocks from here."

"No disrespect, Mr. Boudreau, but perhaps you can give me the address and I'll just catch a cab. I'll need one anyway to take me back to the hotel, so it'll simplify things." Dakota tried to hide her discomfort about traveling with a stranger.

"Je comprend. I weel call one for you, yes? There are few cabs in theese part of the quarter."

"Thanks!" Dakota said, grateful he hadn't attempted to persuade her to go with him. Boudreau made her nervous. She wanted to spend more time asking him questions but decided discretion was a wiser choice. Granted, his quiet demeanor and manners made him appear harmless, but she had learned to rely on her instincts. At the moment, they were raising several flags.

After making a quick call, Boudreau motioned for her to leave the office and locked the door behind them. Within minutes, a taxi pulled up. Boudreau gave the driver the address and walked away without saying a word.

"It's always the quiet ones," Dakota mumbled, climbing into the cab. The driver, a young black man, turned to look at her and smiled brightly. "Howdy."

"Well, howdy," she said, returning the smile.

"Just sit back and relax, ma'am. We'll be there shortly."

Before she could reply, she felt herself jerked backward as the cab took off, wheels squealing.

"How about slowing it a bit so we get there in one piece?" she suggested.

"Sorry, ma'am, but time is money."

"True and so are tips, so if you want one, slow it down."

The driver immediately slowed to a more reasonable pace. "Better?" he teased.

"Much better. Thanks."

The drive to Mambo Lucretia's home was uneventful despite the cabbie's enthusiasm for dodging around slower vehicles. Once there, Dakota saw several cars parked along the street. A small group of people was standing on the corner talking while others scurried about. Boudreau was leaning against a black limousine, his arms crossed.

"Would you mind waiting for me? It should only be about

twenty minutes," Dakota asked her driver.

"It'll cost you extra, but I need to go buy some cigs, so how about I come back?"

"That's fine." She paid the fare and tip.

"See you soon." With squealing tires, the taxi disappeared down the road.

Hope he doesn't have an accident on the way. Dakota walked to where Boudreau was standing and waited for him to speak.

"Theese eez her home," he said, pointing to a large two-story house protected by a five-foot-high brick fence and large wrought iron gates.

Dakota approached the gates and peered through them into a secluded garden. Huge live oak trees blocked the sunlight, making it dark and eerie. Most of the area was covered in plants and shrubbery that had been allowed to grow wild, giving it a natural look, as well as providing a visual barrier preventing the curious from having a clear view of the house.

"Rather gloomy, isn't it?"

"Oui! Mambo Lucretia, she likes her privacy."

"Apparently. Does she ever do interviews?"

"Rarely, but..."

Dakota waited for him to continue. "But?" she prompted.

"Pardon, Mamselle Devereaux, but I have already asked Mambo Lucretia eef she would see you. I hope you are not angry."

"No, not at all. I wasn't aware you even knew her."

"Oui, I know her. Ma grandmère...uh, you say grandmama... know her."

Frowning, Dakota wasn't sure what to think. "Why didn't you tell me?"

"I don't know you. Perhaps you mean her harm. I must first learn who you are." He shrugged.

"But I explained that I was doing a story for my magazine. I'd have thought that and my credentials were enough proof of who I am."

"I'm sorry, mais I do not trust your kind."

"My kind? Oh, you mean journalist. I can understand that. So do I get an interview?"

"Oui. Mambo Lucretia say she can talk to you now, eef you weesh."

As if on cue, the iron gates opened and a tall, handsome black woman strolled toward her. Sunglasses concealed her eyes, but the slight smile was warm and friendly.

"Bonjour. You must be Mamselle Devereaux."

"Yes, I am. It's a pleasure to meet you. How should I address you?"

"You may call me Lucretia, of course."

"I'm Dakota. Thank you for meeting me on such short notice. I really didn't expect this."

"Nor I. You are a respected journalist. I was curious why you would weesh to write about me."

"Actually, the story is on voodoo, but while I was at the library doing some research, then in the French Quarter, I overheard your name a few times. You're well known here, so I thought it would add more color to my article."

Lucretia laughed. "I doubt I am eenteresting." She motioned for Dakota to accompany her into the garden. Nodding to Boudreau, she guided Dakota down a path and onto a small, secluded porch. Dakota didn't notice Boudreau talking to the cab driver who had returned from his errand nor the small salute the cabbie gave him as he accepted the money that was handed to him.

Leading her into a small living room, Lucretia pointed to a small settee near the fireplace.

"Please…sit. May I offer you coffee or tea? I do not keep the soft dreenk. They are bad for the health."

"Tea would be fine, thank you."

Lucretia smiled and left the room. Minutes later, she returned carrying a small tray containing a teapot, two small cups, creamer, and a sugar bowl. Setting it on the round coffee table, she poured Dakota a cup and handed it to her. Leaning back in her chair, she folded her hands on her lap and waited for her to take a sip.

"Is eet satisfactory?"

"Mmm. Good. Thank you."

"Bien. Now what would you like to know?"

"I'm doing this article on voodoo, its history, and modern practices. I'm particularly interested in learning a little about your background and New Orleans voodoo."

"There eez not much to tell about me. My family move here when I was a young woman."

"Then you're not Cajun?"

Lucretia laughed and shook her head. "No, I am French, but thees eez my home."

"How did you get involved with voodoo?"

"I was chosen."

Dakota realized Lucretia was reluctant to discuss her personal life and decided to change the subject. "I understand New Orleans voodoo is different from Haitian or African."

"Perhaps a leetle bit, but not much. The roots are the same. The spirits are the same. We sometimes call them by different names, but that eez all. May I ask what purpose thees article?"

"Purpose?"

"Oui," Lucretia said, motioning toward the magazines on her coffee table. "I see you write about thees Illusionist. She eez, how you say, fascinating and most beautiful."

"Yes, she is," Dakota agreed, assuming a nonchalance she didn't feel. "She just finished her last performance here, and I thought I could kill two birds with one stone, so to speak. My editor will be impressed if I can give him something new to publish."

Taking another sip of her tea, Dakota felt slightly dizzy. Hands shaking slightly, she placed the cup and dish on the table and massaged her temple.

"Are you not well?" Lucretia asked, leaning forward in her chair to stare unblinkingly at Dakota.

"No, no, I'm fine. Just felt dizzy for a moment. I probably should be going, though. I have a dinner arrangement this evening."

"Perhaps another time then, oui?" Lucretia rose to her feet.

Smiling, Dakota nodded and stood also. "That would be great. Thank you for your time."

As Lucretia led her toward the door, Dakota again felt the dizziness. Her legs were heavy as if her blood had turned to syrup. Placing her hand on the wall, she leaned heavily against it trying to regain her equilibrium. A warm arm circled her waist.

"Let me help you. I theenk you should lie down for a while, oui?"

Unable to refuse, Dakota could only nod as she was helped to the couch and lowered onto it. Lucretia picked up her ankles and turned her feet so Dakota was lying down, then placed a knitted comforter over her.

"Eez there anyone I should call to come and get you?"

Dakota could barely open her eyes. Frowning, she tried to think. She knew her lover would be worried and come looking for her.

"My...my friend," she murmured, feeling worse as the waves of dizziness increased, followed by nausea. "If you could...call Ms. Lysanne... and tell her."

"Certainment. How weel I contact Ms. Lysanne?"

Dakota mumbled the hotel and room number before closing her eyes. Moments later, she lay unconscious on the couch.

Lucretia pulled the small medallion from Dakota's neck. "I have no doubt your Ms. Lysanne weel be here very soon."

Dialing the hotel's number, Lucretia asked the receptionist to inform Yemaya that Dakota had been involved in a small accident at a warehouse near the waterfront and needed her assistance as soon as possible.

After giving the location, she hung up and called Boudreau. Ten minutes later, he arrived at her house in the black hearse. Lucretia handed him a small package and gave him his instructions. Nodding respectfully, Boudreau drove away.

Returning to the unconscious woman, Lucretia summoned several of her servants and ordered them to carry Dakota to a small room in the basement that was furnished with a bed, table, and lamp.

"Make sure she eez comfortable and guard her well," she ordered. "Eef she eez harmed or escapes, I weel be most unhappy."

Bowing, two of the servants picked Dakota up and hurried away. Neither of them wanted to think about the implied threat of their mistress's words.

CHAPTER THIRTY-TWO

Yemaya!" a warm, sultry voice whispered. "Wake up! We need to talk."

Groaning, Yemaya rolled over and pulled the blanket over her head.

"Yemaya, Dakota needs you."

Stirring restlessly, Yemaya struggled against the exhaustion that was holding her captive. Dakota needed her. It was all she could think about as she fought her way to consciousness. "Dakota?"

"No, daughter, it's Mari."

Opening her eyes, she gazed into the pale blue eyes of her ancestor.

"Mari, what happened?" She sat up and rubbed her eyes. Around them was a glorious meadow filled with thousands of flowers. It was a place she had visited before in the spirit world whenever Mari or Maopa needed to speak to her.

"Dakota is in trouble. Maopa can feel her distress, but we can't locate her. Something blocks her energies from us."

"How can that be? I thought the spirits could see everything."

"Even we have limitations. Spirits feel only that which is of their own."

"But you are the Earth Mother. Everything living is of your own making."

"Not everything. The Earth has evolved. She has become the creator of life and occasionally its destroyer. Even I no longer control her."

"What can you tell me about Dakota?"

"Only that she is unconscious and drugged. Because of this, she doesn't dream, so we're unable to reach her mind. Whatever it is, it's strong and suppresses almost all her mental activities."

"Fuck! What about Sarpe? Or Ekimmu? Can either of them

help?"

"Not with this, but Sarpe has gone to Ekimmu to let her know of Dakota's disappearance. I know they'll do whatever they can."

"Thank you. Let me know if you find anything. I have to go."

"I will. Now go! I'm meeting with Intunecat. He may know something. He sees more than I, and he has a special connection with Dakota."

Nodding, Yemaya lay down and closed her eyes. She didn't care for the last remark but knew it was true. As she drifted off, she felt the warm lips of her ancestor press gently against her cheek.

"Be safe, daughter."

Yemaya awoke to the sound of her phone ringing. Hoping it was Dakota, she lunged for it, knocking it onto the floor.

"Damn!" she swore, grabbing it. "Hello?"

"Ms. Lysanne, I'm sorry to disturb you, but we just received a message that Ms. Devereaux has been in an accident and needs you to meet her. She gave an address."

"The call was from Ms. Devereaux?"

"It doesn't say. I'm sorry, Ms. Lysanne. The message was just passed to me by our reservation clerk."

"Give me the address."

Within minutes, Yemaya was in a taxi heading to the Warehouse District. Once there, she paid the driver and walked quickly toward the address left on the message. A light shone through the office window indicating someone was inside. Knocking on the door, she stepped back as it swung open. A large black man stood staring at her for a few moments.

"Ms. Lysanne?"

"Yes, where is Ms. Devereaux?"

"Please come inside, mamselle," he said, stepping back and motioning for her to enter. "I weel explain everything."

"You can explain to me from here."

"Please do not make thees more difficult than eet eez," he replied, holding up the small medallion Dakota had worn. "You must come with me now. Mambo Lucretia say she weel not harm her if you come quietly. I have twenty meenutes to bring you to her home." He glanced at his watch.

"Where?" Yemaya demanded angrily.

Boudreau felt a sudden pressure in his head. Reaching up with his right hand, he massaged his temple. "Ms. Lysanne, we really don't have much time," he grumbled painfully.

"Then we should go" was all she said.

Nodding, Boudreau stepped past her and walked to his car. Opening the back door, he held it for her until she climbed in. Neither spoke during the ride to Lucretia's estate. Boudreau tried to concentrate on his driving while Yemaya fought the inner rage that was again struggling to gain control of her mind.

"We are here."

Looking up, Yemaya merely nodded and opened the door. Boudreau escorted her onto the porch and knocked on the door. When it opened, a tall dark-skinned woman stood before them.

"Ah, Ms. Lysanne. Please come in."

"Where is Dakota?" Yemaya growled.

"She eez safe for now."

"What do you want?"

"You."

"Me?"

"Oui. I get you, and Ms. Devereaux weel be released."

"Why?"

"You have sometheeng I need. You have thees power. I must know what eet eez."

"I have no power. I am an Illusionist. What I do is very scientific and nothing more."

"Pleeze do not take me for the fool. We both know better."

"You know nothing," Yemaya hissed, her eyes burning darkly.

"Mais you are wrong. I know much," Lucretia countered, switching her gaze beyond Yemaya to Boudreau.

Before Yemaya could react, she felt a pain exploding in her head, followed by darkness.

"Tie her and prepare her for the ceremony. I weel have what she has."

Walking to the back of the house, she opened a door beneath the stairwell and switched on the light. Descending the steps, she unlocked another door and entered a small room. A night lamp glowed next to a bed. Dakota lay unconscious, her breathing shallow. Lucretia watched Dakota's chest rising and falling for several moments.

"She eez very beauteeful. Eet eez a shame she must die, but Bondye has ordained thees. I fulfeel my destiny for me and my people."

Hearing footsteps, the priestess turned to see her servant standing in the doorway.

"Qu'est-ce que c'est?"

"What do you want me to do with her?"

"Bring her along. Capturing Ms. Lysanne was too easy. I do not like eet. Either she plays weeth us or she eez not as powerful as I thought. The journalist weel be our security."

"As you wish, mistress."

"Now gather my followers. Tonight weel be a great day for all of us."

Lucretia held the huge snake high above her head displaying it to her followers.

"Regardez, Dambala!"

Looking down at Yemaya, who was tied to a large altar, she smiled smugly.

"Well, Ms. Lysanne. I see you wake up. I regret my rudeness, mais I could not permeet you to use thees power you possess."

"I told you I do not have any powers," Yemaya said, her voice cold and emotionless.

"Naturellment. You are only the Illusionist. We weel see. Maybe yes, maybe no."

Turning to her followers, she forced the serpent's jaws open, exposing fangs almost two inches long. Squeezing the jaws slightly, a drop of venom formed on the tip of one fang and fell to the ground. A slight hiss escaped from the snake when she laid it between Yemaya's spread-eagle legs.

Immediately, it coiled in a figure eight, ready to strike anything that moved. Backing away slowly, Lucretia spread her arms wide and raised them toward the blackened sky.

"Thees woman eez a non-believer. Dambala must decide her fate."

Sensing no immediate threat, the snake slowly uncoiled and began flicking its tongue, tasting the air. Gliding up Yemaya's right leg, it hesitated for a moment and lay still. Yemaya knew not to move. Trying to break the restraints now would only antagonize the snake, possibly causing it to strike. Feeling impotent, she was aware her own *beast* was beginning to awaken, sensing her vulnerability. It would make the situation worse since it lacked the control needed to remain calm. Torn between trying to concentrate on the snake's movements and the awakening of the darkness within her, it was difficult to concentrate on either.

"Perhaps I make a mistake, Ms. Lysanne. Why do you not struggle?" Lucretia asked. Yemaya ignored her. She was more concerned about the serpent. Sensing no immediate threat, it moved across her body searching for the warmest spot to curl up on. Yemaya knew she would have to do something to keep the snake away from her face. A bite there would be fatal.

"Thees is very disappointing." Lucretia sighed melodramatically, interrupting Yemaya's thoughts. "I theenk maybe you need a little incentive, oui?" Motioning to one of her serviteurs, she stepped away from the altar and out of Yemaya's line of sight. From the corner of her eye, Yemaya saw a figure being dragged forward.

"I believe you know Ms. Devereaux," Lucretia said nonchalantly when her servants pushed Dakota to her knees by the altar. Hands tied in front of her and gagged, Dakota was unable to say anything, but her eyes reflected her fear when she saw the huge snake lying on Yemaya's chest. Disturbed by the arrival of more people, the snake again coiled, reared back, and flicked its tongue nervously.

"Stay still, Dakota," Yemaya whispered.

It was the first time Dakota had ever seen Yemaya truly afraid. Sweat ran in rivulets from her lover's forehead into the hair around her ears. Keeping eye contact, Dakota tried to project a calmness she didn't feel. She could feel Yemaya's struggle against her own darkness lurking within the depths of her mind, as well as her attempts to control her fear of the snake. Dakota's presence would inevitably tip the balance unfavorably against her lover.

"Please," Dakota prayed, hoping Yemaya would somehow pick up on her thoughts. "Forget me for the moment. You have to control the rage."

Nodding slightly, Yemaya closed her eyes and concentrated, knowing already there was no chance of freeing either of them. Almost her entire life had been spent perfecting the art of escape. The slightest move would cause the snake to strike. Because it was exceptionally large, it could produce enough venom to kill several people and Yemaya couldn't be assured it wouldn't strike at Dakota, who was only a few feet away and on her knees almost eye level with the serpent.

Like a computer, her mind quickly considered different scenarios, but they were just as quickly discarded because of the risks to Dakota. Eventually, she realized she had only one choice. If she released the *beast*, rather than fight it, there was a chance it could break the bindings holding her.

Yemaya knew it was able to produce an almost inhuman amount of strength. She would take her chances with the snakebite. The alternative was that she and her lover would die. Opening her eyes, she looked longingly at Dakota, hoping she would understand why she was surrendering to the darkness within her.

"Forgive me," she whispered, her eyes beseeching her lover to trust her.

Dakota frowned, momentarily confused. Only when she saw Yemaya's dark gray eyes morph to black did she understand her meaning.

"No," she cried, ripping off the gag, guessing Yemaya's intent. *This can't be happening*, she thought. "Mari, Grandma, where are you?" she silently cried out, praying the spirits would come to their aid.

CHAPTER THIRTY-THREE

Mari and Maopa stared into the Eternal Flame. The spirit world was unnaturally quiet. The Earth Mother and her chosen were furious over the treatment of their mortal descendents but were unable to intervene.

"What was I thinking?" Mari stormed, ignoring the brilliant streaks of lightning bouncing around them from the angry energy flowing from her essence.

"We wasn't. I neva trusted that dark un," Maopa grumbled. "These be our own. We should a taken care of 'em and that demon woman ourselves."

"I know! They're our responsibility, not Intunecat's. I should have trusted in myself instead of listening to his reasoning. As strange as it seems, I do trust him. I've known him a long time. He's many things, but he has never lied or deceived me."

"There may be truth in that, but I'd feel better knowin' I were the one lookin' after my kin."

"So would I."

A flicker to their right interrupted the conversation. Vyushir and Arbora appeared simultaneously. The wolf spirit lay by the flames, yawning tiredly as the warmth of the fire wrapped itself around her weary body. The purple-haired woodland spirit gave Mari and Maopa quick hugs before sitting on a log and glancing at the images of the two mortals.

"They sure do get themselves into situations," she mused. "I think you two are going to have a lot of worries over the next sixty or seventy human years if your children keep this up."

"I can't believe you find this amusing," Mari growled, glaring at Arbora.

"Of course not. However, I seem to have a lot more trust in the Dark One's word than you two. Besides, Sarpe said she'd keep an eye on them. Surely you don't distrust her?" Arbora asked, making eye contact first with Mari, then Maopa.

"I trusts her more than that there dark un."

"I know they'll do everything possible. I'm just afraid it may not be enough or they'll be too late. Already, the venom is working its way to Yemaya's heart. Even she isn't strong enough to fight the damage it will do to her body. I should never have given my word not to interfere."

"Perhaps, but I have to agree with Intunecat. He is in a better position to handle the situation. You're too close and there's too much at stake for both of our worlds to let you and Maopa charge to the rescue. Most humans are not yet ready to know of our existence. It's fine that they believe we're real. It's not that they know we are. The damage they would do to each of our kin to promote their own agendas would be catastrophic."

"As always, you're right. I'll give him a little while longer, but I'll not sacrifice my daughter for the sake of a reluctant promise."

Maopa nodded in agreement.

"If it comes to that, we'll see," Vyushir said. "The word of the Earth Mother is never given lightly nor is it taken so. If we of our world cannot trust you to keep your word, Mari, who can we trust and what will become of us?"

Realizing Vyushir spoke the truth and that she was a prisoner of the very principles she had established and practiced from her birth, Mari swore under her breath. Looking at her chosen, she felt trapped between the love for her mortal child and her love for those she had shared an existence with for eons.

"We must have faith," she said quietly.

Again Maopa nodded but didn't say anything. The four spirits turned their gazes toward the Eternal Flame.

CHAPTER THIRTY-FOUR

"No!"

Trapped within the dark abyss of her mind, Yemaya heard Dakota's cry and wept. If her decision proved wrong, it would cost her the one person she loved more than life itself.

The *beast* was exuberant. Finally, it had succeeded in its struggle for control. Looking at the serpent coiled on its chest, it snarled and tensed its arms and legs, rejoicing in the feeling of raw power coursing through each muscle.

The movement of the body beneath the snake alarmed it. Rearing back its head, it looked around, unsure of the danger. When an arm snapped loose from its bindings, the startled serpent hissed and struck, sinking its fangs deep into the forearm. Furious at the sudden pain, the *beast* emerged from its cave and struggled to break the bonds holding the other arm.

Dakota caught her breath when she saw Yemaya's right arm rip through the restraint only to be bitten by the snake. The left arm bulged and trembled as it strained to break free. Afraid that the snake would strike a second time, Dakota looked at the high priestess.

"Help her! You have to do something."

"She belongs to Dambala now. Her fate eez in the spirit's hands."

"You're crazy! She's been bitten! She'll die! She needs help now."

"She weel not suffer long. See, already she grows quiet." Lucretia smirked, pointing toward the still figure of Yemaya. "I was right about her. She has great powers. See how she breaks the ropes. Eet eez only a matter of time before she gathers her strength to save you, even though she cannot win against Dambala."

"Why are you doing this?"

"I have needs. She weel fulfill those needs. Eet eez the way of theengs, oui?"

"No. This is never the way. What do you need? We can help you, I'm sure," she pleaded.

"Ah, c'est impossible, mon enfant. There is only one theeng that weel help me et mon petit-neveau—her blood. It eez powerful. It weel cure him of the seekness."

Dakota's eyes widened as she realized what the woman was saying. "This is insane! She's just like you and me."

"Peut-être, but I believe in Bondye. He brought her to me. Mon petit-neveau eez very sick. Thees eez his only chance, et les loas, they promise me immortality in return for her blood. Eet eez a good exchange, eez eet not?"

"It isss not!" a soft voice hissed from the darkness.

Startled and turning together, everyone watched as a tall golden-haired woman stepped from the shadows into the light created by the bonfires. Gasping, the serviteurs crossed themselves and moved rapidly away, unconsciously creating an aisle when she strolled casually to the altar. The drums grew silent as hands hung motionless in the air, stilled by the incredible beauty of the stranger.

"What eez thees?" Lucretia demanded, angered by the interruption. "Who are you to intrude on my ritual?"

"*Your* ritual?" the woman purred ominously, her disdain dripping from every word. "You are missstaken, priestesss. Thisss is *my* ritual. Thisss…" she said, motioning toward the snake coiled on Yemaya's body, "is mine!"

Dakota watched the woman closely when she entered the circle of light. Something about her was vaguely familiar.

Lucretia frowned. No one had ever dared challenge her during her rituals. She realized that if she didn't take control quickly, her followers would lose faith. She would be nothing. There was, however, something about this intruder that radiated power. She would have to be cautious until she knew more about her.

"You must leave thees place. Les loas weel not be pleased."

"No, they won't and neither am I. You make a mockery of the spiritsss, priessstess."

"Who are you to say thees? I weel call Bondye down to punish you. He weel not be pleased," Lucretia threatened, her eyes blazing with anger.

The woman laughed. "Do it. I have no fear of your sspirits. Your threatss are meaningless. *My* words, however, I sssuggest you not take lightly. You will never again misssuse my kin in sssuch a manner. It is an abomination. Continue with your perversions, if it pleasses you, but I take what is mine—*him*." She pointed to the large rattlesnake lying on Yemaya's chest. "Be warned, there is a prisse to pay for what you have done. If you sssurvive thisss night, I will not tolerate further abusse of my ssnakes. You will release all my creatures and never abuse any of them again. Dissobey me at your peril for I promissse you, priestesss, *you do not* want to experience my wrath."

Stepping close to Lucretia, the woman made eye contact with her. Only then did the priestess notice the golden elliptical pupils. Gasping, she stepped back, clutching the amulet around her neck.

"Yess. You ssee the truth. Anger me again and even Bondye will not be able to protect you from my vengeance."

Stepping to the altar, she picked up the snake and stroked its head lovingly. The serpent relaxed in her grasp and began wrapping its long body around her arm until it had worked its length up and onto her shoulders. Releasing the head, the snake settled its head comfortably between her breasts and lost interest in its surroundings. The spirit turned to Lucretia's followers.

"You disssappoint me," she said almost sadly, her gaze lingering on each individual as if memorizing the face. "To sserve a falsse bokor who practicess Petro is intolerable. To use mine to take a life, unforgiveable."

Ashamed and fearful, the people dropped their gazes.

"Good. Your humility pleases me. Be gone from my ssight before I change my mind and sseek retribution."

Trembling, several of Lucretia's followers scurried away, slinking off into the darkness. To discover their priestess practiced dark voodoo was frightening, to have angered Dambala, terrifying, but to have seen her in human form, beyond comprehension. Some swore they would never again participate in such rituals. A few, however, still had doubts and chose to support their priestess.

"Sso be it," the spirit hissed angrily. "Your fate is yours to choosse. Remember well thiss night. I will not forget or forgive."

With those words, she and the large snake disappeared, bringing gasps from those who had remained. Frightened, they looked to their priestess for guidance.

"Do not fear thees loa," Lucretia declared haughtily, regaining her composure. "She eez not the true Dambala but an imposter, a minor loa. See how queekly she left? Her powers are weak. Would she not have cured thees one of the poison or taken them with her? Eet eez a test of your faith and you have passed. My people, you are strong. Bondye rewards true believers for their loyalty," she promised. The serviteurs looked pleased. Their bokor spoke truth for surely if the woman was the true Dambala, she would have destroyed Mambo Lucretia and freed the two women.

Turning her attention back to Dakota and Yemaya, she smiled, switching back to English. "I hope thees small intrusion deed not get your hopes up."

Motioning to Boudreau, who had been standing in the shadows, she held out her hand. His unquestioning loyalty gave her confidence and she made a mental note to reward him for it. Perhaps she would give him immortality. It would be good to have such a trusted servant travel the years with her.

Boudreau stepped into the light, his hands extended toward her. A large knife with a white bone handle carved in the shape of a serpent lay across his palms. Seeing the carving, Lucretia frowned but then picked it up and displayed it to her followers.

"Behold! Proof! The false loa has left the sacred knife. Dambala would take eet weeth her, would she not?"

Several nodded. It was true. The real serpent spirit would have taken the powerful symbol.

Grasping it in her right hand, Lucretia signaled for Boudreau to hold Dakota.

"I theenk you weel make a good servant, Ms. Devereaux, so I weel not keel you. Perhaps, Boudreau would like you for himself, would you not, my loyal friend?" she asked, looking at her servant. Boudreau smiled and licked his lips, a rare display for her normally stoic servant.

"Over my dead body," Dakota snarled, trying to shake off his hands.

"All in good time, ma petite, but I have many potions to make you more, how do you say, ameenable?"

Yemaya heard the words but was helpless to do anything. The

venom coursing through her veins burned, making it difficult to breathe. The pain was excruciating, causing the raging *beast* to surge forward, angry and desperate to locate the source of the attack. Now it was in complete control of her. Survival was its only goal. When the spirit had appeared, the *beast* quieted and listened. It knew that knowledge was power. It would use everything within its power to retain the hard-won control over Yemaya's strong will. By giving in to the rage voluntarily, Yemaya had handed it everything it needed to stay in power.

"Have faith," a soft voice whispered. "All isn't what it sseemss."

"Sarpe?"

"I have done all I can. The venom is being neutralized even as we sspeak, but it is a sslow process. Repairing the damage will take longer. I'm ssorry I can't do any more than thiss, but it iss our way not to interfere in matterss that do not conssern uss. I have already oversstepped those boundaries, but others are coming. You musst be ready."

"Thank you. You have already done enough." Yemaya could feel the poison dissipating, as did the *beast*. Recognizing a power far beyond its own capabilities, it remained quiet, waiting for the spirit to leave. Restraint was the best strategy. Once it was gone, it reasserted itself.

Walking to stand beside the altar, Lucretia stared into Yemaya's black eyes that were clouded with pain. Yemaya was barely aware of the priestess's presence.

"You have great powers. Your eyes speak for you."

"I think not," the *beast* growled. "They say nothing," it hissed, wanting nothing better than to destroy the arrogant human. The muscles in Yemaya's arm and legs bulged as they strained against their bindings. Her free arm struggled to release the restraint around her other wrist.

Shrugging, Lucretia raised the knife high above Yemaya's prone body. The drummers pounded furiously, the tempo increasing rapidly in anticipation of the sacrificial kill. Dakota's scream was drowned out by the drumbeats as the knife plunged toward her lover's chest. The priestess felt the adrenaline rushing through her body. She could almost taste immortality.

"*I think not,*" a low voice murmured from slightly behind the priestess and to the right. The downward momentum of her arm was suddenly halted when a force gripped her wrist tightly, holding it stationary. Pulling hard, Lucretia was unable to move her arm. The grip tightened painfully.

"Release me!" the priestess ordered angrily. Her arm was pulled slowly away from Yemaya's body and forced down to Lucretia's side. The pressure increased. Groaning, she dropped the knife. Rubbing her wrist, she glared at the dark-skinned woman standing next to her.

"Who are you?" Lucretia snarled, frustrated by the second interruption but not sure if the new intruder was another loa or human.

The woman smiled. It was the kind of smile that put fear in its recipient. Even white teeth with elongated canines gave Lucretia the feeling she was looking at a wild animal, but the eyes made her step back. Pale blue and gleaming, they glowed brightly; flames danced wildly behind the icy pupils.

"Mon Dieu!" the priestess exclaimed, backing away. "Vous etes un d'eaux!"

The smile broadened and Lucretia shivered. "Yes, and you are a murderess. You killed Ramus. Why?"

Lucretia wasn't sure what to say. In spite of the incredible strength the woman had displayed, she appeared calm and non-threatening. There was no anger in her voice, although her eyes burned with a curious intensity.

"We know about your kind. You are immortal. Your blood eez potent, good medicine. Eet cured mon petit-neveau from the seekness and eet weel give me immortality. I weesh for no more than what you have."

Ekimmu's laughter held little humor. "You're a fool! We're not immortal. We live and we die as you yourself have already proven. My people live long, but they suffer the same inevitable end as all living things."

"Your kind leeve off the blood of humans. The one I keeled has destroyed many lives. I don't theenk he weel be missed and I weel achieve my desires. Surely, you don't fault me for wanting what you take for granted? You have used us, now I use you."

Ekimmu couldn't fault the priestess's logic. Nor could she

condemn her for wanting the same thing her own people wanted. The Gebians had made the same choice in ancient times for the same reason. Still, the taking of a life was unacceptable. It was ironic Ramus had died as he had lived. Even more so that he had become a victim to someone coveting the very gift he had squandered. Ekimmu couldn't bring herself to feel angry. At least not on Ramus's behalf.

"I understand your reasoning, but it doesn't explain this," she said, motioning toward Dakota and Yemaya.

"She eez one of yours."

"She isn't Gebian."

"Bah! C'est impossible! Look at the eyes. They are black. They are like..." Lucretia hesitated, confused. Ekimmu's eyes were blue, much like Yemaya's before the ritual had begun. "Yours! Thees eez how your people survive," she accused. "You change the color to deceive us."

"I have always had blue eyes. An anomaly, some say. It's true my people have black eyes. This woman isn't one of us. No matter, your search for immortality through her or us is a waste. These deaths won't cure your nephew or bring you immortality."

"You lie!"

"Do I? Have you given your nephew your potion, priestess?"

"Yes and he eez better. The seekness, eet eez gone."

"And what sickness is this?" Ekimmu asked curiously.

"AIDS. He was *indescrete* in his youth. Mon petit-neveau enjoys the company of young men. Now he pays the price. I have cured him."

Ekimmu laughed. "And you think her blood will do the same for you?"

"I do not need a cure. I dreenk the potion. I weel live forever. Thees woman's blood weel give me power. She eez a great sorceress. Her blood holds much magic."

"Perhaps," Ekimmu agreed, glancing at Yemaya. Her eyes were as black as the darkest night. It was easy to understand why Lucretia would mistake her for a Gebian. "But hers is not yours to take, nor is Ms. Devereaux yours to give to another. You have unwisely chosen the wrong path, priestess. Age and ambition have made you foolish, and power will make you greedier than you already are."

"If that eez so, immortality weel bring me wisdom, don't you theenk?"

"You mean like it did for Ramus?" Ekimmu countered. Turning to Boudreau, her eyes narrowed ominously. She hadn't missed his momentary display of lust. His anticipation at being given Dakota angered her, but now wasn't the moment to teach him a lesson. "Release her," she ordered. *Later,* she thought.

Unquestionably loyal, Boudreau glanced at Lucretia for confirmation, angering Ekimmu even more.

"I admire your loyalty," she hissed, "but not your stupidity. Do it!"

Shrugging, the priestess waved her hand flippantly. The entire evening was already ruined. Still, her servant's loyalty and obvious defiance of the woman gave her some satisfaction.

"Let her go. She eez of little use to me now."

Once free, Dakota ran to the altar and kneeled by Yemaya. Yemaya's eyes were closed and her breathing slow and even, as if asleep.

"Yemaya?" Dakota whispered, shaking her lightly. When she received no response, she looked at Ekimmu for help.

"Be patient! She fights another battle. This is a journey she must make on her own, Dakota. You can't always be there for her."

"I know." Dakota sighed, unconsciously stroking Yemaya's hair. "I just wish..." She was unable to finish the sentence as the tears streamed down her cheeks. She laid her head on Yemaya's chest and silently wept, feeling completely helpless.

Ekimmu said nothing. Unwilling to intrude on Dakota's sorrow, she refocused her attention on Lucretia.

"This is over, priestess! Take your people and go. There will be no more sacrifices. No more deaths, now or ever."

"You cannot dictate to me or my people how we honor les loas. I am Mambo Lucretia, high priestess to Bondye," she declared arrogantly. "Eef he eez displeased weeth me, let him tell me now."

Her followers gasped. To call upon Bondye was reckless. Only the most powerful bokor would summon his actual presence. An eerie silence followed as they waited nervously. Lucretia smiled smugly, enjoying the stillness. Such a proclamation would ensure the loyalty of those who had remained. She was confident of her position as high priestess and bokor.

"See! Bondye does not come. He eez pleased with my loyalty," she announced boldly.

The leaves rustled faintly as a breeze moved through the trees. At first, no one noticed. Then small gusts fanned the fires causing them to dance wildly. The large bonfire in the middle of the group flared high. From its center emerged a tall figure shrouded in a long black cape and hood. Red eyes gleamed brilliantly from the shadowed face.

"You called my name, priestess," he said, his voice cold and unfeeling.

Terrified, Lucretia and her followers fell to their knees and bowed their heads. Some crossed themselves and began mumbling quiet prayers.

"Rise, woman, and answer me. I have no time for trivialities," he commanded.

"Master!" she stammered, awed by his presence and impressive height. "Forgeeve me, my lord, but theese strangers dishonor you. They intrude on our ritual. I breeng gifts to pleeze you," she added, motioning toward Dakota and Yemaya.

Acknowledging her gesture, the shadowy figure walked slowly to the altar and looked at the two captives. For several moments, he remained quiet, deep in thought. Finally, he leaned close to Dakota and smiled.

"So at last we meet in person, Little One."

Stunned, Dakota tried to think of something to say but could only stammer one word. "Intunecat?"

The slight nod and low chuckle was his only response before he turned to Ekimmu.

"I see you have finally found someone worthy of your attentions, queen."

Ekimmu frowned, thinking he must be talking to someone else.

"You are the last of Isis's bloodline, are you not?" he asked impatiently.

"If our history is correct, yes," she replied, unsure where the conversation was going.

"It is as correct as need be," he said. "You may choose not to take your rightful place amongst your people, but you cannot abdicate your heritage. Even if you choose to ignore your obligations, your people still hope. They have waited a long time for you to fulfill your destiny. You have found that which you seek, have you not? There are no excuses left to you now," he admonished gently.

Ekimmu couldn't think of an adequate reply. It was apparent Bondye knew more about her and her people than even she did.

"As it should be" was his response to her thoughts.

Next he glared at the serviteurs, kneeling before him on the ground.

"*Be gone!*" he commanded angrily, his voice colder than death itself. "You displease me. I have no use for you."

Scurrying away in all directions like startled roaches, everyone but Boudreau disappeared into the darkness. To suffer the wrath of Bondye was to be cursed in life and a guaranteed suffering after death.

"You, priestess! What say you? You defile my name, corrupt my people, and pervert these rituals. You slay the innocent and offer blood sacrifices to Petro, a perverted creation of your imagination, then dare to proclaim yourself *my* high priestess," Bondye berated, his red eyes flaring with barely suppressed anger. "Explain yourself."

"My lord!" She wiped her sweating palms on her thighs. "I have always served you faithfully."

"You have served only yourself," he scoffed. "Once there was a time when you were mine and served me well. For that, I will be lenient and let you live, but from this moment on, you are nothing to me. Be warned, though, there will be a price to pay when the darkness comes. You have condemned yourself and your nephew to great pain and misery in this world. It is nothing compared to your afterlife."

Throwing herself at his feet, Lucretia moaned and begged for mercy.

"Leave this place, *Charogne,* and pray that I rethink my decision should you again prove yourself worthy of my attention."

Afraid for her life and her soul, Lucretia literally crawled from the clearing before getting to her feet and running. Faithful to the last, Boudreau followed his mistress, unwilling to abandon her even at the cost of his own soul. Both were followed by the haunting laughter of their god.

"What about, Yemaya?" Dakota demanded, glaring at the dark

spirit. "No one seems to be helping her."

"We have helped her as much as possible, Little One. Sarpe has neutralized the venom. Ekimmu has protected her physical body while she struggles with her inner demon, and I have removed any immediate threat so she can battle her darkness freely. I think you know she wouldn't appreciate my interference. Now you must stand aside also. If it is meant to be, she will find the solution to her problem. Be patient."

"Be patient! That's all everyone keeps saying," Dakota grumbled, looking like a small child. "I've been patient. I am patient. I'm tired of being patient. I've used up every ounce of patience I've ever owned."

Intunecat chuckled at her unintended dramatics. He had grown fond of her during their brief exchanges. "It is a renewable resource, Dakota," he teased, using her name for the first time. "I have confidence you will discover you have plenty left after this. You will need it. Now I believe I am finished here."

Before Ekimmu or Dakota could say anything more, he vanished.

"I take it you know him," Ekimmu said.

"Not really. He helped me once. He pops up every now and then when things get tough. I'm never sure what to make of him. At first, I thought he was evil. Then he goes and does something like this. Now I don't know what to think, but I don't trust him."

"He is what he is, I guess," Ekimmu reasoned. "A spirit. I sometimes think good and bad don't come into it when spirits are involved. They have an agenda of their own and our rules simply don't apply when dealing with them, as I'm quickly discovering."

"Yeah! That's what Arbora said."

"Arbora?"

"Another spirit I met a while back."

"I take it you have these spiritual encounters often?"

"If you only knew!" Dakota sighed, feeling exasperated. "If you only knew!"

"Knew what?" a low, sultry voice whispered.

"Yemaya?" Dakota cried, grabbing and hugging her.

"Easy, my whole body feels like it has been run over by a truck."

"Sorry! Are you okay? What happened?"

"I am not sure."

"Can you walk?"

"If we go slowly."

Dakota and Ekimmu helped Yemaya sit up. For several minutes, Yemaya didn't move, other than to flex her legs and arms.

"I think I can make it now. Hopefully, we are not far from the highway," Yemaya said tiredly, looking at the dark forest surrounding them.

"I have a car a short distance away," Ekimmu said. "I'll get it."

Smiling, Yemaya nodded gratefully. Several minutes later, they heard a car engine and saw the headlights.

"How about we go back to the hotel?" Yemaya suggested wearily. "Then you can tell me what happened here. Would you like to join us, Ekimmu?"

"Perhaps another time," Ekimmu said, looking at her watch. "The sun will be up in a few hours and I have to meet with someone."

Dakota and Yemaya grinned knowingly.

"With a certain spirit, I take it," Dakota teased.

"Mind your manners. Now let's get you two back to your hotel so I can keep my appointment," Ekimmu said, hoping her flush wasn't visible in the dim firelight.

They helped Yemaya to her feet and moved slowly away.

CHAPTER THIRTY-FIVE

A t the hotel, Dakota helped Yemaya undress, then get into the hot tub.

"The more the spirits involve themselves in our lives, the more confused I get," she said. "Mari and Granny, I understand because they're family. Arbora is just plain nice. Sarpe surprised me tonight, but Intunecat leaves me uneasy. I don't know what to make of him."

"I would have to agree. Whatever his agenda is, it is well beyond my comprehension. Perhaps Mari or Grandma Dakota can give us some insight into him, but not tonight. I just want to hold you close and sleep."

"Me too, love. Speaking of which, I wonder why they didn't help us. I can't believe they'd just let all of this happen, not that I expect them to come to our rescue all the time."

"I suspect Intunecat had something to do with that."

"No doubt. Let's get you to bed. We both could use a good night's sleep."

Standing, Dakota stepped from the tub and motioned for Yemaya to follow. Grabbing a towel, she quickly dried her lover and nudged her into the bedroom.

Once settled, Dakota pulled Yemaya's head onto her chest, cradling her in her arms.

"Yemaya, did you know this was going to happen?"

"No. At least not on a conscious level, but..."

"But?"

"I can see why you ask. It was a little too coincidental, the show and this evening. Even I find it strange."

"Yeah! Then again, the past year has been somewhat unusual, but it's been the best year of my life."

"For me too," Yemaya mumbled, her words slightly slurred

from exhaustion.

Before Dakota could say anything else, she heard Yemaya sigh softly, then felt her relax and snuggle closer. Within seconds, she was asleep. Kissing her lightly, Dakota rested her cheek against her lover's head.

"Oh, Yemaya," she whispered tenderly. "When we're together, I'm the person I was meant to be, not the person I thought I was. You have given me everything I could have ever dreamed of and more. I love you so much."

Closing her eyes, Dakota joined her lover in the dreamworld Mari and Maopa had created especially for them, a world free of barriers and restraints but filled with everything the mind could imagine and a few things it couldn't. The smile on the faces of the two sleeping lovers spoke more than words or gestures.

After taking Lucretia home, Boudreau hurried back to his place, hoping his grandmother was still awake. The appearance of the spirits had left him shaken. Ancelin would know what to do. She had always been his mentor, even as a young boy.

Knocking on her bedroom door, he waited anxiously for an answer. When none came, he sighed heavily, unwilling to wake her. Unable to sleep, he went to the kitchen to fix a sandwich. The sun would be up shortly and his grandmother was always an early riser.

Three hours later, growing impatient, he went to check on Ancelin. Again, he knocked on her door. When she didn't answer, he pushed it open and peeked inside. In the darkened room, he was barely able to make out her silhouette on the bed. Tiptoeing closer, he leaned down to touch her, only to discover her withered body curled in a fetal position, stiff with rigor mortis.

Falling to his knees, he pulled her gently into his arms and wept. She had been the one person he had loved unconditionally and now she was gone. Her frozen expression told him she had been in tremendous pain.

Boudreau imagined how she must have called out to him for help. How awful it must have been when he didn't come, he thought, feeling an overwhelming guilt. She had always been there for him and yet, he had failed her in her last moments of life. She had died alone. Boudreau was a broken man.

CHAPTER THIRTY-SIX

The burning pain returned. Like a hot knife slicing through his gut, it seared his insides, causing him to writhe back and forth as he clutched his stomach. Mayhew could do nothing but lie on his bed and hope the pills kicked in quickly.

"What have you done to me?" he gasped, thinking of his aunt's brew and remembering the conversation with his doctor earlier in the day.

"I'm not sure what to say," Dr. Kinnelly said, rubbing the back of his neck nervously. "You were showing signs of improvement and the lab work indicated your white cell count was increasing at a fairly good rate."

"So why do I feel so tired now and have these horrible stomach cramps? I can't sleep or eat and feel weak all over."

"I don't know what's happening, but you're tired because you barely have any T-cells left. It's like they've been almost totally eradicated from your system. I can only imagine the cramps are from your digestive system shutting down. Have you done anything different since your last visit?"

Not wanting to get his aunt in trouble, Mayhew shook his head.

"Okay. I'm going give you a shot to help with the pain and prescribe a strong analgesic for the stomach problem. My nurse will schedule you to come in for a transfusion in the morning, then a complete blood exchange next week. We need to get those T-cells up or replace them quickly. Without them, your whole body is going to turn on you. I've never seen anything like this before. I'll check with some of my colleagues to see if they've heard of anything similar to this. Hopefully, one of them will have a suggestion."

Mayhew sat silently, saying nothing. What was there left to say?

"Now, you go home and rest...and don't do anything or go anywhere until my nurse calls. I want you on call and ready to come in the minute you hear from her."

Numb from the realization that he was dying, Mayhew stumbled to his car and drove home. It was time to call Cornelius. His lover would call their friends to organize his farewell bash. It didn't take a genius to know his doctor was only delaying the inevitable.

Whatever his aunt had given to him had apparently backfired, causing the virus to proliferate at a phenomenal rate. Her *cure* had gone horribly wrong, but Mayhew didn't feel any anger toward her. Out of love, she had tried her best to help him in the only way she knew how, and for that, he was grateful. He carried that belief in her and his love for her to his grave a month later.

Lucretia stood silently beside the headstone, her head bowed. Behind her, Boudreau held a large umbrella, shielding his mistress from the rain while she wept over her nephew's grave. Water poured down his face and neck, soaking his shirt under the raincoat, but he stood very still, making sure the priestess was well protected from the weather. Tears, mixed with raindrops, slid unnoticed down his cheeks.

She is dying, he thought sadly. *Her heart is broken and I can do nothing for her but watch her wither away.*

"Venez, maîtresse," he said softly to Lucretia, noticing her shivering. "Vous êtes froide et il commence à faire noir." He took her gently by the arm and led her away from the gravesite to the limousine. Frail and in poor health, the cold night air was causing her to shiver uncontrollably.

"Il est mort, Boudreau," she whispered, her voice weak from crying. "Je l'ai tellement aimé"

"I know!" he agreed sadly. *We all loved him*, he thought.

"Je l'ai tué," she whispered. "He was so young and I keeled him," she added.

"No! Eet was the seekness, nothing more. Eet was God's weel." Boudreau tried to comfort her. For more than twenty years, he had served her faithfully and would continue to do so. Nothing could change that.

Nodding, Lucretia didn't argue. It was easier to believe her servant than to face the horrible truth.

As the car left the cemetery, the priestess stared at her hands, searching for signs of the sickness that was now ravaging her own body. The thin skin couldn't hide the enlarged veins protruding across their backs nor the emaciated condition of her hands. Quickly tucking them in her coat pockets, she leaned back in the seat and closed her eyes. A dark, humorless laughter danced momentarily across her mind sending a chill through her body.

"Ramus," she thought, finally understanding his final words to her. She had doomed her nephew and herself to a horrible death.

EPILOGUE

After dropping Yemaya and Dakota off at their hotel, Ekimmu called Om Loh Rehn and gave her a brief summary of the events. Pleased, Constance agreed to meet with her the next evening for a complete report.

Throwing the keys on the stand, Ekimmu opened the bedroom door and stepped inside. The television was on, but the sound was turned low. A documentary about crocodiles was playing with the narrator explaining what a fantastic species they were.

Laughing, Ekimmu walked over to the bed and stared at the large orange and black snake coiled up on the bedspread watching the program.

"Setting the proper atmosphere?" she asked, raising her right eyebrow.

"Yess and ssaving my energy for things to come."

"You'll need it!"

Laughing, the snake morphed into human form. "Oh, I know. Believe me, I know," the spirit grinned mischievously.

"I love a woman with a lot of spirit," Ekimmu chuckled, removing her clothes and climbing onto the bed.

Giggling, the two women dove beneath the sheets and proceeded to wrestle for dominance.

The *beast* lay in its lair, bruised and battered. The rage quieted temporarily but wasn't defeated. The arrival of the first spirit had made it cautious. She was too powerful for it to challenge.

When the dark spirit arrived shortly afterward, the *beast* knew the time wasn't right to take control. With the realization that victory would have been impossible came the decision to retreat once again. It was growing more powerful and wiser. The presence of the spirits had made it cautious. Each encounter taught it patience and something else. It would never be able to subdue Yemaya without the assistance of someone or something else.

"You need only ask," a dark seductive voice whispered.

The beast snarled unhappily knowing it was true, but at what cost?

ABOUT THE AUTHOR

Fran Heckrotte lives in sunny South Carolina. Some of her interests include motorcycling, boogie boarding, scuba diving, gardening, and watergardening.

She spent three years in Alaska, enjoying hiking, camping, gold panning and working part time at a local ranch. After moving to the South with her husband, she became a policewoman for five years, as well as a guest instructor at the Criminal Justice Academy.

She eventually left law enforcement to become a carpenter, building houses. Now she owns a residential property management company. As time permits, she likes to travel to Montreal, Canada, and South Beach Miami with her gal pals to enjoy the nightlife.

OTHER TITLES FROM INTAGLIO

A Nice Clean Murder
by Kate Sweeney; ISBN: 978-1-933113-78-4

Accidental Love
by B. L. Miller; ISBN: 1-933113-11-1

Assignment Sunrise
by I Christie; ISBN: 978-1-933113-40-1

Code Blue
by KatLyn; ISBN: 1-933113-09-X

Compensation
by S. Anne Gardner; ISBN: 978-1-933113-57-9

Crystal's Heart
by B. L. Miller & Verda Foster; ISBN: 1-933113-24-3

Define Destiny
by J. M. Dragon; ISBN: 1-933113-56-1

Gloria's Inn
by Robin Alexander; ISBN: 1-933113-01-4

Graceful Waters
by B. L. Miller & Verda Foster; ISBN: 1-933113-08-1

Halls Of Temptation
by Katie P. Moore; ISBN: 978-1-933113-42-5

Incommunicado
by N. M. Hill & J. P. Mercer; ISBN: 1-933113-10-3

Journey's Of Discoveries
by Ellis Paris Ramsay; ISBN: 978-1-933113-43-2

Josie & Rebecca: The Western Chronicles
by Vada Foster & BL Miller; ISBN: 1-933113-38-3

Misplaced People
by C. G. Devize; ISBN: 1-933113-30-8

Murky Waters
by Robin Alexander; ISBN: 1-933113-33-2

None So Blind
by LJ Maas; ISBN: 978-1-933113-44-9

Picking Up The Pace
by Kimberly LaFontaine; ISBN: 1-933113-41-3

Private Dancer
by T. J. Vertigo; ISBN: 978-1-933113-58-6

She Waits
By Kate Sweeney; ISBN: 978-1-933113-40-1

Southern Hearts
by Katie P Moore; ISBN: 1-933113-28-6

Storm Surge
by KatLyn; ISBN: 1-933113-06-5

These Dreams
by Verda Foster; ISBN: 1-933113-12-X

The Chosen
by Verda H Foster; ISBN: 978-1-933113-25-8

The Cost Of Commitment
by Lynn Ames; ISBN: 1-933113-02-2

The Flip Side of Desire
By Lynn Ames; ISBN: 978-1-933113-60-9

The Gift
by Verda Foster; ISBN: 1-933113-03-0

The Illusionist
by Fran Heckrotte; ISBN: 978-1-933113-31-9

The Last Train Home
by Blayne Cooper; ISBN: 1-933113-26-X

The Price of Fame
by Lynn Ames; ISBN: 1-933113-04-9

The Taking of Eden
by Robin Alexander; ISBN: 978-1-933113-53-1

The Value of Valor
by Lynn Ames; ISBN: 1-933113-04-9

The War Between The Hearts
by Nann Dunne; ISBN: 1-933113-27-8

Traffic Stop
by Tara Wentz; ISBN: 978-1-933113-73-9

With Every Breath
by Alex Alexander; ISBN: 1-933113-39-1

Forthcoming Releases

Preying on Generosity
By Kimberly LaFontaine
May 2007

She's The One
Verda Foster & BL Miller
June 2007

Revelations
Erin O'Reilly
July 2007

Away From The Dawn
MK Sweeney
August 2007

The Gift of Time
Robin Alexander
September 2007

Heartsong
Lynn Ames
October 2007

… And Many More

You can purchase other Intaglio Publications books online
at www.bellabooks.com, www.scp-inc.biz or at
your local bookstore.

Published by
Intaglio Publications
Walker, LA

Visit us on the web: **www.intagliopub.com**